ON · FOOT · IN · THE · PENNINES

38 Walks in The Peak, The Yorkshire Dales, The North and South Pennines and Northumberland

ROLAND SMITH

With photographs by John Cleare

Maps by Mark Richards

GE

Greenwich Editions
Unit 7
202–208 New North Road
London N1 7BJ

To the fond memory of
Tom Stephenson, who did it his Way

First published 1994

This edition published in 1996 by Greenwich Editions,
Unit 7, 202–208 New North Road, London N1

A catalogue record for this book is available from
the British Library.

ISBN 0 86288 062 9

Printed in Italy by New Interlitho SpA
for David & Charles
Brunel House Newton Abbot Devon

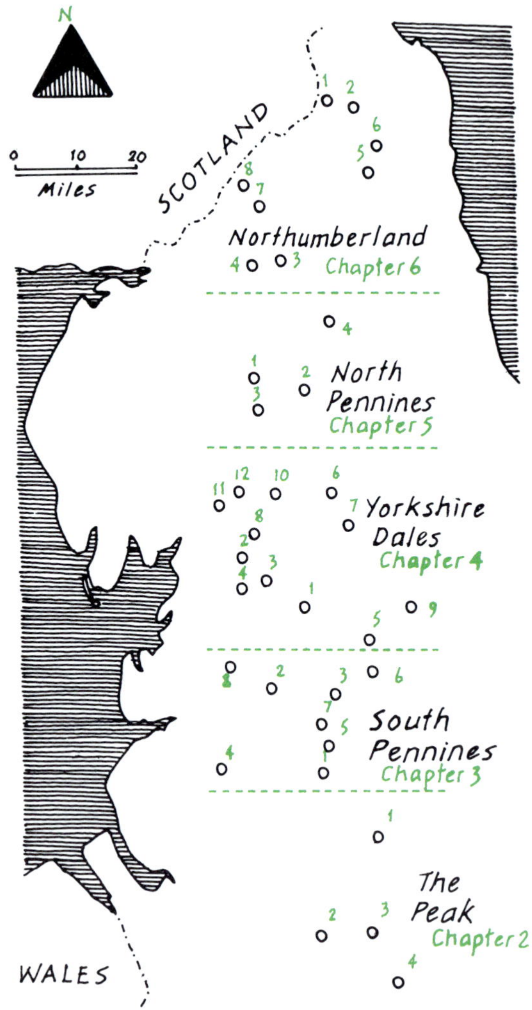

CONTENTS

1 INTRODUCTION 5

2 THE PEAK: A Free Man on Sunday 13
- Walk 1 Bleaklow 19
- Walk 2 The Roaches 23
- Walk 3 Lathkill Dale 27
- Walk 4 Roystone Grange 31

3 THE SOUTH PENNINES: The Great Escape 35
- Walk 1 Blackstone Edge 40
- Walk 2 Pendle Hill 43
- Walk 3 Haworth Moors 46
- Walk 4 Winter Hill and Rivington Pike 48
- Walk 5 Stoodley Pike 51
- Walk 6 Ilkley Moor 55
- Walk 7 Hardcastle Crags 58
- Walk 8 Forest of Bowland 60

4 THE YORKSHIRE DALES: The Striding Dales 63
- Walk 1 Malham 69
- Walk 2 Kingsdale 73
- Walk 3 Ingleborough 77
- Walk 4 Ingleton Glens 81
- Walk 5 Bolton Abbey 85
- Walk 6 Gunnerside Gill 89
- Walk 7 Aysgarth 93
- Walk 8 Dentdale 97
- Walk 9 Brimham Rocks 100
- Walk 10 Wild Boar Fell 103
- Walk 11 The Howgill Fells 106
- Walk 12 Cautley Spout 108

5 THE NORTH PENNINES: England's Last Wilderness? 111
- Walk 1 Cross Fell 115
- Walk 2 Upper Teesdale 119
- Walk 3 High Cup 123
- Walk 4 Blanchland 126

6 NORTHUMBERLAND: The Land of Far Horizons 129
- Walk 1 The Cheviot 135
- Walk 2 Hedgehope Hill 138
- Walk 3 Steel Rigg 141
- Walk 4 Walltown Crags 144
- Walk 5 The Simonside Hills 147
- Walk 6 Rothbury 150
- Walk 7 Tower Knowe 153
- Walk 8 Bakethin Reservoir 155

BIBLIOGRAPHY 158

INDEX 159

1

INTRODUCTION

'Swale, Ure, Nidd, Wharfe, Aire, Calder, Don.' My favourite geography lessons at school were often illuminated by the litany of this little mnemonic which stuck in my receptive young mind.

I will never forget that oft-repeated recital of the rivers which flowed east from the Pennine Chain into the maw of the mighty Humber and out into the North Sea. Thirty years later, it is still with me as I drive up the A1 – more romantically known as 'The Great North Road' – which crosses each of those rivers in turn.

The Pennines were always known as 'the backbone of England', the rugged, knobbly vertebrae that run down the spine of northern England, giving the nation its industrial strength, and the power which drove the wheels of the Industrial Revolution.

My earliest view of the Pennines was inevitably coloured by southern influences. I imagined that the rural landscape was bleak, harsh and gritty; covered by damp, misty moorlands and populated mainly by grimy sheep. The powerful evocation of the brooding Pennine moors in Emily Brontë's classic novel *Wuthering Heights* must also have helped to shape my childhood perception; one similar to Daniel Defoe's early eighteenth-century view that this was 'the most desolate, wild and abandoned country in all England'. My parents regarded the north of England as a place apart, almost like another country, and our family holidays were always taken at the seaside.

The essential Pennine landscape as seen in Nentdale, near Alston in the North Pennines

School trips provided me with my first visits to the Pennines. My first youth hostels were Buxton, in the misty Peak, and castellated Grinton Lodge, perched high above savage Swaledale. I had never seen hills like these before, and boy, were they impressive! Up until then, I had had to imagine my mountains and lakes in the sweeping skyscapes of East Anglia, but this was the real thing. Most of the time, summits like Blea Barf, Greets Moss and Gunnerside Moor (strange, wild, northern-sounding names) seemed to be in the clouds, which served to make them seem even higher.

They reminded me of a poem, 'The Moorland Map' by Ivor Brown (read in a school prize book) which seemed to encapsulate the hard, native candour of the north country:

Our maps are music and our northern
  titles,
Like wind among the grass and heather,
  grieve.
Our maps are candid charts of desolation
And wear the Pennine weather on their
  sleeve.

There's Howl Moor, Wetshaw,
  Winterings and Gutters,
Mirk Fell and Dirty Pool and Hagworm
  Hill,
Fog Close, Cold Syke, Ravock, and
  Crooks Altar,
And Loups and Wham and Whaw and
  Rotten Gill.

Many years later when I returned to Swaledale, perhaps the most beautiful of all the Yorkshire Dales, the magic was still there. Although the apparent size of the hills had diminished with my age and experience, I quickly learnt to love their rhythmic limestone/shale/grit geological succession; the complex pattern of walls and barns; and the perfect little villages like Gunnerside, Muker and Thwaite, which seemed to grow almost organically out of the friendly grey rocks from which they had been built. And as I later tramped the hills above the dales on mile-hungry long-distance walks, I

Crossing the saddle between Great Whernside and Tor Mere Top, Wharfedale, Yorkshire Dales

began to share W. H. Auden's feelings for 'the one landscape that we, the inconstant ones, are constantly homesick for'.

DEFINITIONS

What then, are these magnificent, macho hills, the Pennines? Perhaps we should start with some definitions. In the world of walking, the Pennines are usually accepted to be that range of hills stretching north from Edale, in the Peak of Derbyshire, to the gypsy village of Kirk Yetholm, beyond the Cheviots, just across the Scottish border. Tom Stephenson's 250 mile epic long-distance footpath, the Pennine Way, follows this route, sticking roughly (and rough is the right adjective for this toughest of mountain marathons) to the watershed.

The geologist will have none of this, insisting that the range starts in the south with the Weaver Hills of north Derbyshire, or Dovedale at the very least, and finishes at the Tyne Gap where the Roman Wall rides the switchback of the Great Whin Sill. The geologist would not include the volcanic mass of the Cheviots, nor the smooth Silurian slates of the Howgills. Although the Howgills form part of the Yorkshire Dales National Park, geologically speaking they belong to the Lake District fells across the Lune Gorge and the snarling ribbon of the M6.

We will take Tom Stephenson's model for the purposes of this book, which is, after all, aimed at the walker. There is also a historical precedent dating from the last years of the sixteenth century, when the range was first described. The inclusion of the Cheviots and the Howgills is unavoidable if the full range of walking possibilities is to be explored. I trust those of a geological inclination will see fit to forgive me, a mere Pennine pedestrian.

The name of the Pennines is actually a devious literary forgery, perpetuated in the eighteenth century by an English professor teaching in Denmark. Charles Julius Bertram (1723–65) claimed to have discovered a medieval chronicle, written by a fictitious cleric named Richard of Cirencester, which described Britain in Roman times. The ingenious Bertram invented many Roman-sounding names, among which was 'Alps Penina' describing the long range of hills which dominated the North of England. Presumably it was supposed to correspond with the Apennines back in the Romans' Italian homeland. Before the forgery was uncovered, two pioneer geologists William Conybeare and William Phillips had perpetuated the myth by naming the range of hills 'the Penine Chain' in 1822. The name, with the modern addition of another 'n', has been in use ever since. The earliest description of the Pennines comes from William Camden, the Elizabethan historian and antiquary, who described in his *Britannia*, first published in 1586, a range of hills in northern England which ran:

> like as Apennine in Italy, through the middest of England, with a continued ridge, rising more and more with continued tops and cliffs one after another ever as far as Scotland. Here they are called 'Mooreland,' after a while the Peake, Blackstone Edge, the Craven, the Stainmore and at length Cheviot.

Four centuries later, all these names are still familiar. The Staffordshire Moorlands on the western edge of the Peak has, since local government reorganisation in 1974, been officially recognised as the name of the local district council. The Peak, southernmost extremity of the Pennines, became Britain's first national park in 1951; Blackstone Edge, which Defoe dubbed 'the English Andes', still frowns bleakly down upon Rochdale and the mill chimneys of industrial west Lancashire; Craven is still the name of the glorious limestone country of North Yorkshire; Stainmore, the ancient pass where Eric Bloodaxe met his death in AD954, is now threaded by the A66 between the Eden valley and the Vale of York, but is still an impressive, lonely, moorland pass; and the Cheviots are still the bald-domed, peat-bogged, battle-scarred boundary between the English and Scots.

Camden's Pennines were still largely unexplored territory, and most of the earliest travellers who ventured across this 'howling wilderness', as Defoe described it, did so with fear and trepidation. Celia Fiennes, who bravely rode sidesaddle across the hills of Derbyshire in 1697, claimed that the county was 'full of steep hills, and nothing but the peakes of hills as thick one by another is seen in most of the County which are very steepe which makes travelling tedious, and the miles long'. She added, in a famous description of the Pennine landscape: 'you see neither hedge nor tree but only low drye stone walls round some ground, else its only hills and dales as thick as you can imagine'.

Ask people what the most impressive physical feature of the Pennines is, and the chances are they will plump for those dales. 'The whole

On top of the Pennines: the view south towards Cross Fell from Melmerby Fell, North Pennines

gift of this country is in its glens,' wrote John Ruskin a century ago. 'The wide acreage of field or moor above is wholly without interest; it is only in the clefts of it, and the dingles, that the traveller finds his joy.' If you dare to go to Dovedale or Malham on a bank holiday weekend, you will see that many modern tourists still seem to agree!

EARLY WALKERS

Walking on the moors has long been a tradition for northern workers, and Yorkshireman J. B. Priestley described it perfectly in his *English Journey* (1933):

> However poor you are in Bradford, you need never be walled in, bricked up, as around a million folk must be in London. Those great bare heights, with a purity of sky above and behind them, are always there, waiting for you.

Bradford folk, he said, had always gone streaming out to the moors, and they had bred a race of mighty pedestrians who thought nothing of tramping between thirty and forty miles every Sunday.

But this breed of formidable walkers were not merely pedestrians. Tom Stephenson, progenitor of the Pennine Way and a mill lad himself, recalled their keen interest in, and knowledge of, natural history. He quoted a writer who in 1873 had revealed that: 'Nothing could be more remarkable than the way in which love for plants developed among the operatives of Lancashire towards the close of the last century and the first half of the present century.' Many of these self-taught naturalists were quite prepared to walk fifteen or twenty miles in search of specimens after a day's work in mill or factory. It was, according to the British Association for the Advancement of Science, 'one of the most remarkable manifestations of popular science which had ever been recorded.'

The weekend trips 'across t'moors' had become part and parcel of everyday life. The Pennine hills, so near and accessible by public transport, acted as lungs for the industrial north, revitalising a population which often lived in grinding poverty and worked under appalling conditions. A modern poet, Glyn Hughes, has expressed it well in *Millstone Grit* (1975):

> The Pennines thrill with a powerful, special beauty. Out of some old neglected industrial town, you may climb a hill and be in a world that seems pristine, utterly untouched. In the ever-changing light, the shifting peat bogs that are formless as putty seem like the soft and shapeless mass of the earth before anything was created upon it.

Limestone walls and emerald pastures: typical White Peak country near Roystone Grange

Northern walkers on the Weardale Way on Allendale Common, with Allendale in the background

Patrick Monkhouse recalled the weekend exodus from Manchester in 1932 in his *On Foot in the Peak*:

> The movement which has brought young townsfolk out on to the moors has hardly a parallel elsewhere in Britain. For an hour on Sunday mornings it looks like Bank Holiday in the Manchester stations, except that families do not go to Blackpool for Whit-week in shorts. South-countrymen gasp to look at it.

Alfred J. Brown, in *Moorland Tramping in West Yorkshire* (1931), estimated that twenty thousand ramblers left Manchester every Sunday morning for the moors.

Even today, the well-equipped walker in anorak, breeches and boots and toting a rucksack does not merit a second glance in Manchester's Piccadilly, The Headrow in Leeds, or The Moor in Sheffield, whereas such a figure would certainly attract attention in London or Bristol.

The presence of the Pennines has made walking something of a religion in the north, to be followed by its loyal aficionados at any time of the year and whatever the weather. G. H. B. (Bert) Ward, king of the famous Sheffield Clarion Ramblers' Club, used to make this annual exhortation to those attempting the tough, 12 hour New Year Revellers' Ramble: 'We go, wet or fine, snow or blow, and none but the bravest and fittest must attempt this walk. Those who are unwell, unfit, inexperienced, or insufficiently clad, should consult their convenience, and ours, by staying at home.' Ladies, on this occasion, were also 'kindly requested not to attend'.

THE GREAT OUTDOORS

It was from the mills and factories that the great outdoors and access to the countryside movement of the 1930s sprang. The story of that long and bitter battle, culminating in the famous mass trespasses in the Peak District, is well known. The fact that ramblers were prepared to go to prison to exercise their 'right to roam' goes some way towards illustrating the passionate interest in walking in the Pennines which still exists in the cities of northern England. It can still manifest itself as something approaching fanatical fervour, especially if those hard-won rights are threatened or when moves are made to deprive walkers of access to the moors.

There can be no doubt that the huge 'access to mountain' rallies held in the Pennines in the 1930s were one of the most important catalysts for the long-awaited legislation for national parks in 1949. The first national park in Britain was set up in the Peak District in 1951, protecting an area where protection was most needed, between the spreading conurbations of Manchester, Sheffield, the Potteries and West Yorkshire. The Yorkshire Dales National Park followed in 1954 and Northumberland, taking in the Roman wall, in 1956.

These special areas, the jewels in the country's conservation crown, are administered by local planning authorities charged with ensuring that their superb landscapes and associated wildlife are protected against harmful change, and that opportunities for quiet, outdoor recreation are provided for visitors. In 1990 over thirty million visits were made to the Pennine parks, proving their perennial popularity. These precious landscapes have been further protected by the second-tier designation of Area of Outstanding Natural Beauty (AONB) conferred on the Forest of Bowland in the west; the North Pennines between the Dales and the Tyne Gap; and the imminent designation of the Nidderdale Moors, to the south and east of the Yorkshire Dales. In addition, seven local authorities on either side of the South Pennines have combined to form the Standing Conference of South Pennine Authorities (SCOSPA) with the aim of improving facilities for recreation, conservation and tourism in the South Pennines.

Many conservationists believe that the landscape and heritage qualities of each of these areas merit nothing less than full national park status, and forceful arguments have been put forward both for the designation of the North Pennines as a national park in its own right, and for Nidderdale's inclusion in the adjacent Yorkshire Dales National Park. Perhaps one day, echoing Tom Stephenson's dream of 'a long green trail', we will have a Pennine National Park protecting the whole of this magnificent hill country.

Many areas of the Pennines are also designated national or local nature reserves by English Nature or the local naturalists' trusts to give special protection to their wildlife. The Pennines have a rich variety of plant and animal life, some of which, like the unique Arctic and Alpine flora of Upper Teesdale, is virtually unchanged since the Ice Age. In other places, the Pennines are at the crossroads between highland and lowland Britain, showing a fascinating mixture of species of both these varied habitats.

Despite appearances, few Pennine landscapes can truly claim to be real wildernesses. Every moor, dale and fell exhibits some human influence, and only the steepest crags where grazing is impossible can truly be called 'natural'. Government assistance is given to maintain the traditional farming methods and systems which have largely created the 'field and barn' landscape we admire today in the Pennine Dales and the South-west and North Peak Environmentally Sensitive Areas (ESAs).

Wildernesses they may not be, but the Pennine landscapes should never be underestimated. The highest Pennine summit, Cross Fell on the western escarpment, does not top 3,000ft (900m), but the vast, featureless expanses of peat bog and moor of the Pennines, and the often severe weather conditions they attract, still claim victims among the unwary every year. If you are setting out to explore the Pennines on foot, as I hope this book will encourage you to do, you *must* go properly prepared and equipped. That means a good sound pair of boots in all but the driest of summer conditions; wind and waterproof clothing (the layer system has much to commend it); sufficient food and emergency rations; an Ordnance Survey map and a compass and, most importantly, the ability to use them. If your group gets into difficulties, leave someone with the injured party, find the nearest telephone and dial 999, asking for the mountain rescue service.

I have often set out from a Pennine dale in glorious spring sunshine, only to be beaten off the summit by a driving blizzard and whiteout conditions a couple of hours later. A common saying in the Pennines is that they have six months of winter followed by six months of rain. Another is that if you can see the view it's going to rain, and if you can't, it's raining already. There is more than a little truth in both.

The aim of this book is to give the walker, in words and pictures, a flavour of the superb walking country provided by the Pennines. The regions are described in turn, from the Peak to the Cheviots, touching on their natural and human history, but always concentrating on their walking opportunities. Suggestions are then made for walks in each district. I must emphasise that this book is *not* designed for use in the field, and the descriptions of the routes and the sketch maps are only suggested ideas for walks. If you want to follow any of them, and I hope you will be tempted to explore for yourself, you should always use the appropriate 1:25,000 (2½in to the mile) or 1:50,000 (1¼in to the mile) Ordnance Survey map, as noted at the start of each walk. Fortunately, most of the best walking country in the Pennines is well covered by the excellent 1:25,000 Outdoor Leisure series.

Tom Stephenson's hidden agenda for creating the Pennine Way was to open up the then-forbidden grouse moors of the Pennines, particularly the most jealously guarded in the Peak. But today this proposed 'long green trail' is an over-used, severely eroded bog-trot for much of its length, a sad testament to the over-promotion of long distance routes, and to the modern boom in 'challenge' walks. For these reasons the Pennine Way will be avoided, wherever possible, in this book.

I hope that by going on foot in the Pennines, you will end up echoing the fervent wish of that indefatigable moorland tramper Alfred Brown, expressed in his book *Four Boon Fellows*, published in 1928:

A walkers' paradise – the view from Whinstone Lee Tor, looking across the Ladybower Reservoir in the Peak

There *must* be dales in Paradise
Which you and I will find,
And walk together dalesman-wise
And smile (since God is kind)
At all the foreign peoples there
Enchanted by our blessed air!

2

THE · PEAK

A · FREE · MAN · ON · SUNDAY

In the introduction to *High Peak*, their classic history of walking and climbing in the Peak District published in 1966, Eric Byne and Geoffrey Sutton expressed the opinion that the Peak was 'by far the most important hill playground in Britain or perhaps anywhere else.' And they added unequivocally: 'Today more people walk and climb in the Peak than in all the other hills of Britain put together.'

This is probably still the case, and with the tremendous increase in the popularity of walking, and hill walking in particular, which has taken place over the past twenty-five years, that means an awful lot of bootprints for the fragile landscape to absorb. Going for a walk of a couple of miles or more is the number one outdoor attraction for the twenty-two million annual visitors to Britain's first and Europe's most popular national park.

There are times on a summer Sunday or bank holiday weekend when the Stepping Stones in Dovedale become submerged under a rising tide of trippers, paddlers and picnickers. But the majority of those visitors go no further than dipping their toes at the Stepping Stones, and every walker knows that in the less-visited upper reaches of the Dove, the isolated reef knoll hills of Chrome and Parkhouse still stand inviolate.

Rambling in the Upper Dove, looking towards the serrated reef limestone ridge of Chrome Hill

Further north in the Dark Peak, the erosion problems faced on the southernmost stretches of the Pennine Way across the peaty plateaux of Kinder Scout, Bleaklow and Black Hill are enormous. Full-time maintenance teams are employed on this one footpath, the first and most popular of the long-distance routes, or 'National Trails' as they are now known. However, you can still enjoy that 'tremendous silence, older than the world' as described by E. A. Baker, in many a less-frequented clough on Kinder or Bleaklow's craggy sides, if you are prepared to walk off that officially designated, and consequently well-beaten track.

There are several very good reasons for the Peak's phenomenal popularity among walkers. Between Dovedale in the south and Black Hill in the north, The Roaches in the west and the East Moor on the other side of the Peak, are some of the finest walking opportunities in Britain, whatever your taste. Few places have such a splendid variety of scenery in such a small compass, from the gentle riverside strolls in the limestone dales of the White Peak, to the stamina-sapping slogs across mile after mile of featureless peat hag and moorland, which is the joy of the dedicated (some would say masochistic) Peakland bog-trotter.

In between there are the delightful footpath ways between the lovely villages of the historically rich limestone plateau, and the glorious panoramic promenades provided by the famous Peakland gritstone 'edges', overlooking the softer beauties of the shale-grit valleys of the Derwent and the Wye, where the great houses of Chatsworth and Haddon dominate the landscape.

And it is all *so* accessible. It has been estimated that half the population of the country lives within sixty miles of the centre of the Peak District. And this delectable countryside is served with a well-maintained and signposted network of over 1,600 miles of rights of way. In addition over eighty square miles of moorland, mainly in the north and east of the 555sq mile (1,438sq km) National Park, are covered by over twenty access agreements negotiated by the National Park Authority with landowners. These allow the rambler the

freedom to roam at will – subject only to a commonsense set of byelaws and brief closures in times of fire emergency or during the grouse-shooting season. Nowhere else in Britain has such a fine record in the provision of public access, and nowhere else was it more badly needed than on the once-forbidden grouse moors of the Peak.

After the Enclosure Movements of the mid-eighteenth to the mid-nineteenth centuries, large areas of once-common moorland came into the hands of big estates or public agencies. Ramblers were excluded on the pretext of potential interference with the rearing of red grouse for shooting for sport, and the 'sterilisation' of land for water-gathering in reservoirs. But with such superb walking country so tantalisingly close and yet so frustratingly forbidden, another 'sport' soon became popular among ramblers from the surrounding cities during the rambling craze of the twenties and thirties: the activity described by one of its greatest exponents, Bert Ward, as 'the gentle art of trespass'.

The whole thorny problem of access to the Peak's moors came to a head on 24 April 1932 – the day of the celebrated Kinder Scout mass trespass. After a party from the Communist-inspired British Workers' Sports Federation had been unceremoniously thrown off Bleaklow by gamekeepers, a group of activists

The author on the icy ramparts of Crowden Tower, on the southern edge of Kinder Scout

led by twenty-year-old out-of-work mechanic Benny Rothman, resolved that if there were enough trespassers, no band of landowners' lackeys would stop them.

About four hundred ramblers attended a well-publicised rally in a disused quarry at Bowden Bridge, east of Hayfield. Benny Rothman told them that the hills were theirs by right, and had been stolen so that 'Lord Big Bug and Lady Little Flea' could enjoy their annual slaughter of the grouse. With that, the procession moved off along White Brow by the Kinder Reservoir and into William Clough, following a right of way established as early as 1897 by the Hayfield and Kinder Scout Ancient Footpaths Association.

At a given signal about half-way up the clough, the ramblers broke ranks and headed straight up the steep slopes of Sandy Heys, where a line of over twenty gamekeepers was waiting. A few undignified scuffles followed, during which one keeper injured an ankle. The ramblers marched triumphantly on to reach the edge of the Kinder plateau near Ashop Head, where they met up with another party from Sheffield, who had come across Kinder's summit from Edale.

Heads held high, the victorious trespassers marched back down into Hayfield – and into the arms of the waiting constabulary. Five people were later charged with riotous assembly and breach of the peace and received prison sentences totalling seventeen months.

The mass trespass has now entered into the realms of rambling folklore, but there can be little doubt that it acted as a catalyst both in the establishment of our national parks and in gaining greater access to the countryside for all.

Looking south-east from Stanage Edge down the Derwent Valley

Ramblers can now walk freely over the once-forbidden moors of Kinder Scout (2,088ft/636m), access agreements giving dedicated Peak District 'bog-trotters' the chance to exercise their addictive hobby at will. These aficionados are formidable walkers: their eyes light up at the mention of any of the bog-trotters' test pieces, such as the 40 mile

Derwent Watershed, which encircles the watershed of the mightiest Peakland river, or the 25 mile Marsden–Edale, the classic one-day marathon across the Peak's three highest summits of Black Hill, Bleaklow and Kinder Scout.

Because the Peakland summits are so modest in terms of altitude, they are often underestimated by those who do not know them. There are many tales of would-be Pennine Wayfarers setting out from its southern terminus at Edale – well-equipped, eager and fit – who return dishevelled and utterly demoralised after a day at 'the Kinder caper'. Unless you have experienced Kinder Scout in all its moods, it is impossible to appreciate how such a relatively low plateau can tempt and ensnare the unwary. I have known and loved Kinder for twenty-five years, but it was not so long ago that I found myself walking in a complete circle in mist on the plateau, simply because I thought I knew it well enough not to consult my compass.

Yet Kinder Scout and the northern moors have a wild, untamed beauty all their own. The weird gritstone tors which punctuate the edges of Kinder, Bleaklow, the twelve miles of the Eastern Edges, and the Ramshaw Rocks/Roaches syncline to the west, have a sculpted, almost artistic quality. In mist, the strange, smoothly-shaped rocks of places like the Woolpacks on Kinder's southern edge, can feel quite threatening, even malevolent. Small wonder that one of their alternative names is Whipsnade.

Peveril of the Peak: Peveril Castle, Castleton, from the slopes of Cave Dale

The contrast between walking in the Dark and White Peaks could not be more pronounced. The Dark Peak is a brooding, sullen landscape, not to be taken lightly nor underestimated, while the contrasting limestone White Peak is an altogether softer, more gentle country.

If the grit is the land of the brave, then the limestone is the land of the romantic – a place of gently rolling contours and narrow, path-threaded dales fed by the crystal-clear waters of some of Britain's purest rivers. This is the country which inspired Lord Byron to enquire of a friend: 'Was you ever in Dovedale? I assure you there are things in Derbyshire as noble as in Greece or Switzerland.'

Dovedale is still the most popular of the dales, but it is a place to be avoided in the height of summer, and there are many other dales every bit as beautiful as that of the Dove. The parallel Manifold Valley, just across the hill to the west, has some of the finest limestone scenery south of the Yorkshire Dales, yet it never seems to be crowded. The lovely Lathkill gets many people's vote as the most beautiful Peakland dale; even the Dove-loving Charles Cotton regarded it as 'by many degrees, the purest and most transparent stream I ever yet saw, either at home or abroad.'

If you like your walking to be fairly sedate and level then the converted railway lines of the Tissington, High Peak, Manifold and Monsal Trails are for you. They are also ideal for introducing younger or less able people to some of the best of the rolling White Peak landscape.

Prehistory is everywhere in the White Peak, where the word 'low' paradoxically almost always describes a high point and indicates a prehistoric (usually Bronze Age) burial mound. The most famous 'low' is Arbor Low, the so-called Stonehenge of the North.

For many people the lasting impression of a first visit to the Peak is the incredible network of often crumbling drystone walls. It has been estimated that there are some twenty-six thousand miles of drystone walls in the White Peak alone, a lasting monument to the industry of the Enclosure Movements.

But in this walkers' paradise, the martyrs of the thirties who first stood up against the landowners will never be forgotten. When the veterans of the 1932 mass trespass gathered to mark the sixtieth anniversary of the historic event at Bowden Bridge Quarry in April 1992, the words of Ewan MacColl's rousing ramblers' battle hymn once again rang round the watching hills:

I'm a rambler, I'm a rambler, from
  Manchester way,
I get all my pleasure the hard moorland
  way,
I may be a wage slave on Monday,
But I am a free man on Sunday.

B L E A K L O W

Map OS Outdoor Leisure Sheet 24, The White Peak

Start Monyash GR 150667

Length About 10 miles

Time Allow 4–5 hours

Difficulty Easy dales strolling, can be muddy

THE WILD HEART OF BLEAKLOW

Bleaklow has been dubbed Britain's only true desert, and accurately described by John Hillaby as land at the end of its tether. Here, less than a dozen miles from the city centres of Manchester or Sheffield, you can experience true solitude and enjoy a real wilderness experience.

For the dedicated Peakland bog-trotter, Bleaklow remains the ultimate test. This strenuous ten-miler is for experienced walkers only, and should not be attempted by those unskilled in map and compass; but it reveals the true wild heart of Bleaklow and a spectacular landslip for the wild-country connoisseur.

Giving a fair impression of Suilven from Lochinver, The Tower, Alport Castles, emerges from the mist

Start at the large layby and forestry works area at Westend Forest Gate, ¾ mile west of the Howden Dam on the minor no through road north of the Fairholmes Visitor Centre in the Upper Derwent Valley. Note that although public access has traditionally been allowed into the Westend valley, there is no public right of way until the access point on Ridgewalk Moor. During most weekends, the valley road north of Fairholmes is closed to traffic, but a minibus service is in operation.

Passing through the quiet, mature forest of Fagney Plantation on the well-made forestry track, the route eventually emerges at a clearing where stood Blacklow Court, now in ruins. This is where grouse shooters gather to share out their spoils at the end of the day. Turn right across the sturdy bridge crossing the Westend and start the gradual ascent of Ridge Upper Moor. This is a shooters' track, engineered in the hillside for the passage of Land Rovers, so easy enough for walkers. The views which open up in front are more reminiscent of the Scottish Highlands than Derbyshire, and Bleaklow Stones stand out challengingly on the horizon.

Crossing a number of fords through streams issuing from Ronksley Moor above to the right, the track climbs steadily with the constant music of the River Westend below and to the left for accompaniment.

Passing the normally inaccurately named Dry Clough, the track turns steeply up the hillside in a zig-zag to reach the top of the ridge. From here, the bog-trotting really begins, but if the weather is clear, the next objective of Grinah Stones in view to the left provides encouragement. It is a question now of picking the driest route along the 1,650ft contour towards the beckoning stones on the skyline.

The gritstone boulders of Grinah Stones are curiously pockmarked, like Gruyère cheese, and they take their name from the Old Norse *grein*, meaning a small valley forking off another. The stream issuing from beneath their weathered ramparts is known as Grinah Grain, a delightful piece of etymological tautology. Also nearby are Deep Grain, Grains in the Water (the source of the Alport) and Near and Far Fork Grains. The view from the headland of Grinah Stones is one of the finest and wildest in the Dark Peak. It extends southwards across the deep valley of Grinah Grain down the

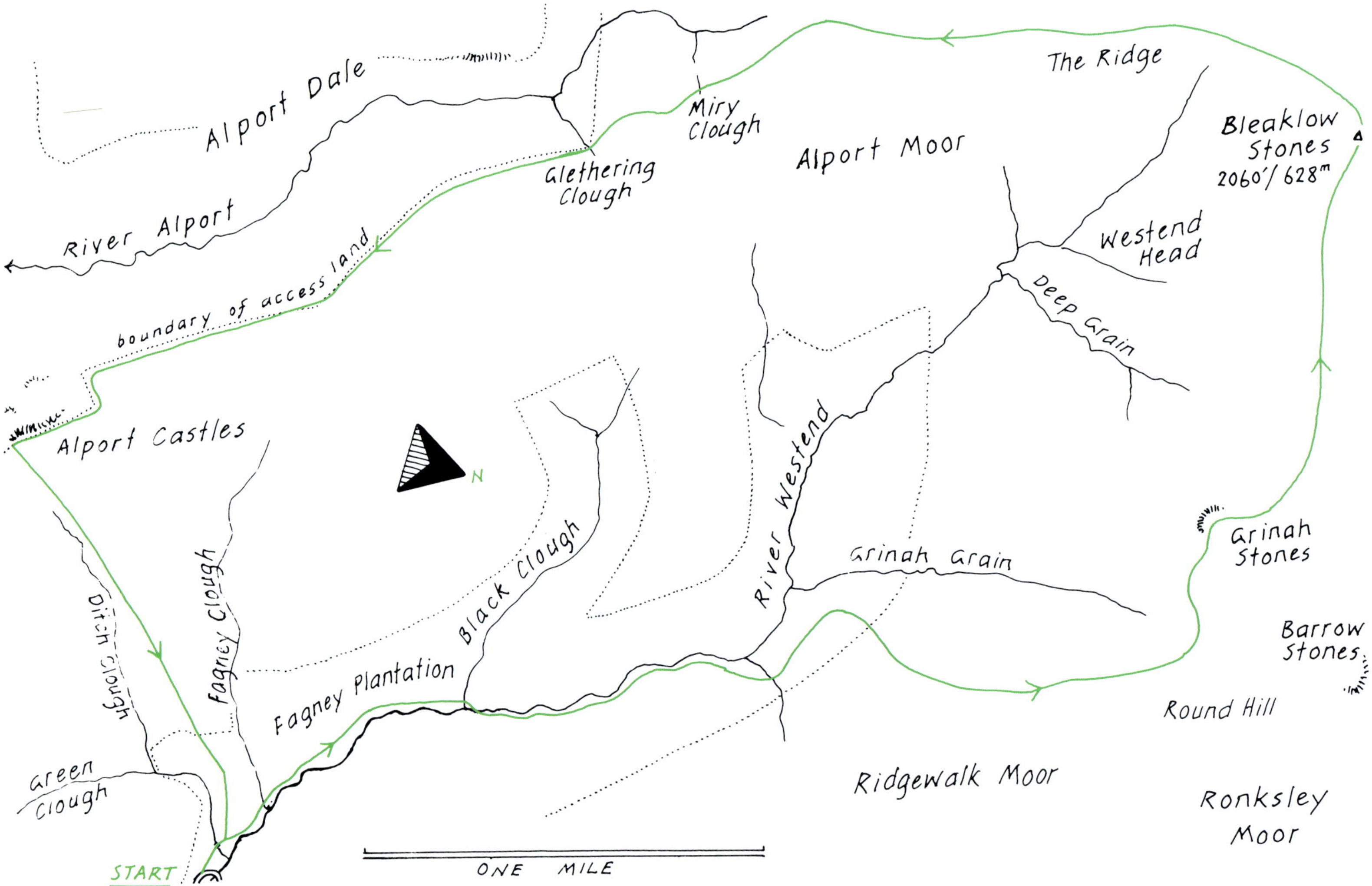
Alport Dale
River Alport
boundary of access land
Alport Castles
Glethering Clough
Miry Clough
Alport Moor
The Ridge
Bleaklow Stones
2060′/ 628m
Westend Head
Deep Grain
N
River Westend
Grinah Grain
Grinah Stones
Barrow Stones
Round Hill
Black Clough
Fagney Plantation
Fagney Clough
Ditch Clough
Green Clough
START
ONE MILE
Ridgewalk Moor
Ronksley Moor

length of the Westend Valley to the tiny glinting triangle of the Ladybower Reservoir, nestling beneath the prow of Bamford Edge. To the east, the whole of the Eastern Edges from Howden to Stanage are revealed, while the long level Kinder plateau stretches out from Crookstone Knoll to Fairbrook Naze in the west. A perfect lunch stop, and a place to linger and reflect.

There is a choice of routes from Grinah Stones: either to turn north and take in the curious rocks of Barrow Stones above Swains Greave, the source of the mighty Derwent, or to follow the well-trodden path around the head of the valley to reach Bleaklow Stones, another fantastic collection of wind and frost-eroded gritstone tors. Prominent here are the Trident Stones, a huge block weathered into three prongs, especially impressive when viewed from below. Among the rocks behind the main edge, is the Anvil Stone, which looks as though it may have been forged by the Gods for use by Vulcan himself.

The view from Bleaklow Stones opens up to the north across the deep chasm of Longdendale to the thin needle of the Holme Moss television mast, threading the clouds above Black Hill, with the Hawarth Moors beyond. Northeast lie the tower blocks and suburbs of Huddersfield.

From this 2,060ft (628m) summit, turn due south down the tawny-tinted rank moor grass of The Ridge towards the deep trench of Alport Dale which is prominent ahead, marked by the block of forestry plantations in its lower reaches. This indistinct track is rough going, and is very wet under normal Bleaklow conditions, so be prepared.

Eventually, you will join a narrow track which leads down the eastern bank of the Alport, one of the quietest and most beautiful of Bleaklow's dales. A series of delightful waterfalls – a rarity in the Peak – mark its length, and the path sticks to its precipitous flanks, giving a bird's-eye view into the gorge.

After the deep notch of Glethering Clough (the name means 'sheep-gathering') opposite Grindlesgrain Tor, strike up to gain the lonely trig point on Westend Moor at 1,661ft (506m). From here, the path is followed to Birchin Hat, and the celebrated landslip of Alport Castles, one of the wonders of the Peak, whose tottering towers of millstone grit suddenly appear as the land dramatically drops away to the green recesses of Alport Dale beneath.

It is thought to be Britain's largest landslip, formed as water and frost forced their way in through the unstable shales and levered the blocks of gritstone away from the cliff face. The finest views of the Castles, with The Tower prominent, are from beneath, in the climb up from Alport Castles Farm.

From Birchin Hat turn northeast to descend on the right of way which follows the gentle spur between Fagney Clough and Ditch Clough into Ditch Clough Plantation. The path steepens here and emerges a short distance from the starting point.

A glimpse of the Howden Reservoir on the grassy track down from Birchin Hat

THE · ROACHES

Map OS Outdoor Leisure Sheet 24, The White Peak

Start The Roaches layby GR 004621

Length 9 miles

Time Allow 4½–5 hours

Difficulty Easy moorland and woodland paths

THE ROACHES ROUND

You are left in no doubt that you've reached the Pennines as you drive east out of Leek on the A53 and take in the first startling sight of The Roaches as you cross Blackshaw Moor. A serrated skyline of jagged rocks seems to brush the clouds as Hen Cloud, The Roaches and Ramshaw Rocks burst into view, throwing out both a threat and a challenge to the red-blooded hill-walker. Once attained, the view from the top extends over the verdant Cheshire Plain to the distant glint of the Mersey.

The dramatic gritstone overhang of The Sloth seen from Rockhall Cottage, The Roaches

Our route, which also takes in the mysterious chasm of Lud's Church, starts in the shadow of The Roaches on the minor road which winds beneath their craggy heights, northwest of the hamlet of Upper Hulme. There is roadside parking and an experimental park-and-ride system operates from Tittesworth Reservoir.

Take the gravel track which leads up towards the col between The Roaches and the isolated summit of Hen Cloud. (Cloud is a locally common and entirely appropriate Old English word meaning rock or hill, while The Roaches is said to come from *roches*, the French for rocks.) The Gibraltar-like summit of Hen Cloud at 1,345ft (410m) is the apex of The Roaches syncline. Protected by overhanging rocks to the left under the first tier of The Roaches is Rockhall Cottage, formerly a gamekeeper's cottage and the home of the eccentric Doug Moller (self-styled King of the Roaches), which has now been converted into a low-cost climbers' bothy.

Pass in front of the cottage and through a scrubby plantation of firs to ascend to the crest of The Roaches via some steps. Once at the top, the views across the Cheshire Plain are outstanding, with the upturned saucer of the Jodrell Bank radio telescope usually visible in the middle distance, and Tittesworth Reservoir glinting in the foreground. The red-tinged Roaches gritstone was the scene of some of the most outstanding rock climbing of the 1950s, when Manchester apprentices Joe Brown and Don Whillans, both later to have outstanding Himalayan careers, pushed standards to new extremes. Many of their most famous first ascents, such as The Sloth, took place on the fearsome Roaches overhangs. The Sloth was so named because of the amount of time the climbers spent suspended upside down, like the creature of the same name. One of the most famous, and photographed, views of The Roaches takes in the stupendous overhang of The Sloth, with the peak of Hen Cloud in the background.

Continue along the crest, passing the mysterious dark and peaty tarn of Doxey Pool, reputedly the home of a gruesome seaweed-haired monster and mentioned in Domesday. Eventually, the 1,658ft (505m) summit and trig point of The Roaches is reached. The rocks here show distinct evidence of cross-bedding in the Roaches grit, laid down three hundred million years ago in the delta of an enormous river system flowing from the north. Carved and shaped by aeons of wind and frost, the

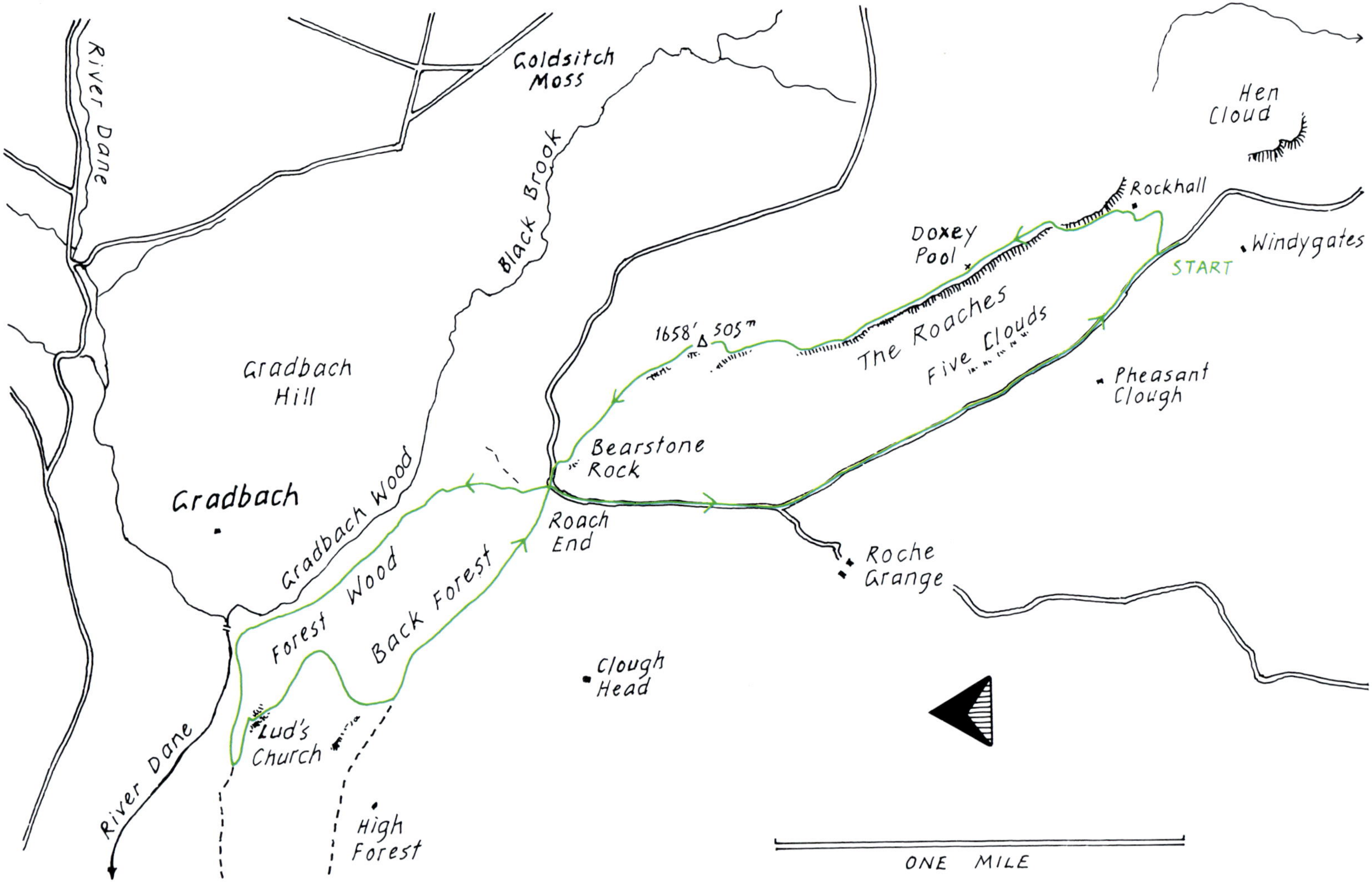

Goldsitch Moss
River Dane
Black Brook
Hen Cloud
Rockhall
Doxey Pool
Windygates
START
1658' 505m
The Roaches
Five Clouds
Gradbach Hill
Pheasant Clough
Bearstone Rock
Gradbach
Gradbach Wood
Roach End
Roche Grange
Forest Wood
Back Forest
Clough Head
Lud's Church
River Dane
High Forest
ONE MILE

rocks and boulders show every shape and form – a wonderland of nature's architecture. The view north from the summit takes in the shapely cone of Shutlingsloe (1,679ft/512m), rising proudly over the coal-bearing bogs of Goldsitch Moss, and the moors of Axe Edge, where both the Dove and Wye rise.

Descend through a heather-fringed avenue of sculpted stone to the outcrop of Bearstone Rock and the minor road at the aptly named Roach End. Turn right here and then almost immediately left over a squeezer stile on a gently descending stone-paved trod into the trees of Forest Wood. Follow this pleasant path through the mixed woodland with the musical chattering of Black Brook far below on the right. This path gently drops to a ruined forge at Forest Bottom, where a footbridge to the right leads off to the village of Gradbach; but our route is to the left, uphill again on a good track with views of Tagsclough Hill on the right.

The path emerges at the rocky outcrop of Castle Rocks, with fine views across the Dane Valley to Tagsclough and Allgreave Hills. Turn sharp left here, and after about 200 yards look out for the partly concealed entrance to Lud's Church in the trees on your right.

Lud's Church is a natural gritstone chasm, about 50ft (15m) deep, 100ft (30m) long and 20ft (6m) across, formed as the result of a landslip. It is a place full of myths and legends; its name is said to have derived from Walter de Lud-auk, a follower of William Wycliff, who used the remote spot for illicit church services in the fourteenth century. There is a legend that his beautiful granddaughter was killed in this outdoor church after a raid by the king's troops.

Lud's Church has also been identified as the Green Chapel of the Arthurian early medieval alliterative poem, 'Sir Gawain and the Green Knight'. It was here, according to a detective essay in literary geography by Ralph Elliott of Keele University, that the unknown poet set the dramatic showdown between the chivalrous Knight of the Round Table, Gawain, and the supernatural Green Knight. Apart from the similarity in the North Midland dialect used by the author, many of the geographical descriptions seem to fit the scenery of the north Staffordshire moors, especially that around The Roaches.

Leaving the myth-haunted, fern-draped confines of Lud's Church at its southern end, ascend the gently rising path through the birches to meet a concessionary path leading off to the right. This emerges through knee-high heather to the crest of the Back Forest ridge, an ancient trackway. This is followed left alongside a recently repaired drystone wall back to Roach End, with good views of Shutlingsloe, the scene of the denouement of Alan Garner's classic childrens' thriller *The Weirdstone of Brisingamen*, to the rear.

Reaching the road again at Roach End, follow the gated minor road right, back below the gulley-split tiers of the Five Clouds which outcrop beneath the main escarpment of The Roaches. Two miles of easy walking on this quiet lane, with good views to the right, completes the Roaches round.

Hen Cloud from the north-west

LATHKILL · DALE

Map OS Outdoor Leisure Sheet 24, The White Peak

Start Monyash GR 150667

Length About 10 miles

Time Allow 4–5 hours

Difficulty Easy dales strolling, can be muddy

THE PUREST STREAM OF ALL

Charles Cotton, writing as 'Piscator' in the second part of the seventeenth-century classic *The Compleat Angler*, described the River Lathkill as 'by many degrees, the purest and most transparent stream that I ever yet saw either at home or abroad'. And it bred, he added, 'the reddest and the best Trouts in England'. Three hundred years later, the Lathkill remains one of the purest streams in Britain, a fact which was recognised in 1972 when it was included in the Derbyshire Dales National Nature Reserve (NNR).

The author rests by the side of the tufa dam at Carter's Mill in Lathkill Dale

The Lathkill (or Lathkin, as Cotton knew it) is a rarity among British rivers, because it is one of very few whose entire catchment and course is over Carboniferous limestone. This not only gives it the clarity and purity so admired by Cotton and his friend Izaak Walton, but also the nationally important limestone flora and fauna which has resulted in its special official protection.

Lathkill Dale has not always been such a haven of peace and tranquillity. Like most other Pennine rivers, it has had to earn its living, and during the eighteenth- and nineteenth-century lead-mining boom, the dale became a hive of industry, filled with the sounds of men at work.

Walkers are fortunate that they can enjoy the delights of Lathkill Dale, thanks to a concessionary path which runs through its entire 3 mile length. On the Thursday of Easter week, a toll of 1p per person can be applied – a small price to pay for sharing such beauty.

Our walk starts in the former lead-mining village of Monyash (its name means 'many ash trees') at the head of Lathkill Dale. Follow the 'Limestone Way' signs out of the village, through the churchyard and straight ahead on a broad, stone-walled track at Manor House Farm.

This leads on past the head of dry Fern Dale on the left, and over the broad White Peak plateau to One Ash Grange, which was founded as a penitentiary for errant monks from Roche Abbey, near Rotherham. This well-cared-for farm now houses a National Park camping barn, providing basic, low-cost accommodation for walkers (no penance required!).

Bearing left through the farmyard, follow the yellow waymarks down a steep flight of steps which descends into the wooded upper part of Cales Dale. Our route follows the Limestone Way signs again up and out of the dale across the fields towards Calling Low, surrounded by its shelter belt of sycamores. Passing through the farmyard, follow the waymarks through the stiles across the fields through the edge of Low Moor Plantation, to reach the Long Rake road near Bee Low. Turn left along the lane, and left again after about half a mile where a public footpath sign points to the village of Over Haddon, visible across the wooded defile of Lathkill Dale ahead. There are fine views from this path across the valley of the River Wye to the right, dominated by the wooded escarpment of Manners Wood above Bakewell.

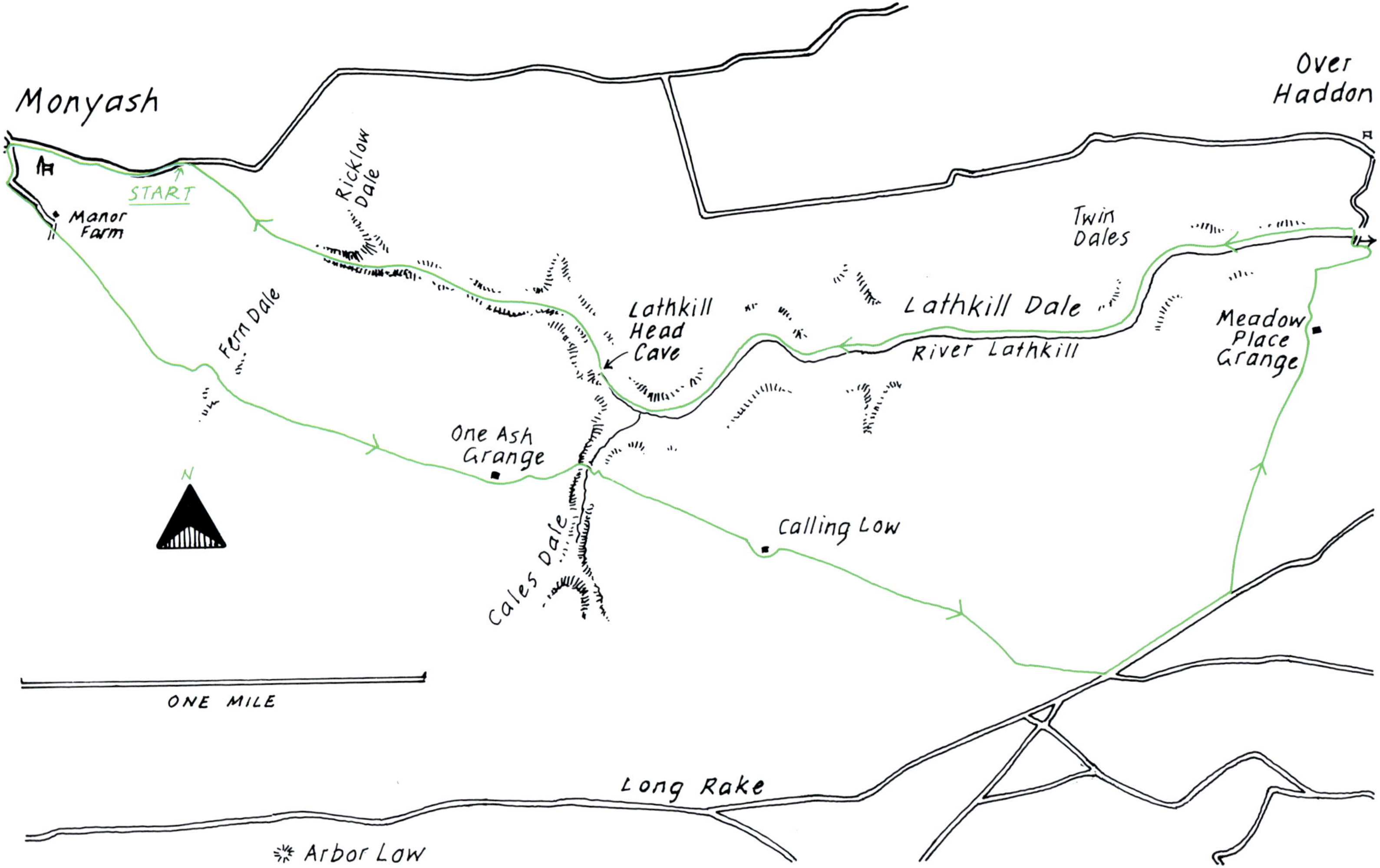
Monyash
START
Manor Farm
Ricklow Dale
Fern Dale
Lathkill Head Cave
Lathkill Dale
River Lathkill
Twin Dales
Over Haddon
Meadow Place Grange
One Ash Grange
Cales Dale
Calling Low
N
ONE MILE
Long Rake
Arbor Low

At Meadow Place Grange, descend into Lathkill Dale through the woods, bearing sharp left at the railed clapper bridge at Lathkill Lodge. Over Haddon, up the hill, provides refreshment.

The return route passes through the most beautiful section of Lathkill Dale, past a series of weirs and falls constructed to provide breeding grounds for Cotton's 'reddest Trouts'. Such help has always been necessary because the Lathkill is one of the Peak's 'disappearing' rivers, darting underground through the limestone at the slightest opportunity. The lead miners of Lathkill had to 'puddle' the river bed with clay in order to use the water to power the pumps which kept their mines dry, and it is a task which still has to be undertaken periodically.

Entering the woodland, the remains of the Mandale Lead Mine, which ceased operations in the 1860s, are revealed at the foot of Twin Dales to the right. The large ivy-clad structure was the main retaining wall of the Cornish beam-engine house, and the trees which now cloak the workings date only from the closure of the mine.

The thick ash woods of Meadow Place and Low Wood on the other bank (to which there is no access) represent some of the finest climax ashwoods in Britain, and are the home of several rare species such as pink mezereon, dogwood and geulder rose. Entering Palmerston Wood the path runs by the side of the river where kingfisher, dipper and grey wagtail are sometimes seen. The Lathkill is also home to the rare freshwater crayfish, known locally as a 'crawkie'. This lobster-like crustacean will only tolerate the clearest, cleanest waters, and is yet another sign of the outstanding pollution-free quality of the Lathkill.

Eventually, the path emerges from the woodland and into the open upper reaches of the dale. Invasive hawthorn scrub which has spread due to less intensive grazing, threatens this valuable grassland habitat, where up to fifty-four species of plants per square metre have been found.

The route continues west over a stile by the site of Carter's Mill, a former corn mill, where a pretty cascade tumbles over a dam formed of tufa, or re-formed limestone deposited by the clear, calcium-rich water held back in the millpond. Passing the entrance footbridge to Cales Dale on the left, the dale swings to the north under increasingly impressive crags (or scars) of white limestone.

The Lathkill is, by now, often little more than a trickle under the thick undergrowth, and it normally disappears completely by the collapsed lead mine adit of Holmes Groove. In winter conditions, especially after heavy rain, the river bursts impressively out of the hillside at Lathkill Head Cave, on the left-hand side of the path. The crag opposite is known as Parson's Tor, after an unfortunate Monyash cleric who fell to his death here in 1776.

Now the dale narrows dramatically, and the great scree slope coming down from the right marks the spoil from the disused Ricklow

Ruins of the Mandale Lead Mine

Quarry, which produced fashionable 'figured marble' from the fossiliferous limestone in Victorian times. A scramble round this boulder choke leads out into the meadows of the upper dale and on to the B5055 Bakewell–Monyash road. It is now only a short step left to Monyash, grouped protectively round its ancient market cross.

THE PEAK · WALK 4

ROYSTONE · GRANGE

Map OS Outdoor Leisure Sheet 24, The White Peak

Start Minninglow Car Park GR 194582

Length 4 miles

Time Allow 2½ hours

Difficulty Easy trail and field walking

A WALK INTO THE PAST

The dry, crag-rimmed dale occupied by the eighteenth-century buildings of Roystone Grange, near Ballidon, is typical of many which dissect the rolling White Peak limestone plateau. The 'grange' element indicates that it once supported an outlying farm serving a medieval abbey, in this case that of Garendon in far-off Leicestershire.

There are nearly fifty 'granges' in the Peak – evidence of the extensive sheep ranches run by the ecclesiastical entrepreneurs of the Middle Ages – but Roystone Grange is the only one which has been systematically studied and excavated, to reveal an astonishing story of the continuity of human life extending over six thousand years. That fascinating story is now told in the Roystone Grange Trail, a thrilling example of 'public' archaeology, and the subject of this White Peak walk.

The 4 mile trail starts at the National Park's Minninglow car park on the High Peak Trail. This former railway line, opened in 1830 as the Cromford and High Peak Railway at the very dawn of the Railway Age, is now a popular traffic-free walking and riding route through some of the finest White Peak landscapes. A few steps south of the start the first cuttings and embankments of this impressive civil engineering project come into view.

The easy trail leads south over soaring embankments, revealing a wonderful panorama of tree-topped limestone hills, criss-crossed by a network of drystone walls. Prominent in front is the important Neolithic chambered tomb site of Minninglow, with its distinctive spindly crown of beeches, visible from so many viewpoints in the White Peak. In the valley to the right is Minninglow Grange, and just beyond a deep, tree-lined cutting, we come to Minninglow Quarry, a source of building stone and lime in the early 1900s.

A little further on to the right is a well-preserved Victorian brick-kiln complex, restored by the excavators of Roystone. There is a good geological reason for a brick-kiln here in this remote spot. Silica-rich sands outcrop here and at nearby Friden, and were used in the manufacture of refractory furnace bricks for the steelworks of Sheffield and elsewhere. The chimneys of the brickworks at Friden can be seen clearly on the northwest horizon.

Just before the brickworks and in the shadow of Minninglow Hill to the left, leave the High Peak Trail, turning left to climb ancient Gallowlow Lane between high drystone walls. This follows the line of the medieval grange estate boundary. After a few more steps, turn right over a high ladder stile and descend through the fields via the tunnel beneath the High Peak Trail. High on the hillside to the right as you pass through the tunnel are the remains of a Bronze Age burial mound, topped by an early nineteenth-century wall.

The walls in these parts were the subject of an award-winning study by local farmer and amateur archaeologist, Martin Wildgoose, and published in Richard Hodges's *Wall to Wall*

Approaching Roystone Grange along the line of a boundary first constructed in Roman times

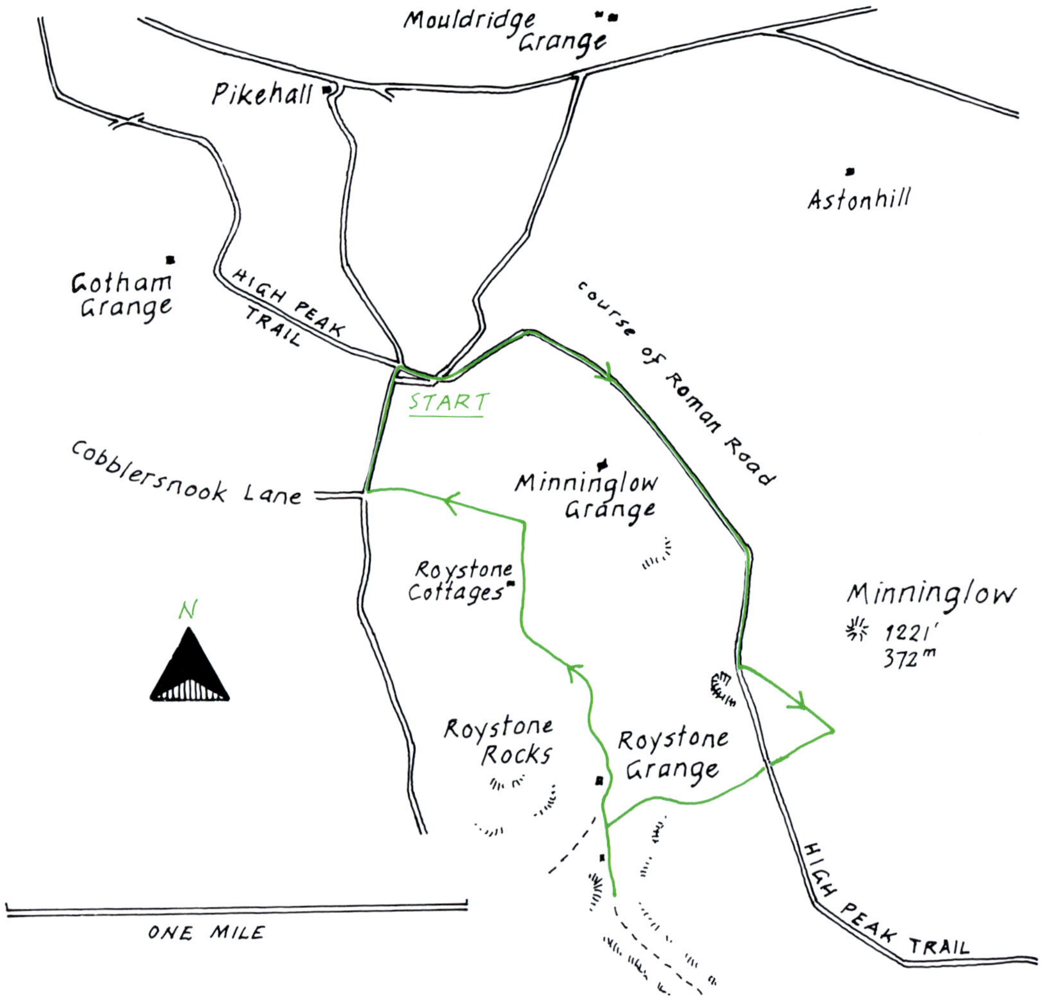

History (1991). By investigating the methods of construction, he dated many of the walls round Roystone to the Romano-British period. Several are still in use today.

Descend the field to the squeezer stile at the bottom, and turn right into a walled lane which winds down towards the buildings of the modern Roystone Grange. Up on the hill to the right is the curious Nissen-hut shaped store where explosives were kept for use in the quarries. Head for the chapel-like building of the pump house, where a great steam engine once sent air up to the pneumatic drills used in the quarries.

You are now in the heart of the Roystone Grange complex, where people have lived and farmed for thousands of years. Just behind the pump house, where an interpretive board tells the story, the main excavation of the medieval grange has taken place. A dairy, probably used by the monks of Garendon Abbey, has been investigated along with other farm buildings, below the spring which lies hidden behind a wall in the trees above. It was probably the presence of the spring which induced the first farmers to build here, and later, in the twelfth century, the farm, then known as Revestones, was granted to the Cistercian abbey of Gardendon, which used it as a sheep ranch.

Down the dale beyond the pump house the low boulder foundations of a Romano-British sheep pen can just be discerned. Amazingly, sheep are still sheared on the same spot some two thousand years later.

Further down the dale, the outlines of Romano-British field systems can just be made out (especially in evening light, or after snow) as terraces on the steep eastern side of the dale. On the opposite side of the track is a nineteenth-century lead vein adit. Other evidence of lead mining, which also goes back to Roman times, can be seen in the crater-like depressions which run across the hillside to the right as you return to the pump house.

Back at the grange site, walk up towards the eighteenth-century farmhouse, solidly built from local stone, with an impressively large barn. Pass through the farmyard and walk up to the disused dairy shed, where another board explains how the Roman period settlement was uncovered in the slope of the hillside to the left. The second-century Roman manor was an impressive bow-walled building, sheltering in the lee of the hill. Archaeologists estimate that this farmstead and others like it may have supported a population of at least fifty people in this remote and isolated valley.

Follow the lane past the farm cottages to its junction with Gallowlow Lane, where you must go left for half a mile to reach the minor road to Parwich. Turn right here and follow the road along the shelter belt of Cobblersnook Plantation back to the High Peak Trail and car park.

Walking south on the embankment of the High Peak Trail, approaching the spindly crown of trees on Minninglow in the distance

3

THE · SOUTH · PENNINES

THE · GREAT · ESCAPE

Few places in Britain can show the same sort of startling contrasts as the South Pennines. A short, sharp walk of less than an hour can take you from a dingy industrial town or city of decaying and now largely empty mills and factories out onto the open moors, where the wind blows clean and free and you can walk for miles, your only companion the plaintive, bubbling call of the curlew.

But, as the Pennine poet Glyn Hughes has pointed out, there are always reminders of the everyday world you left behind you in the valley:

> Through the apparent silence, you distinguish, beyond the song of lark or call of grouse, a continuous hum so constant, monotonous and quiet that you had mistaken it for silence. It is the day-and-night noise of Lancashire and Yorkshire, as incessant as the flow of a river.

Generations of mill and factory workers from the cities which were the birthplace of the Industrial Revolution have found solace in these hills. However hard the labour, however bad the conditions, the moors were always there waiting: the 'Great Escape'.

Remote and deserted, Upper Ponden Farm stands high on Haworth Moor in the heart of 'Bronte Country' near Haworth

Dismissed by the National Park architect John Dower as 'The Industrial Pennines', and just failing to achieve national park status, the South Pennines became a kind of environmental no man's land, fringed by industrial cities and properly designated, protected landscapes, yet highly valued with a ferocious loyalty by the artisans who used them every weekend for recreation.

Then in 1974, following an abortive initiative by the former West Riding of Yorkshire County Council, the Standing Conference of South Pennine Authorities (SCOSPA) was set up jointly by the local authorities for Bradford, Burnley, Calderdale, Kirklees, Pendle, Rochdale and Rossendale, plus North-West Water and the Pennine Parks Association. The aim of this unique partnership is to promote and improve facilities for informal recreation, conservation and tourism in the loosely defined area of the South Pennines, and it has succeeded in giving this underrated area the recognition which it has needed for so long.

The South Pennines is traditionally that area between the Forest of Bowland and the Lancashire fells to the west; the Peak and Yorkshire Dales National Parks to the south and north, bounded by Standedge and the River Aire respectively. To the east, the West Riding wool towns of Halifax, Leeds, Bradford and Huddersfield mark the boundary. The highest point is Pendle Hill, at 1,832ft (559m), but generally speaking the highest continuous ground is found on the western scarp of the Pennines on the Blackstone Edge escarpment, which is followed by the Pennine Way. This was the highest point of the great Armorican anticline of some 280 million years ago, when the highest points of the South Pennines probably matched the present summits of the Alps. Aeons of erosion have reduced these lofty eminences to the moors and edges we see today.

The moors slope away more gently to the east towards the Aire and Calder valleys. The isolated, heather-clad boss of the Forest of Bowland in the west is separated from the main mass of the Pennines by the rivers Wenning and Ribble, but geologically speaking is part of the same system.

Pendle, Boulsworth and Black Hameldon Hills north of Burnley are the highest ground today, because they are formed of the more resistant Pendle Grit, which has withstood the powers of erosion far better than the Kinder Scout grits of the western escarpment.

About ten thousand years ago, rushing meltwater from the Ice Age glaciers to the north and east gouged out the steep-sided gorges and dales which intersect the gently sloping plateau, where early man first settled on dry, commanding sites such as Ilkley Moor (Walk 6). It was these fast-flowing rivers which attracted the first industrialists, anxious to find a cheap and reliable power source to run their mills; but the woollen industry had been established in the South Pennines long before these forerunners of the Industrial Revolution arrived.

No one knows when the first spinning wheel or hand loom was installed in the South Pennines, but certainly by the early sixteenth century many households were making a few pieces of cloth for domestic use and local sale. This period saw the emergence of the first yeoman clothiers, middlemen who supplied the raw wool to self-employed handloom weavers, and then collected the end product for sale at the local Piece or Cloth Halls, which were built in most sizeable towns. Probably the best preserved is Halifax's magnificent colonnaded Piece Hall, built in 1779.

The gloomy eastern portal of Standedge Tunnel, on the Huddersfield Narrow Canal at Tunnel End, Marsden

The cottages of these early weavers are a common feature in South Pennine towns and villages, easily recognisable by the long continuous rows of south-facing mullioned windows at first-floor level, designed to allow maximum light to the looms inside. In villages like Wycoller, Golcar and Heptonstall, long terraces of this kind of cottage are built up the hillside. Seen from the rear, they look like bungalows, but at the front, the full height of up to three storeys is realised. These long rows of windows in weavers' cottages foreshadowed the design of the textile factories which were to follow. Later 'top and bottom' houses which climb up the hillside in places like Hebden Bridge, were built by millowners or millworkers' associations.

Out on the moors, evidence of this early industry remains in the form of tenterhooks or tenterposts set in drystone walls, which were used to stretch cloth and allow it to dry; and in so-called 'wuzzing holes', shallow, finger-sized holes used when the washed yarn was spun-dried by 'wuzzing' it round in a basket on a pole inserted in the hole. The traditional woollen industry in Lancashire was gradually replaced by cotton as the first imports of the new textile came in from America. By 1800, it was largely confined to the Rochdale and Rossendale districts, while over the border in Yorkshire, many went over to worsted spinning.

As the textile industry grew in size, communications became more important, and by the mid-seventeenth century, the first turnpike trusts began to appear. These often followed the much earlier packhorse routes which were the first trunk routes to cross the Pennines, apart from the one or two 'Roman' roads, such as that which apparently follows the line of the much later Blackstone Edge causeway (Walk 1).

The South Pennines is well served by these traditional packhorse causeways (or 'causeys' as they are know locally) which, because they were built to last of local gritstone, make fine walking routes for the modern rambler. When action was taken in 1992 to combat the serious erosion being suffered on the Pennine Way, it was significant that the Countryside Commission turned to the traditional causeway-stone

A South Pennine landscape of reservoir, plantation, walls and barns at Widdop, near Heptonstall

FOR SALE

method for the reconstruction of the pathway across the soft peat moors.

Originally, these causeways were used by trains of up to forty packhorses which carried goods across the hills and were led by men known as 'jaggers'. There are several Jagger's Cloughs or Gates in the Pennines, and the name is thought to have originated from the German Jaeger ponies which were sometimes used, alongside the more popular Galloway ponies. Guideposts or stoops and the distinctive low-parapeted packhorse bridges, designed to let the swinging panniers pass unobstructed, are another reminder of the days when the jingling bells of packhorse trains were a common sound on the moors. Good examples are the much-photographed bridges at Wycoller, and Lumb Bridge across Crimsworth Dean (Walk 7) on the Boulsworth to Halifax Limers' Gate. Many of the later turnpikes, built between the mid-seventeenth and mid-nineteenth centuries, were constructed by John Metcalfe, 'Blind Jack of Knaresborough' or John Macadam, the great Scottish-born road builder.

By the middle of the eighteenth century, the packhorse was still the mainstay of the trans-Pennine transport system, but following the construction by former millwright James Brindley of the Duke of Bridgewater's first canal between Worsley and Manchester in 1761, and the discovery that one horse towing a barge could pull six hundred times the load that the same horse could carry on its back, plans were soon laid for the first trans-Pennine canals.

Weavers' cottages and cobbles in Heptonstall, a typical hill-top textile village

It was during the later Industrial Revolution that the South Pennines really earned its 'muck and brass' reputation, and Blake's 'dark, Satanic mills' still spring to mind when the industrial Pennines are mentioned. Much has been done to clean up that Victorian image, but the view from Blackstone Edge, for example, still shows a fair number of gaunt factory chimneys puncturing the sky.

This was also the age of the great Victorian philanthropists, and a time of great civic pride – some of the profits from that phenomenal period of industrial growth going to patriotic projects like the monument on Stoodley Pike (Walk 5).

But still the moors remained inviolate, and they inspired some of the finest literary talent ever seen in one family among the strange, introverted Brontës of Haworth. Haworth is a typical South Pennine cobbled mill town, spreading up the hillside from the Worth valley, and now the centre of a burgeoning Brontë industry.

When the Reverend Patrick Brontë and his family moved here in 1820, Haworth was nothing more than a hillside hamlet above the hills and factories of the Worth valley. His talented daughters swiftly fell in love with the area and few writers before or since have captured the spirit of these South Pennine moors better than Charlotte, Emily and Anne Brontë.

Perhaps the finest novel that the sisters produced was Emily's *Wuthering Heights* published under the pseudonym of Ellis Bell in 1847. In her preface to the 1850 edition, her sister Charlotte describes how to Emily 'her native hills were far more to her than a spectacle; they were what she lived in, and by, as much as the wild birds, their tenants, or as the heather, their produce.' The novel's close observation of the moors testifies to Emily's love for them. She was never happy when away from them, sometimes becoming physically ill if separated for too long. Charlotte wrote: 'She found in the bleak solitude many and dear delights; and not the least and best-loved was – liberty.'

That is a sentiment with which many South Pennine ramblers can identify. Perhaps the great escape which this land of hills and mills still provides was best described by Linton Heathcliff in *Wuthering Heights*. He told Cathy that his 'most perfect idea of heaven's happiness' on a hot, still July day was:

> lying from morning till evening on a bank of heath in the middle of the moor, with the bees humming dreamily about among the bloom, and the larks singing high up overhead, and the blue sky and bright sun shining steadily and cloudlessly.

BLACKSTONE · EDGE

Map OS Outdoor Leisure Sheet 21, The South Pennines

Start The White House Inn GR 969179

Length About 2 miles

Time Allow 1 hour

Difficulty Easy moorland walking, but can be exposed and wet in places

TO THE 'ROMAN' ROAD

The beautifully paved and graded roadway which sweeps up from Littleborough, near Rochdale, across the craggy heights of Blackstone Edge before dropping down to Ripponden and Halifax in Yorkshire has long been marked on maps as a 'Roman Road'. Generations of guidebook authors and photographers have perpetuated the myth, some even claiming that the groove down the centre of the paving was worn by the brake-poles of Roman chariots!

The well-engineered roadway could well be on the line of a former Roman road linking the forts at Littleborough and Aldborough. But the present surface most probably only dates from a 1734 Turnpike Act, which gave the authorities powers to 'widen the existing road over the craggy mountain of Blackstone Edge'.

The Blackstone Edge road is twice the width of the normal Pennine 'causey' used by the long lines of packhorse trains which were the juggernauts of the eighteenth century. Its method of construction is similar to many others across the Pennines, and leaves no doubt that it dates from that period as a sort of packhorse dual carriageway. Our walk takes in the best section of the so-called Roman road, and mounts the aptly named gritstone outcrop of Blackstone Edge, which commands fine views down into the industrial mill towns of central Lancashire in the valley below.

The White House Inn is a well-known staging post on the A58 Rochdale–Halifax road, which mounts what the eighteenth-century traveller Celia Fiennes called the 'formidableness' of Blackstone Edge with consummate ease. Park here and carefully cross the busy A58, descending the hill slightly to meet up with the sign for the Pennine Way (south).

The route heads south past a series of quarries the stone from which was used to build the reservoirs of Blackstone Edge, White Holme, Light Hazzles and Warland, northward along the line of the Pennine Way.

The well-used path soon brings you out on to the cotton grass and peat-hagged moor of Blackstone Edge, and you continue to follow the line of the Pennine Way across this barren and blasted heath. Soon you come across another paved causey which leads unerringly up to the ancient Aiggin (pronounced 'Ajjin') Stone, which has fancifully been related to the Roman word *agger* for an earthwork. The fallen stone may have been first named after the Saxon god, Aigle, but no one knows for sure.

From the Aiggin Stone traverse right, across the moor to ascend the craggy crest of Blackstone Edge itself, with its commanding views over the glinting waters of Hollingworth Lake, constructed at the end of the eighteenth century as a feeder lake for the Rochdale Canal, and now a popular country park for the people of Rochdale. The OS trig point perched on top of the rocks (1,550ft/472m) is a fine viewpoint, and the strangely jumbled and wrinkled outcrop a few steps further to the south is known as Robin Hood's Bed.

Retrace your steps to the Aiggin Stone and turn left down the old packhorse route into

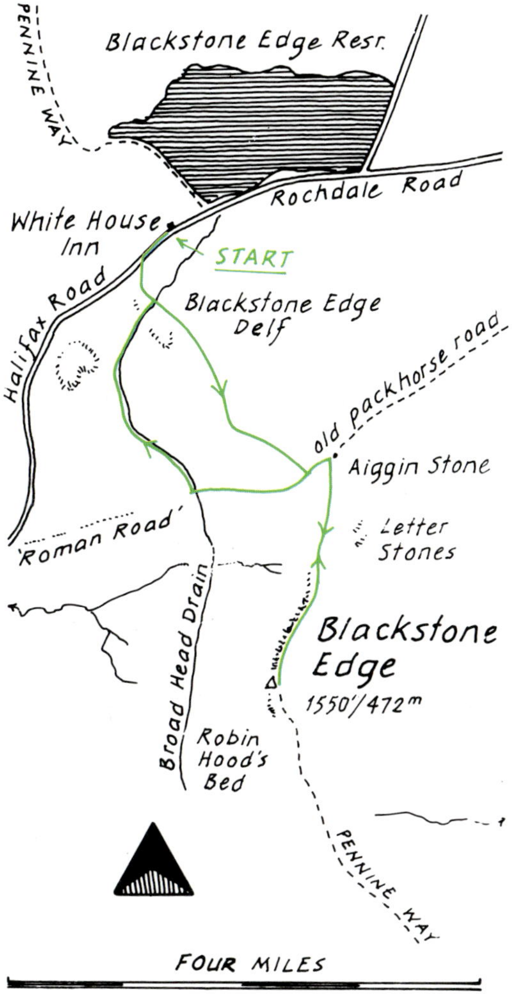

On the Blackstone Edge 'Roman' road, descending towards Littleborough

Lancashire to inspect the 'Roman Road' which is reached just below the crest of the hill. It is an impressive sight. Nearly 18ft (5m) wide, the causeway is made of carefully smoothed and worked gritstone paving slabs, with clear raised kerbs, cut-and-cover drains, and that mysterious grooved section running down the centre. The most likely explanation for this appears to be that it acted as a drain for the frequent downpours of rain on these misty moors. After inspecting this marvel of eighteenth-century road engineering take the Broad Head Drain waterworks road which follows the concrete-lined reservoir-regulating drain contouring across Blackstone Edge Pasture back to the A58 and Blackstone Edge Delf quarry, near the White House Inn.

PENDLE · HILL

Map OS Pathfinder Sheets SD83/93 and SD64/74, Burnley and Clitheroe and Chipping

Start Nick o' Pendle GR 772386

Length About 6 miles

Time Allow about 3 hours

Difficulty Moderate moorland walking, boots essential

WITCHES AND QUAKERS

Although only 1,832ft (557m) high, Pendle Hill dominates the Lancashire cotton towns of Accrington, Burnley, Nelson and Colne every bit as much as the Matterhorn does Zermatt. So much does it impose its presence that for many years it was believed to be one of the highest hills in England.

Pendle's witch-haunted summit is a place of pilgrimage for many Lancashire hillgoers, and it is a place full of history, myth and legend, as well as being one of the finest viewpoints in this part of the Pennines.

Looking south towards Barley and the Ogden Reservoir from just below the summit of Pendle Hill

Most people ascend Pendle by the broad track which runs from the pretty village of Barley up what is known as its 'Big End'. This is the shortest and most direct route, but suffers from the fact that the stupendous view is at your back for most of the climb. We will make the longer but more interesting climb up from the celebrated Nick o' Pendle, the highest point on the minor road between Sabden and Whalley. As we start from about 1,000ft (297m) it gives an easy ascent, but one which can be tricky in mist or bad weather.

Park in one of the parking spaces among the upturned gritstone slabs on the Sabden side of the Nick, and take the broad cart track which leads off through rocky outcrops over Apron-full Hill, where the Devil was supposed to have dropped an apronful of stones.

This stony track leads over Pendleton Moor to the springs at Badger Wells, which feed down to Sabden Brook in the valley to the right. An easy ascent takes you over Black Hill, with increasingly good views behind over the Hodder Valley towards the dark heights of the Forest of Bowland to the north. Now you meet the steep-sided Ogden Clough, winding up from the right. If the weather is clear, you may just be able to spot the top of Pendle peeping over Barley Moor straight ahead.

The track narrows here to a path which winds along the edge of the heathery clough. Gradually, the clough levels out, and you drop down to cross the stream and bear right on an increasingly wet and peaty track over the moor. The going here can be a little sticky and arduous in the best traditions of a Pennine peat moor, but your reward is soon at hand, and you emerge at the bare stony summit of Big End to a magnificent view over the patchwork of fields and farms of Twiston and Rimington Moors.

The village of Barley, clustered protectively around its green, is down to the right, between the Ogden and Black Moss Reservoirs which are surrounded by the dark cloaks of conifer plantations. To the south, the great rounded bulk of Boulsworth is prominent.

Northwest along the summit escarpment just through a gap in a drystone wall is Robin Hood's or Fox's Well. The first name is thought to have nothing to do with the legendary outlaw, but was named after the Celtic deity, Robin Goodfellow. Its other name refers to the founder of the Quaker movement, George Fox, who climbed to this summit in

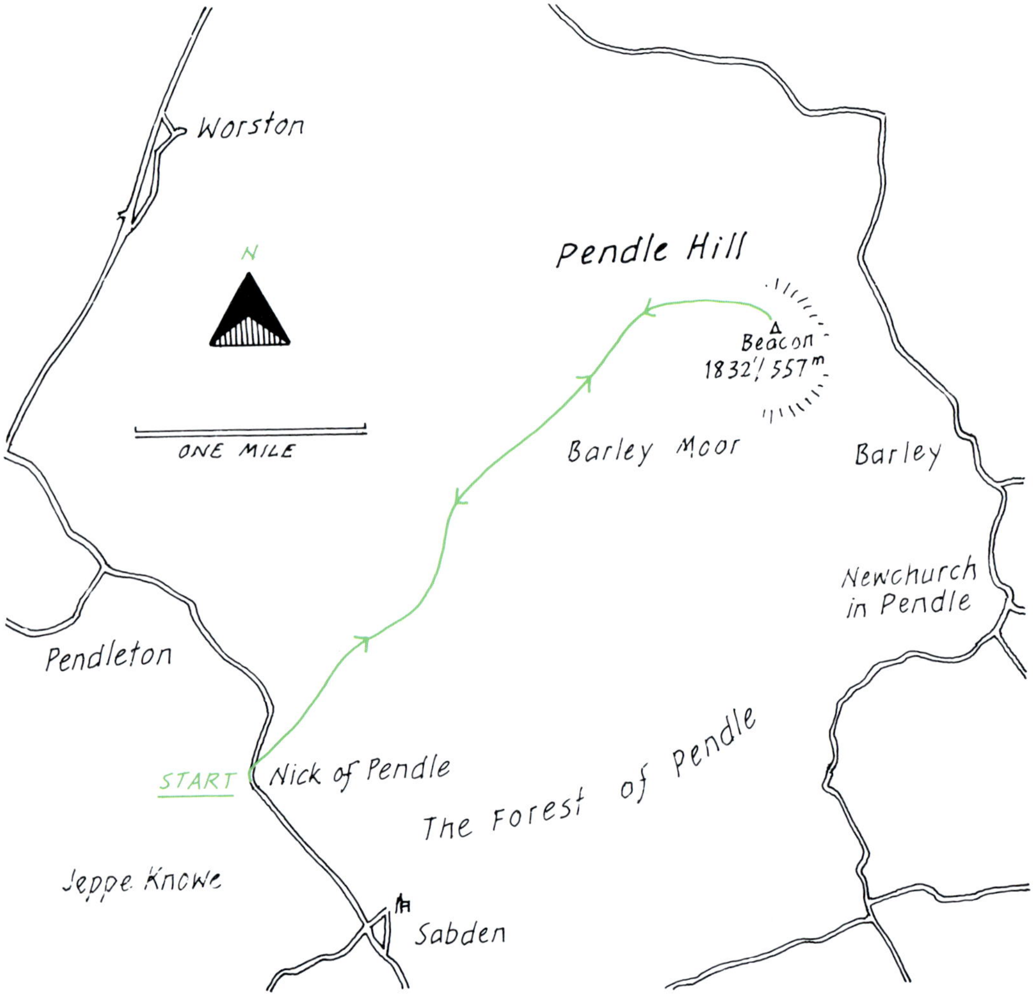
Worston
N
ONE MILE
Pendle Hill
Beacon
1832'/ 557m
Barley Moor
Barley
Newchurch
in Pendle
Pendleton
START
Nick of Pendle
The Forest of Pendle
Jeppe Knowe
Sabden

1652 and drank from its waters. Fox's Well is now a place of pilgrimage for Quakers and others every Good Friday, for it was here that Fox experienced the revelation which was the inspiration for his Society of Friends. He later described how he was 'moved of to sounde ye day of ye Lorde & ye Lorde lett mee see a top of ye hill In what places hee had a great people'.

Another regular 'pilgrimage' to Pendle's windswept summit is made by torch-bearing walkers at midnight every Hallowe'en in the hope of meeting up with Pendle's most famous ghosts: the witches who featured in William Harrison Ainsworth's popular Victorian melodrama, *The Lancashire Witches – A Romance of Pendle Forest* (1854) which was based on the trials of the witches of Pendle in the seventeenth century.

Ainsworth's description of the view from Pendle's Big End was suitably melodramatic: 'Dreary was the prospect on all sides. Black moor, bleak fell, straggling forest, intersected with sullen streams as black as ink, with here and there a small tarn, or moss-pool, with waters of the same hue ...' Just the place, you might think, for stories of witchcraft and black magic, and this part of Lancashire was a hotbed of the Old Religion at the time. Old Mother Demdike, Old Chattox and Alice Nutter were among nine women from the area who were tried and executed at Lancaster Castle in 1612, on charges of communing with the Devil, and committing sixteen murders (Old Mother Demdike, an eighty-year-old half-blind beggar, actually escaped the gallows by dying in gaol before her sentence was passed).

Retrace your steps, taking care in mist to head due west off the summit, back down Ogden Clough. Leave the clough where it starts to bend to the left and rejoin the broad cart track which leads unerringly down to the Nick o' Pendle and your starting point.

The eastern end of Pendle Hill from Padiham Heights across the valley of Sabden Brook

The author crosses Pendleton Moor on the ascent of Pendle Hill from the west, with Ribblesdale in the background

HAWORTH · MOORS

Map OS Outdoor Leisure Sheet 21, The South Pennines

Start Haworth GR 029372

Length About 6 miles

Time Allow 4 hours

Difficulty Some boggy moorland tracks, boots recommended

THE BRONTË TRAIL

The extraordinary flowering of talent which emerged from the grim parsonage in the hillside town above the Worth valley of West Yorkshire is unique in British literature; and anyone who reads the powerful novels of Charlotte, Emily and Anne Brontë cannot fail to see where their inspiration arose. The wild and forbidding moors which surrounded their home were to be a constant backdrop to their writing. Few areas are so closely associated with the literature they inspired.

Top Withins – the model for 'Wuthering Heights'?

We will follow the Brontë Trail from the soot-blackened walls of their parsonage home in Haworth. Walk up the cobbled lane which leads up past the parsonage and take the paved path to Haworth Moor, across the fields to West Lane. Take the left fork after about 50 yards to meet the road which leads to the Penistone Hill Country Park, the childhood playground of Cathy and Heathcliff described in Emily's classic *Wuthering Heights*. The trig point on the summit provides a good viewpoint to the hilltop village of Stanbury, across the waters of the Lower Laithe Reservoir.

Cross Moor Side Lane and follow the signs to the Brontë Waterfalls, passing over a cattle-grid and into a derelict stone-walled lane. You pass several sadly abandoned farmhouses, many of which carry the name 'intake', showing that they were won from the moor in relatively recent times.

The path, which can be boggy in places, passes high above the tree-fringed shores of the Lower Laithe Reservoir before dropping down into the confines of South Dean Beck, and the famous clapper bridge (inevitably known as the Brontë Bridge) restored with the help of an RAF helicopter. The Brontë Falls, known to the sisters as 'the Meeting of the Waters', tumble down from Harbour Hole to the left. Across the valley from this popular picnic place is the windowless face of Virginia Farm.

Cross the bridge and follow the right bank of the South Dean Beck upstream, along the slopes of Sandy Hill, past a series of deserted circular sheepfolds. By now, the dark, truncated shape of Top Withins has appeared on the skyline ahead, and you must cross the beck again, and climb up past two more deserted farms, also called Withins (the name probably means wet land where willows once grew). Eventually you join the Pennine Way coming in from the right, and the way is now clear to the sadly ruined farmhouse of Top Withins, said to be the inspiration for Emily's *Wuthering Heights*. The site is superbly situated and so accurately described by the northern adjective 'wuthering', which means cold and windy.

Follow the Pennine Way back down to its junction with the South Dean Beck, and then east over Withins Slack and Stanbury Moor. Passing over Flaight Hill, you reach Upper Heights Farm, where you leave the Way and turn left to descend to Far Slack Farm and Lower Slack, on the banks of the Ponden Reservoir. On a promontory to the left stands Ponden Hall, thought to be the model of Thrushcross Grange from *Wuthering Heights*.

Turn right and walk along the banks of the reservoir to the dam wall where the path climbs up past Rush Isles to join the Stanbury road. Passing through this one-street, ridge-top village, turn sharp right to take the minor road which runs down and across the wall of the Lower Laithe dam. Bear left at the end of the dam and walk up the track with the water treatment works in the valley below to the left. This track joins the Haworth road near to the cemetery and brings you back into the village.

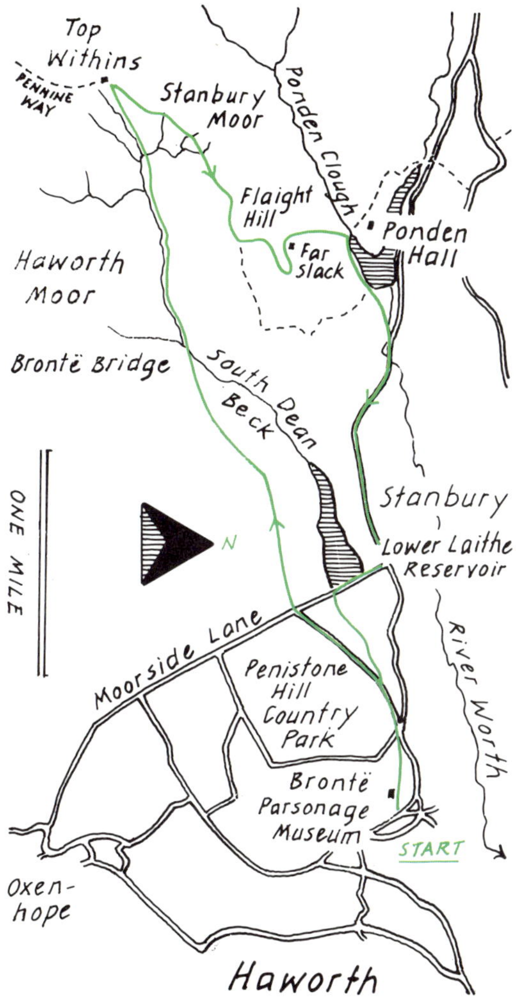

WINTER · HILL · AND · RIVINGTON · PIKE

Map OS Pathfinder Sheet SD 61/71, Bolton (North)

Start Rivington Hall Barn car park GR 633145

Length About 8 miles

Time Allow 3½–4 hours

Difficulty Easy ascents, but can be very wet and muddy. Boots recommended

BEFORE THE MAST

The television mast on Winter Hill and the tower on Rivington Pike are well-known landmarks on two of the very finest viewpoints on the western edge of the Pennines.

Rivington Pike (1,198ft/365m) is part of Lord Leverhulme's Rivington estate, and the Tower, built in 1733 as a shooting lodge on the site of an ancient beacon, is a Grade II listed building. The terraced gardens and grounds are well served by a visitor centre at the Great House Barn near Rivington Reservoir.

Winter Hill, at 1,498ft (456m) is the highest point of the West Pennine Moors, and is crowned by the 1,000ft (305m) tubular television mast. The other, earlier masts on Winter Hill are used by the police and British Telecom.

This walk takes in both of these prominent summits which require very little effort in return for their wonderful views. These extend from Rivington as far as the Clwydian and Carneddau Hills of Wales looking south, Blackpool Tower and Morecambe Bay to the west, and the Lakeland mountains to the north.

Park at Rivington Hall Barn on the Rivington estate north of Horwich and take the track which leads off to the right, behind the main buildings. Passing a stone cottage, go left up a stony lane leading into the woods. After about 200 yards, the path, which is signposted to the Terraced Gardens, goes through a gate into an open field with woodlands clothing the steep hillside ahead. The prominent dovecote on the skyline is your next destination.

Entering the woodland, ascend every staircase you encounter, turning to the left at every fork. The rustic staircases become grander as they ascend through the mixed ornamental woodland, eventually leading over an arch to

The Tower on Rivington Pike was erected in 1733, originally for use as a shooting lodge

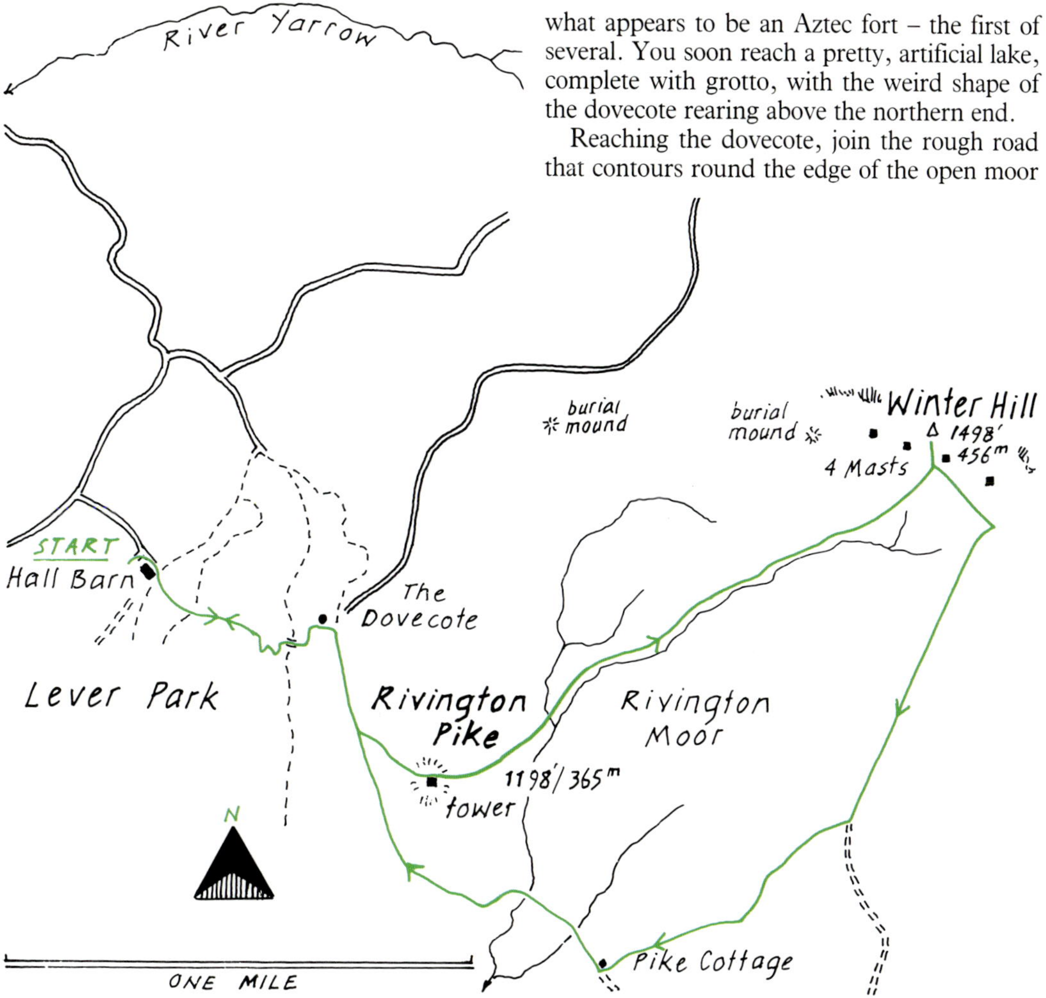

what appears to be an Aztec fort – the first of several. You soon reach a pretty, artificial lake, complete with grotto, with the weird shape of the dovecote rearing above the northern end.

Reaching the dovecote, join the rough road that contours round the edge of the open moor to the squat, castellated tower ½ mile to the southeast on the summit of Rivington Pike. If you are lucky enough to reach the tower in the early evening, you could be rewarded with some of the most wonderful sunset views in the north, extending south to the prow of the Great Orme in Wales, sixty miles away.

Our way heads northeast along a broad, usually muddy track heading straight for the TV mast on Winter Hill, about three-quarters of an hour away. When you reach a road made of railway sleepers, cross it and continue on to a metalled road. Follow this past the television transmission station and the Scotsman's Stump, a memorial to James Henderson, who was apparently the victim of a shooting accident on Rivington Moor in 1803. Go on past the end of the road to the cairn which marks the summit, and another fine viewpoint. There is a small burial mound about ¼ mile west of the cairn.

The easiest and quickest way back to Rivington Hall Barn from here is to retrace your steps to the TV station and follow the metalled road back down towards Horwich. When it starts to bend to the left, just before a large stone cairn ahead, a broad but rather faint track leads off to the right across Twa Lads Moor, named after a now disappeared twin cairn dating from the Bronze Age, and one of many prehistoric sites which have been identified on these hills. Follow this track across the moor down to Pike Cottage, where you turn right to return to Rivington Hall Barn.

STOODLEY · PIKE

Map OS Outdoor Leisure Sheet 21, The South Pennines

Start Hebden Bridge GR 992272

Length About 10 miles

Time About 5 hours

Difficulty Some moorland walking, boots and waterproofs recommended

A NAPOLEONIC LANDMARK

The most prominent landmark in the whole of Calderdale and arguably the South Pennines is the blunt gritstone needle of Stoodley Pike, perched on the edge of the moors above Todmorden and Hebden Bridge. For Pennine Wayfarers, it is a tantalising and constant goal for many a weary mile from the Blackstone Edge escarpment as they skirt the string of reservoirs on Light Hazzles Edge.

The obelisk, replacing a former tower or pike, has had a somewhat chequered history.

On the Rochdale Canal at Hebden Bridge – a landscape of mills and hills

The original was started in 1814 to commemorate the abdication of Napoleon and the Peace of Ghent, but when Napoleon escaped from Elba in 1815, work had to be postponed until after the conclusive Battle of Waterloo later that year. In 1854 the monument collapsed, and the present massive soot-blackened gritstone structure, which stands about 125ft (38m) high, was built two years later.

We approach this dominating landmark from the charming former cotton town of Hebden Bridge. This friendly settlement, squeezed into the narrow confines of the Calder Valley, is now enjoying something of a revival in its fortunes, as young and upwardly mobile incomers move in to the 'highly desirable' double-decker terraces on the hillsides.

Leave Hebden Bridge by Holme Street, turning left at the end of the street to cross the Rochdale Canal (one of the earliest trans-Pennine canals, opened in 1804) and turn right on to the towpath. Crossing the Black Pit Aqueduct over the River Calder, turn immediately left up a flight of steps and left again when you reach the road. Cross the railway bridge and continue past an old warehouse for about 100 yards to a green lane which leads off to the right.

Follow this until it joins a farm road, and at a sharp left-hand bend, cross the stile which leads off right down through Horsefold Wood to join a metalled road which leads up left towards the old hand-loom weaving hamlet of Horsefold. Keep straight on here along a wide grassy lane which brings you to the edge of Beaumount Clough.

Follow the path alongside the trees until it drops down to a bridge, which you cross and head up to the stile which brings you on to the stone-walled and green Pinnacle Lane. Turn right and follow the lane until it reaches the open fields. Continue on, keeping the drystone wall to your left until you reach a stile leading into another walled lane.

Turn left, and after about 300 yards, go through a gate on the right and on to another green lane which you follow towards Swillington Farm, where the lane ends. Here you join the well-trodden highway of the Pennine Way on the right which crosses the lane and climbs steadily up the moor to reach the Stoodley Pike monument. This is a good place to stop for lunch and admire the wonderful view. Behind you Hebden Bridge is embowered by trees.

Continue on the Pennine Way along the edge of the moor, which drops steeply down towards

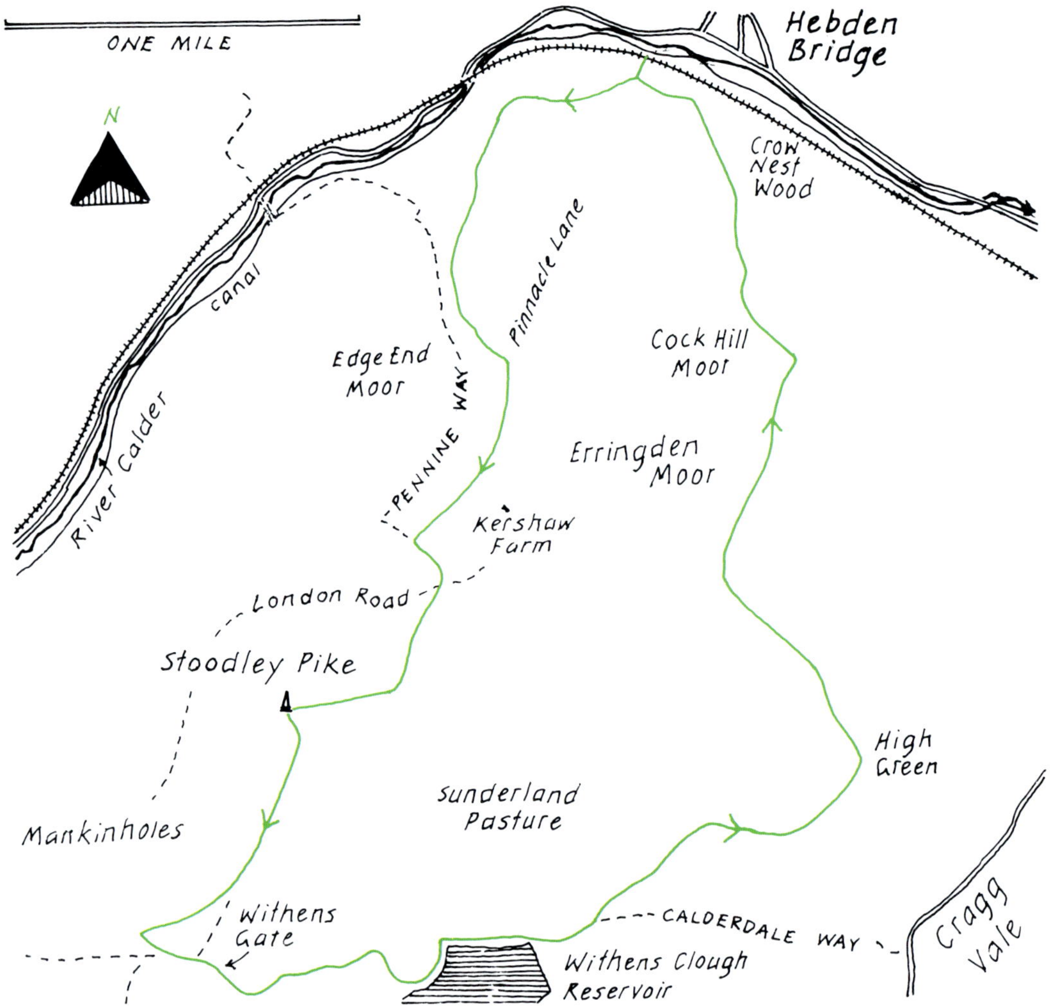

Todmorden off to the west. After a mile or so you reach the large standing stone known as the Te Deum Stone – the highest point of the packhorse route between Cragg Vale and Mankinholes. It is said to have acquired its name from the fact that coffins were rested here on their way to burial at Mankinholes.

Turn left here and follow the causey track, now known as the Calderdale Way, down to the Withens Clough (or Gate) Reservoir. Take the higher Calderdale Way alternative which contours round on a causeway track giving fine views across the reservoir and descends to the car park under the dam wall.

From the car park, a walled lane climbs easily up Law Hill to the left, forking right at the top. This track descends gently to the left past Hill Top Farm, the attractively named Sandy Pickle Farm and Keelham. The track, wet in places, continues across Bell House Moor around the head of Spring Wood and then down across the expanse of Erringden Moor. Enter a green lane below Cock Hill Moor and follow this steep path down towards Old Chamber, passing through a beautiful arched tunnel which takes the track to the house.

Entering Crow Nest Wood, the track zigzags to the bottom, where a left fork brings you back to the road and the green lane to Hebden Bridge.

The solid gritstone exclamation mark of Stoodley Pike, on the moors above Hebden Bridge

ILKLEY · MOOR

Map OS Pathfinder SE 04/14, Keithley and Ilkley

Start Ilkley GR 116477

Length About 3 miles, but can be extended

Time Allow 2½–3 hours

Difficulty Moorland which can be muddy in places, boots recommended

ON ILKLEY MOOR BAHT 'AT

The so-called 'Yorkshire National Anthem' is in fact nothing more than a Victorian music-hall song, written by a songwriter from Lincolnshire to make fun of the local accent! But no visit to the South Pennines would be complete without a visit to Yorkshire's most famous moor, an ever-popular playground for the citizens of Leeds and Bradford.

What is less well known perhaps is that Ilkley Moor, which overlooks the lower reaches of Wharfedale, contains one of the richest collections of prehistoric art in the Pennines. The moor is peppered with examples of the mysterious cup-and-ring marked stones, including one which shows a Sanskrit symbol only found elsewhere in Europe in Sweden and Greece.

On Ilkley Moor looking north-west into the jaws of Wharfedale, with Beamsley Beacon on the right

A full day is needed to investigate the prehistoric landscape of Ilkley Moor thoroughly, with its numerous tumuli, ancient dykes and dramatic natural rock formations. Add to that the fact that the entire moor is common land with free access and enjoys splendid views over the Wharfe and Aire valleys, and you begin to understand the reasons for Ilkley's perennial popularity.

Our walk starts in the busy little township of Ilkley, whose history goes back as far as the Iron Age. The Romans founded their township of Olicana here to guard an important ford over the Wharfe on their road between Ribchester and Tadcaster. Ilkley later enjoyed a brief spell as a health spa after the discovery of mineral springs on the moor in the eighteenth century.

From the central car park, cross to Brook Street and at the T-junction at the top of the road enter Wells Parade, opposite the central gardens. Follow the path left of the stream which runs through the park, crossing the stream by the footbridge and leaving the park by the gate in the top right corner. Cross the road and walk up the unmetalled Linnburn Mews and through the gateway at the end, passing the rear entrance to the campus of the Bradford and Ilkley Community College.

Through another gate, take the path along the right bank of the stream, and at the road in front of the college keep straight ahead, turning left at the No Through Road sign and on to the open moor.

Take the grassy path right, over a bridge which leads to the track on the edge of the moor. The houses of Ilkley and the reservoirs are spread out below. Follow this panoramic walk west to the dip where the track crosses Heber's Ghyll and briefly enters the ornamental woodlands, paths and bridges created by the Heber family of Hollin Hall in the valley below.

Follow the path along the top edge of the wood past a stone shelter and through a gate back on to the moor. Take the path to the left of the stile bearing right through the heather to rejoin the main path again, heading directly to the Swastika Stone. The original stone is enclosed behind a crude metal fence to keep it safe from vandals, but an exact replica of the

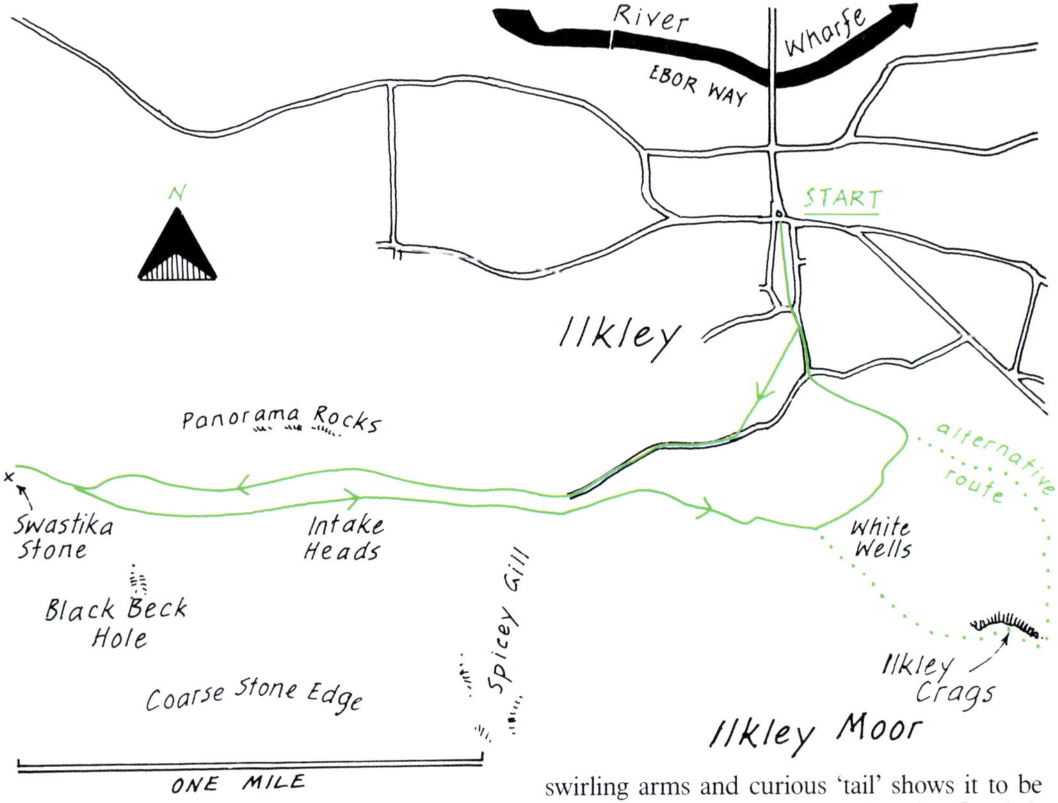

The replica Swastika Stone on Ilkley Moor: could it be a representation of a Sanskrit 'fylfot'?

swirling arms and curious 'tail' shows it to be identical to the ancient *fylfot*, the Sanskrit symbol for eternal life, later tilted and adopted by Hitler's Nazis.

There are fine views from here northwest into the heart of Wharfedale, with heather-clad Beamsley Beacon guarding the entrance to the right and Simon's Seat and Embsay Moor beyond. You now have the option either to extend the walk along the broad track which leads west along the edge of the moor to Windgate Nick, about 1½ miles away following the line of Rombald's Way, or to turn back along the higher level path through the heather, across two wooden footbridges to White Wells and the Tarns.

If you take the latter course, look out for the large rowan tree which marks a hollow leading down to the beautifully restored small square bath-house built in the 1760s by Squire Middleton over Ilkley Moor's most famous mineral spring. Patients were brought up here by donkey from the White Wells Hydropathic Hotel (now the Community College we passed earlier) to be immersed in the icy moorland spring. The Tarn down to the right was landscaped during Victorian times and presents a charming, if artificial, picture.

You can extend the walk from here by going up the steps via Backstone Beck to Rocky Valley and the famous landmarks of the Cow and Calf Rocks on the edge of Ilkley Crags. The Calf is the huge detached block of gritstone which has broken away from the edge. Apparently there was once also a Bull Stone, but this was quarried away by local building entrepreneurs. Several well-worn tracks lead away from the rocks or White Wells back down into Ilkley town centre.

Victorian graffiti on the crest of Cow Rock, Ilkley Crags

HARDCASTLE · CRAGS

Map OS Outdoor Leisure Sheet 21, The South Pennines

Start Hardcastle Crags car park GR 988292

Length About 5½ miles

Time 2½–3 hours

Difficulty Engineered woodland tracks, easy going

CALDERDALE'S PLAYGROUND

Hardcastle Crags are a beautiful reminder of what the rocky cloughs of the South Pennines once were. But even here, there are signs of previous industry in the romantic ruins of Gibson Mill, an early nineteenth-century water-powered cotton mill.

The area is now in the safe hands of the National Trust, and is a popular weekend retreat for the people of Calderdale. The name is a little misleading because it nowadays commonly refers to the whole well-wooded length of Hebden Dale, not just the area of the crags themselves, which are north of Gibson Mill. The rocky outcrops of the crags are well hidden by the abundant woods of beech, birch, oak and Scots pine, many of which were planted during the nineteenth century by the former landowner, Lord Savile.

The Crags are linked to the neighbouring valley of Crimsworth Dean, also partly owned by the National Trust, by the ancient Limers' Gate packhorse track across Shackleton Moor, making a superb circular walk, rich in beauty, history and wildlife.

Start from the National Trust car park at the entrance to the Hardcastle Crags estate, near the junction of Crimsworth Dean Beck with Hebden Water. From the entrance, turn right down to the bridge, climbing the stile and following the pleasant riverside path through the trees. This is also an NT nature trail, and leads easily on for about 1½ miles until you reach Gibson Mill, founded by Abraham Gibson in 1800.

Leaving the mill, continue up the broad track through the woods past the crags below on the left. They are best seen from the valley road near Slack. At a major fork in the track,

Gibson Mill, an early nineteenth-century water-powered cotton mill below Hardcastle Crags

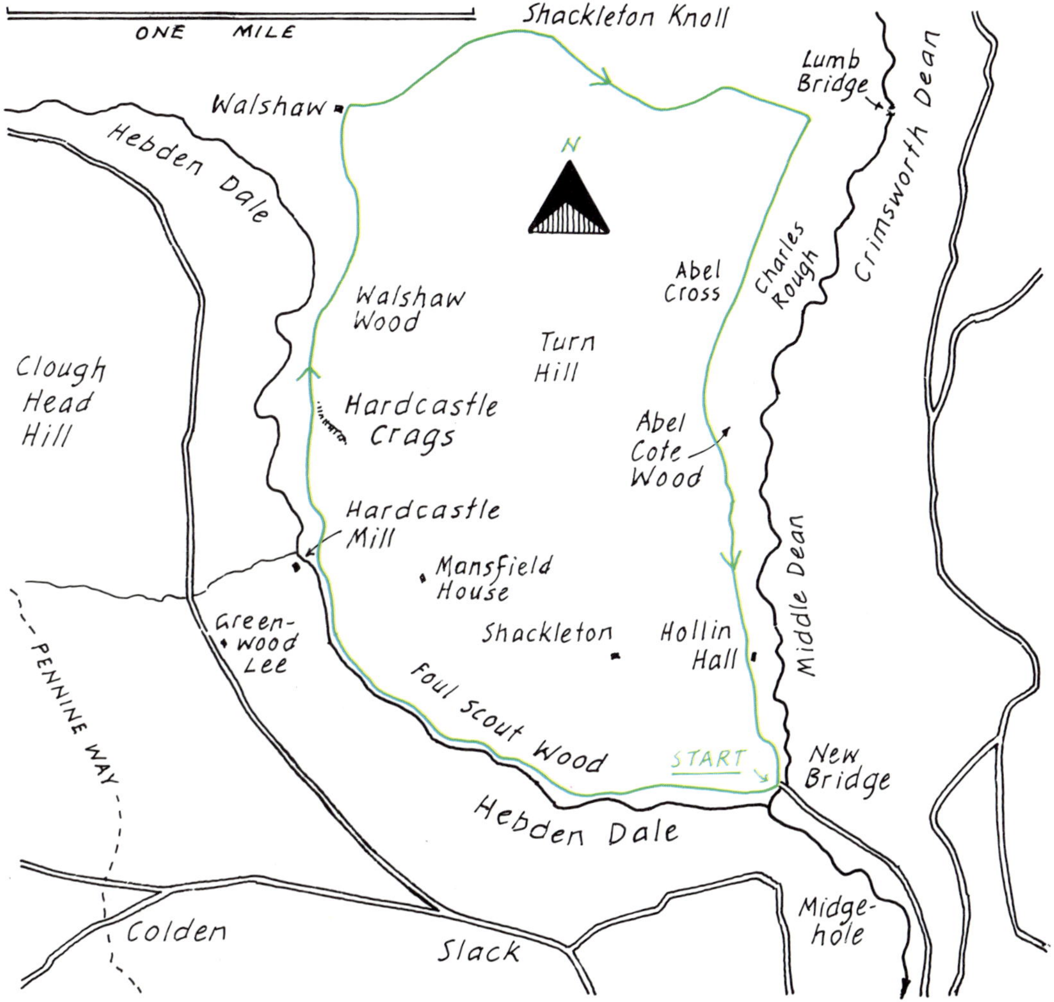

bear right following the main track uphill and where it joins another, go left.

Just before reaching the hamlet of Walshaw, take the gate, sharply right, to follow the signpost to Crimsworth Dean. This path bears right across a field and follows the wall uphill. Pass through this wall via a gate, over the moorland ridge and turn right to follow the enclosed track over the moor. This is Limers' Gate, part of an ancient route between Lancashire and Yorkshire, which is thought to have got its name from the fact that lime was one of the major items carried by the packhorses and used to sweeten the acid Pennine pastures.

At the T-junction, turn right on to the main track which runs along the top of Crimsworth Dean. A worthwhile diversion is to take a left turn at the junction of the tracks for the steep descent past the ruined farmhouse of Sunny Bank to inspect Lumb Bridge, a near-perfect example of a packhorse bridge, idyllically sited near a fine waterfall in Crimsworth Dean Beck.

Back on the main route, the track passes close to the ancient boundary marker of Abel Cross before entering Abel Cote Wood and descending gradually to the valley bottom and the car park. There are fine views on the way, with Heptonstall church prominent on the right, and the Stoodley Pike monument to its left.

FOREST · OF · BOWLAND

Map OS Landranger Sheet 103, Blackburn and Burnley

Start Dunsop Bridge GR 659501

Length 12 miles

Time Allow 5–6 hours

Difficulty Easy riverside tracks followed by some rough pasture and farmland. Boots recommended

WHERE KINGS HUNTED

Effectively bypassed by the M6 motorway, the Forest of Bowland remains a relatively quiet and unvisited corner of Lancashire. This westernmost extension of the Pennines, sandwiched between Ribblesdale and the valley of the Lune, has some longstanding problems of access but nevertheless offers some fine walking.

Originally part of a royal hunting forest used by medieval kings, Bowland gets its name not from bows and arrows, as some of the older signposts in the area suggest, but from 'the land by the bow', probably referring to the bend in either the River Hodder or the River Ribble, which both wind around this upstanding boss of millstone grit.

Our walk starts from the heart of the ancient forest at the hamlet of Dunsop Bridge, where the Hodder joins the Langden Beck at the eastern end of the famous pass known as the Trough of Bowland. Take the private road which leads north from the war memorial up the valley of the River Dunsop between the conifer-clad slopes of Staple Oak Fell to the left and Beatrix Fell to the right. After about two miles, cross the bridge over the Brennand River, which comes in from the left and go up the track which ascends Middle Knoll ahead.

Where the track forks right follow this to contour around Middle Knoll, turning right at Whitendale Farm. Take the waymarked rough track which climbs Dunsop Fell. At the top there are fine views across Croasdale Fell to White Hill and Wolfhole Crag, looking north into the wild interior of the Forest of Bowland.

From the fell-top fence, go through the small gate in the wall and turn right, around the head of the small clough which appears on your left.

Autumn among the plantations of Staple Oak Fell, Dunsop Valley, Forest of Bowland

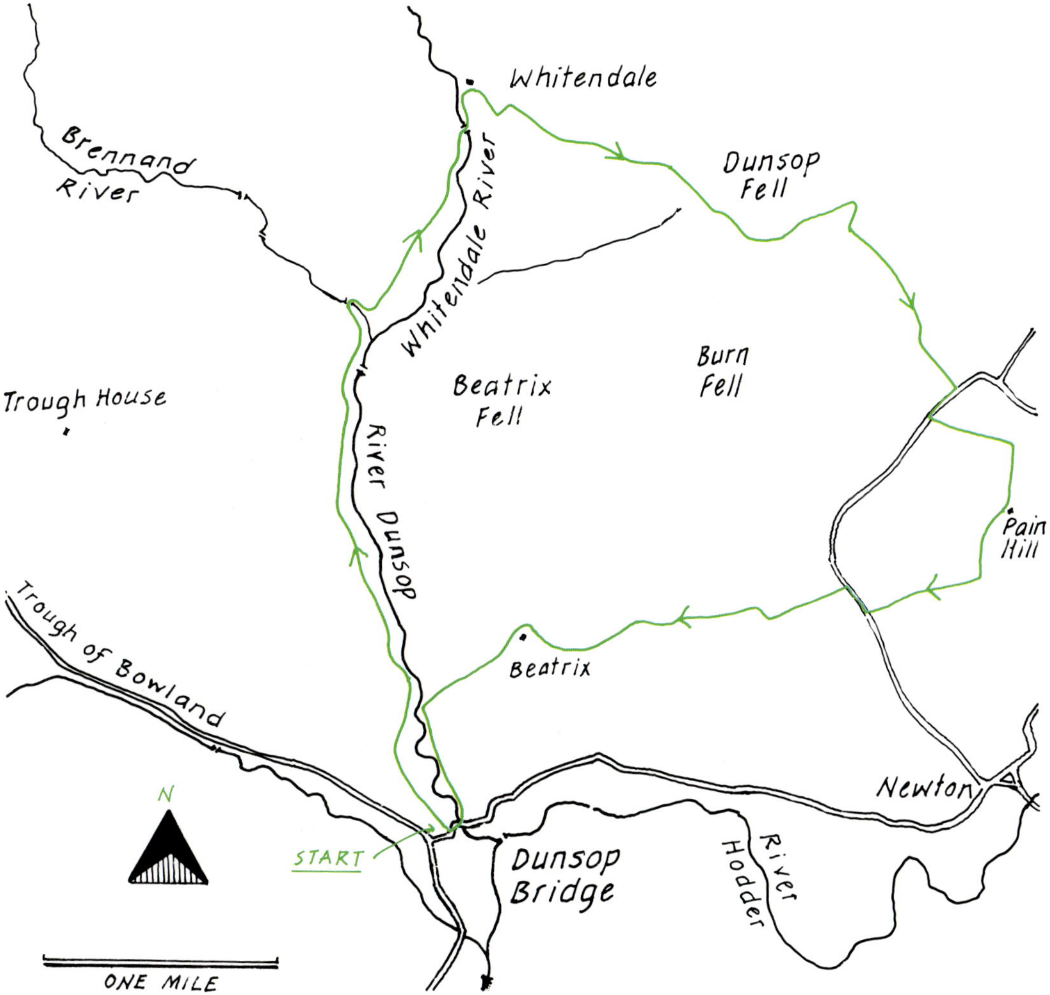

Descend on the right side of this valley, turning right near the bottom and through the second of two gates in the wall on the left.

Head for Burn Side Farm and follow the access road to the farm down to the road near Gold Hill. Turn right here and then left at Laythams, towards Parrock Head Farm. From Parrock Head go over the footbridge, hidden in a dip, to Pain Hill Farm.

Over a wall-stile on the right of the farm buildings, turn right following the wall leading left. Climb the next field and ignore the first stile, heading towards a tree-lined pond. Make for a kink in the wall ahead which reveals another stile followed by two more as you cross the fields to rejoin the road, to the left of a pond.

Turn right and after about 250 yards turn left on to Bull Lane, a walled farm track, which you follow until it peters out into a path which descends to Rough Syke Barn.

Descend to the bridge over the stream passing over a ford through a gate on the left. Climbing up to Back of Hill Barn, continue ahead to meet a track bearing right to Beatrix and an abandoned farmhouse. The conical hill in the valley of the Hodder below is known as Knot or the Sugar Loaf.

Leave the track where the fence on the right ends, keeping parallel with the overhead lines on your right over the hill and down to the stile. Descend from here to the River Dunsop, turning left through a farmyard to return to the village of Dunsop Bridge near the Post Office.

4

THE · YORKSHIRE · DALES

THE · STRIDING · DALES

The late Dr Arthur Raistrick (1897–1991), geologist, historian, conservationist and rambler, was perhaps the greatest dalesman of his time. He personified the character of the Norsemen who settled the upper parts of the dales in the ninth to eleventh centuries, with his sharp features, long legs and no-nonsense manner.

Like those Dark Age Viking invaders, he was also a great thinker. He once said that the Norsemen who settled at the head of the dales 'had nothing to do on the fells but to look after their sheep and think, and they have produced many thinkers.' The area has bred many eminent physicians, mathematicians and scientists, Raistrick among them.

He was an expert on dialect and discovered that the ancient, but still used, Norwegian 'Oldsmol' dialect – probably spoken by those Scandinavian settlers of a thousand years ago – bears a remarkable resemblance to that of West Yorkshire.

The modern rambler listening to dalespeople or looking at the modern map of the Dales will find many of those Old Norse words still in use today: gill or beck (stream); fell (hillside); clint (bare rock); foss (waterfall); seat (mountain pasture); and thwaite (clearing), are common examples.

The author on The Nab, the north-western edge of Wild Boar Fell, looking down on wildest Mallerstang

The Angles and Danes settled lower down the dales, leaving us names of their settlements ending in -by, -thorp or -ley, and a glance at the map shows that generally, these are to the east of the hills, where the dales broaden out into the more heavily wooded, millstone grit and sandstone valleys. The string of 'ley' villages (the suffix means a cleared space in woodland) is particularly noticeable as you travel up Wharfedale on the A65 from Leeds or on the train to Skipton – Armley, Headingley, Guiseley, Burley, Shipley, Bingley, Keighley and Ilkley.

The Norse ancestors of Arthur Raistrick felt most at home at the bleak heads of the dales, where scars of pearly-white limestone break through the surface of the fells, exposing the bare bones of the landscape. This was much more like their Scandinavian homeland and suited their pastoral way of life.

The Yorkshire Dales has perhaps the finest glacio-karst scenery in Britain (a limestone landscape which has been shaped and polished by glaciation). Its limestone pavements, coves and caves, such as Malham, Gordale, Ingleborough and White Scar, are justly famous. Limestone creates landscapes both above and below ground: the action of slightly acidic rainwater slowly broadens the cracks and crevices to create the clints and grikes of the limestone pavements, while the thunderous power of meltwater rivers from receding Ice Age glaciers was responsible for the impressive dry valleys, gorges and caves, like Malham, Kingsdale and Trow Gill; Gaping Gill, Ingleborough Cave and Alum Pot.

The regular sequence of the so-called Yoredale series of rocks, which takes its name from the old name for Wensleydale, gives the characteristic stepped shape of many of the daleshead hills, such as Ingleborough, Pen-y-Ghent and Addlebrough. This shale/sandstone/limestone rhythm is repeated over a dozen times in some places; the more resistant millstone grit 'caps' of such hills providing the noble mountain profiles.

The Howgill Fells in the northwest corner of the Yorkshire Dales National Park, are completely different. Wainwright described these

Limestone clints and grikes at Bar Pot on the southern slopes of Ingleborough

smoothly contoured Silurian hills beautifully, as looking at a distance 'like velvet curtains in sunlight, like silken drapes at sunset'. (He also later described them much more prosaically as being 'like a huddle of squatting elephants'.)

Geologically speaking, the Howgills are part of the Lake District hills beyond the M6. The motorway bursts through the Lune Gorge giving the traveller one of the finest views of British hills anywhere on the network. That the southern half of the Howgills came to be included in the Dales National Park, established in 1954 as the third largest at 683sq miles (1,769sq km), is a quirk of bureaucracy, as is the fact that the equally beautiful northern reaches of the Howgills, the wild Mallerstang valley south of Kirkby Stephen, and the more intimate delights of Nidderdale in the southeast were excluded. Such matters need not trouble us, however, and I include walks in all these areas in this book.

The Dales are pre-eminently walkers' country, and as Halliwell Sutcliffe explained in *The Striding Dales* (1929) 'There is only one road to knowledge of the Dales and Dalesfolk – lifelong intimacy with the rugged scarps, the hidden glens, the homesteads, big and little, perched on the mountains' feet or gathered into grey, comely villages.'

Every dale is different in a subtle, engaging way, and each has its own special attraction. From the north, the rivers running east to the North Sea via the Humber have carved out Swaledale, Wensleydale, Nidderdale, Wharfedale and Malhamdale. On the opposite side of this watershed Lunedale, Garsdale, Dentdale and Ribblesdale run south and west to empty their waters into the Irish Sea.

Swaledale, my own favourite, is the most northern of the Yorkshire Dales. It is the most remote, the wildest and the least touched by human influence, although industry *has* been felt here, as is witnessed by the extensive lead-mining remains around Gunnerside Gill and Swinner Gill (Walk 6). Swaledale is an entity in itself, cut off by unbroken ranges of satisfying hills and occupied in the valley bottom by a string of some of the prettiest villages in the Pennines. With feudal Richmond guarding the eastern entrance, Grinton, Reeth, Gunnerside, Muker, Thwaite and Keld punctuate the dale beautifully on the way to the wild, western expanses of the Buttertubs Pass and Birkdale Common.

Wensleydale could hardly be more different from its northern neighbour. This broad, green dale certainly has its scenic attractions, especially its waterfalls – such as the splendid terraced series of the Aysgarth Falls and the impressive 100ft/30m single drop of Hardraw Force – and Semerwater, the only large natural lake in the Dales. Its villages, like Middleham, West Burton, Askrigg and Bainbridge, and the market town of Hawes, are just as charming as those of its sterner neighbour.

Beyond Hawes, Wensleydale climbs into gritstone country between Great Shunner Fell and the northern end of Great Knoutberry to the summit at Garsdale Head, the highest station on the Settle–Carlisle railway line. But the abiding image of Wensleydale is of sleek, fat, black-and-white Friesian cows grazing in flower-decked meadows guarded by Dales barns, some of which have now been converted to bunkhouses for tourists.

Semerwater is a Dales peculiarity, a glacial lake which has survived, with a legend which may recall the demise of a former Bronze Age community which existed there long before the Iron Age settlers made their home on nearby flat-topped Addlebrough. The Christianised version of the story relates how an angel was refused shelter anywhere save at a shepherd's hut higher up the dale. Next morning, the celestial visitor chanted the incantation still remembered by children in the dale:

Semerwater rise; Semerwater sink:
And swallow all the town,
save this li'le house
Where they gave me meat and drink.

Wharfedale, which includes thirty miles of the Dales Way long-distance path, is perhaps the most populous of the Yorkshire Dales, with tourist attractions like the wooded Bolton Abbey estate, Barden Tower and Grassington dominating its lower reaches. The upper part of the dale beyond Grassington is a limestone lover's delight, with impressive features such as the National Nature Reserve of Grass Wood; Kilnsey Crag, gazing down on the dale like a hooded monk; the former eagle-haunted side-dale of Littondale; and the monastic highway of Mastiles Lane, linking Kilnsey Grange with Malhamdale across the sheep-dotted curlew-

Early morning mist across Malham village and Airedale, from the lip of Malham Cove

KINGSDALE

Map Outdoor Leisure Sheet 2, Yorkshire Dales (Whernside)

Start Twistleton Lane end GR 692760

Length About 6 miles

Time Allow 3 hours

Difficulty Mostly easy tracks, but some limestone pavements and scars to be negotiated, and a final 2 mile road walk

THE VALLEY OF THE VIKINGS

The Valley of the Vikings is not marked on any map, but that indefatigable fellwanderer Alfred Wainwright claimed that the name was used to refer to Kingsdale, north of Ingleton. He wrote in his *Walks in Limestone Country* (1970) that this strange, ruler-straight valley between limestone scars on the southwestern flanks of Whernside was the former home of Vikings, who left an abiding legacy of placenames.

Names like Braida Garth, Yordas Cave and Keld Head Scar have an unmistakably Norse ring, and there can be no doubt that Norse people were among the first to settle permanently in this secluded valley, but the same is true of many other Yorkshire dales.

Kingsdale, however, is also a geological classic: three miles of flat-bottomed green pastures held between straight scars of limestone and terminated by a moraine of glacial drift which must once have held back the waters of a meltwater lake. Add to that an impressive line of open potholes along its western flank, including a forgotten former show cave, and you have more than enough reasons for a thorough exploration.

Our walk starts from the southern end of Kingsdale, where there is parking for a few cars as Twistleton Lane leaves the Thornton-in-Lonsdale to Dent road. A ladder stile leads off to the left across the ankle-twisting escarpments of Low Plain and Keld Head Scar, passing an old limekiln and the huge detached cube of the Cheese Press Stone. This is a 9ft (3m) high limestone erratic left by a retreating glacier and is thought to weigh about 15 tons.

Follow a sketchy path which leads on left of a wall to reach the Turbary Road, a beautiful level track which follows a natural limestone shelf for a couple of miles along the daleside. It gets its name from the ancient commoners' right to collect turfs of peat for fuel in the winter from the Turbary Pasture beneath Gragareth's summit and directly above Yordas Cave.

It also follows the line of the geological divide between the shales of Gragareth's flanks and the permeable limestone beneath. A line of sink-holes and shakeholes marks the boundary, and a series of open potholes gives the walker an insight into the subterranean world of the potholer. The largest of these potholes is Rowten Pot, a huge gaping void to the left of the track reached after about a mile. Draped with rowan trees, it drops a sheer 365ft (111m) and must be approached with caution.

From Rowten Pot there are superb views of flat-topped Ingleborough and whale-backed Whernside, the highest hills in the Yorkshire Dales National Park, across the glacial trough of Kingsdale with the white broken line of Braida Garth and Long Scars between.

Pass through the gate in the wall by Rowten Pot, and you soon see the single tree which marks the entrance to Jingling Pot up the slope to the left. There is a marvellous view down the polished vertical walls of one of the Dales' most beautiful open potholes: but the drop is sheer

Underground Pennines: in the main chamber of Yordas Cave, Kingsdale

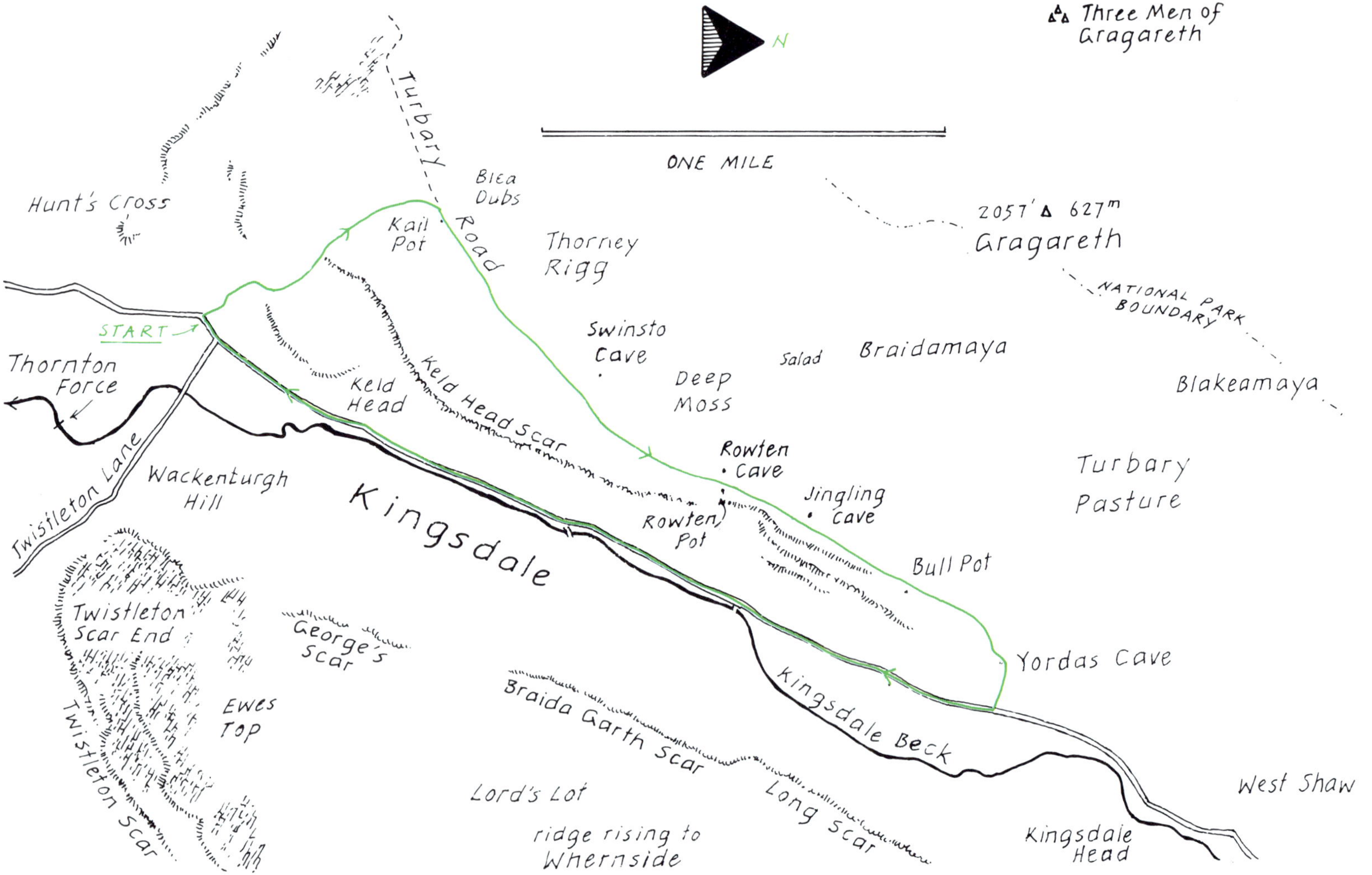
N
Three Men of Gragareth
ONE MILE
Turbary Road
Blea Dubs
Hunt's Cross
Kail Pot
Thorney Rigg
2057' 627m
Gragareth
NATIONAL PARK BOUNDARY
START
Thornton Force
Keld Head
Keld Head Scar
Swinsto Cave
Salad
Braidamaya
Deep Moss
Blakeamaya
Rowten Cave
Jingling Cave
Turbary Pasture
Twisleton Lane
Wackenturgh Hill
Kingsdale
Rowten Pot
Bull Pot
Twistleton Scar End
George's Scar
Yordas Cave
Ewes Top
Braida Garth Scar
Kingsdale Beck
Twistleton Scar
Lord's Lot
Long Scar
West Shaw
ridge rising to Whernside
Kingsdale Head

for 140ft (43m) and it is not a place to slip. Jingling Pot is for expert potholers only.

Returning to the Turbary Road, the next potholes you come across are Bull Pot, covered with iron sheeting, and inevitably nearby, Cow Pot. A faint path leads between the two and down to the right across rough pastures to the trees which mark the entrance to Yordas Cave, just above the road in the valley below. Yordas Cave is thought to get its name from a Norse giant with a liking for devouring small boys, and it was a well-known show cave in Victorian times. Today, however, the low arched entrance to Yordas Cave is unsupervised, but if you have a powerful torch with you, it is quite safe to explore carefully.

The Great Hall of Yordas is 60ft (18m) high, and at the far end on the right the Chapter House is a circular chamber into which usually cascades a fine waterfall which then runs beneath the rocky floor and out the other end of the cave.

From Yordas Cave, follow the path which leads down to the road and turn right for the 2 mile walk back to the starting point along the floor of Kingsdale. Over the wall on the left, you will see the dry bed of the Kingsdale Beck, which later becomes artificially channelled in a straight cut and reappears only at the resurgence of Keld Head, half a mile before Twistleton Lane.

Autumn tints the birches round the gaping chasm of Rowten Pot, on the Turbary Road, Kingsdale

INGLEBOROUGH

Map Outdoor Leisure Sheet 2, Yorkshire Dales (Whernside)

Start Clapham car park GR 745692

Length 8 miles

Time Allow 5 hours

Difficulty Some quite arduous moorland walking after pleasant woodland paths through the Ingleborough Estate. Can easily be shortened

YORKSHIRE'S CROWNING GLORY

Although not the highest hill in the Broad Acres, Ingleborough is generally acknowledged to be the finest in Yorkshire. Every Yorkshireman, it is said, should climb it once before he dies, and such is its presence that some still believe it to be a mile high.

Perhaps this is a dim folk memory of the time when Yorkshire's pride, in the form of the Brigantian tribesmen led by Venutious, made their last stand against the Romans on the large hillfort which crowns Ingleborough's 2,372ft (723m) summit.

Ingleborough is a proud mountain, exhibiting to perfection the classic Yoredale geological sequence of grit/shale/limestone seen on so many of the Dales hills. But it suffers from its own popularity and most of all from being one of the famous Yorkshire Three Peaks.

This 26 mile one-day marathon walk linking the summits of Ingleborough, Pen-y-Ghent and Whernside has been vastly over-promoted, and consequently now poses horrendous problems in erosion control for the hard-pressed Yorkshire Dales National Park authority. It is therefore excluded from this book, but I felt I could not omit a route up Ingleborough because it is such a dominating hill with a fascinating history.

In my view the finest way up Ingleborough is not that used by the 'Three-Peakers', but from the south, from Clapham village. It passes such interesting incidental attractions as the beautiful Ingleborough Estate, Ingleborough Cave, Trow Gill and Gaping Gill, perhaps the most famous pothole of them all.

From the National Park car park in the centre of Clapham, turn right and almost immediately left, over a charming stone packhorse bridge across Clapham Beck. Turn right and go through the woodyard of the Ingleborough Estate, where a small charge is made to use the estate paths up the beckside.

Ingleborough Hall was the home of the botanist Reginald Farrer, who spent much of his life travelling the world and bringing back various exotic plants to his Yorkshire estate. As you walk up the beautifully engineered paths which lead to the ornamental lake, you should not be surprised to see Japanese maple and various multi-coloured azaleas and rhododendrons among the indigenous yew, beech, oak and ash trees.

Springtime in Clapdale Woods sees fine displays of bluebells, primroses, wood anemones and wood sorrel, all signs of original ancient woodland, while the large ornamental lake, complete with boathouse on the opposite shore, was built between 1810 and 1830 by the Farrer family, and water from it powered turbines which gave Clapham street lighting as early as 1896.

Emerging from the pleasant woodlands at a stile, enter Clapdale, passing the clanking ram water-pump which feeds Clapdale Farm on the hillside above to the left. Follow the left bank of

Britain's biggest pothole, Gaping Gill, swallows the waters of Fell Beck on the southern slopes of Ingleborough

Clapham Beck as it narrows between limestone crags and approaches the impressive mouth of Ingleborough Cave, a notable show cavern which has been open to the public since 1837. The stream which emerges nearby at Beck Head is that which plunges into Gaping Gill high on the moorland above.

Beyond Beck Head, the dale is dry, and as it bends to the left, you cross a ladder stile to enter the spectacular little gorge of Trow Gill. With its fringing pines above steeply undercut limestone walls, Trow Gill is a classic glacial meltwater gorge, formed by a retreating waterfall at the end of the last Ice Age. There is an easy little rocky scramble at the end, from which you emerge on to the open moorland of Clapham Bottoms.

A clear path leads off left over another ladder stile and past a number of sealed-off potholes, including Bar Pot on the left, some of which lead into the main cavern of Gaping Gill. That greatest of all potholes is our next objective, and it soon becomes visible on the open moor ahead, surrounded by a flimsy post-and-wire fence. A great grassy crater leads to an awesome hole some 340ft (104m) deep with a cavern at its foot said to be large enough to hold the nave of York Minster.

Our route continues over a wet path to the left of Fell Beck, which gradually ascends the shoulder of Little Ingleborough rising ahead. Once you reach the cairn on the ridge, turn right and follow the clear track which picks its way through the crags and loose stones to reach

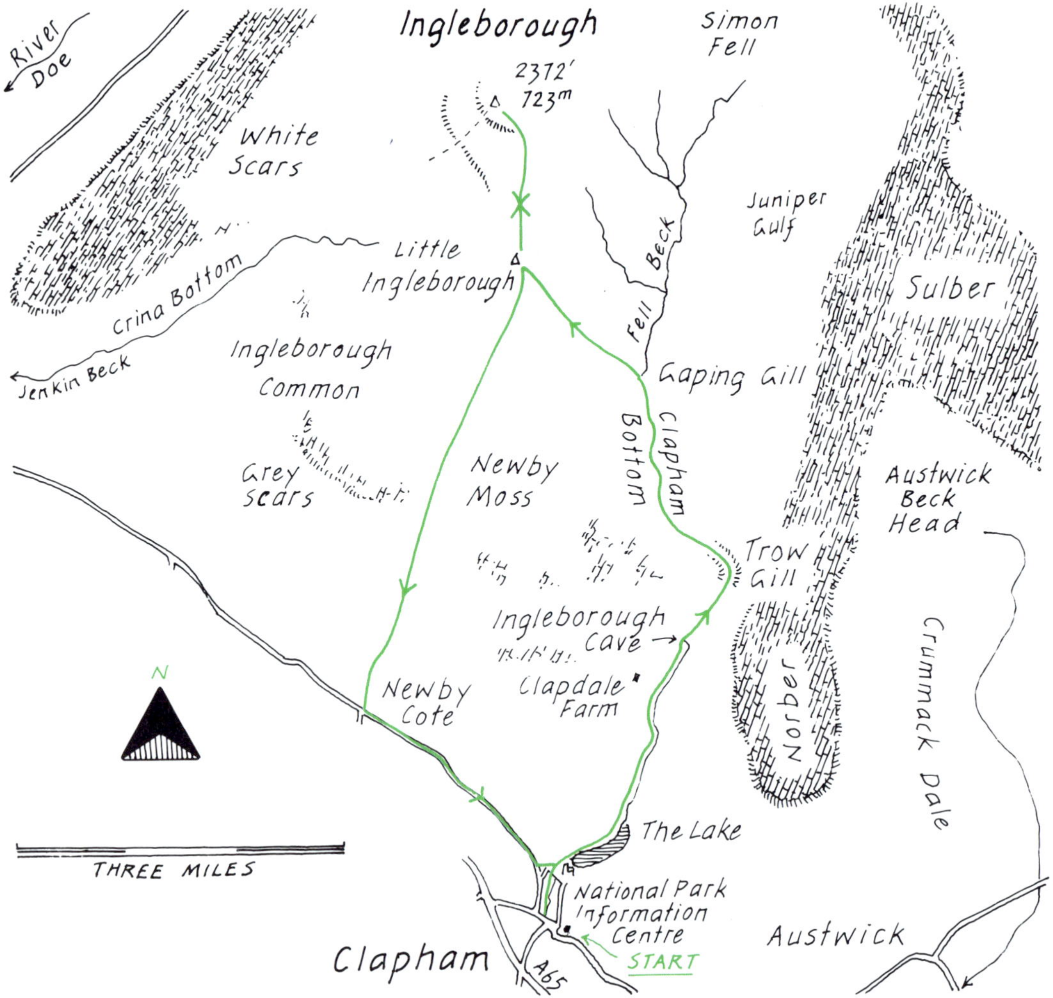

the summit plateau at Swine Tail. Turn left to reach the summit cairn and cross-wall wind shelter, erected by the Ingleton Fell Rescue Team to mark the Queen's coronation in 1953. The remains of Iron Age hut circles can also be traced, in the right conditions, on Ingleborough's broad summit.

The views from Ingleborough on a clear day are wonderful, extending to Morecambe Bay with the misty Lakeland hills beyond, and down Upper Ribblesdale to Whernside and Pen-y-Ghent, with the dim outline of the Forest of Bowland to the west.

Retrace your steps down Ingleborough's southern flank to Little Ingleborough, bearing right from your route of ascent across the featureless expanse of Newby Moss until you reach the shallow valley of Grey Wife Syke. Passing grouse butts and a series of shake- and swallowholes as you traverse the limestone belt, the path leads directly down towards Newby village in the valley below.

Over a ladder stile, enter a walled lane past a disused quarry at the seventeenth-century farmhouse of Newby Cote on the left. The quickest way back to Clapham is to turn left when you meet the road, but it is more pleasant to continue down the lane towards Newby, turning left just before reaching the village into Laithbutts Lane, and then turning right into Clapham.

Beckhead in Clapdale is the resurgence of Clapham Beck from Ingleborough Cave

INGLETON · GLENS

Map OS Outdoor Leisure Sheet 2, Yorkshire Dales (Western)

Start Ingleton GR 694733

Length Just over 4 miles

Time Allow 2½ hours

Difficulty Easy graded paths

AN UNCONFORMING LANDSCAPE

When a walk is described as 'the most delightful of its kind in the country' by the master, Alfred Wainwright, it is difficult to exclude it from any book such as this.

The Ingleton Glens, commonly known as the Waterfalls Walk, is a little gem. Even in this country of waterfalls, this easy stroll is special, as it passes a series of beautiful falls in one wooded valley on the ascent, visits one of the geological wonders of the Dales at Thornton Force, and then descends by an equally lovely waterfall-filled valley back to the starting point.

After heavy rain, peat colours the water of the River Twiss at Thornton Force, at the head of the Ingleton Glens

It is certainly well worth the admission charge.

Start from the large car park and entrance kiosk just under the impressive but disused Ingleton railway viaduct. The path, originally engineered for the benefit of Victorian sight-seers into a series of steps round the falls, leads off left through attractive woodland up the valley of the River Twiss. (Wainwright confused the names of the rivers in his *Walks in Limestone Country* (1970), and referred to this as the River Doe, which we use on our return route.)

The first feature is an impressive little limestone gorge with sheer walls of rock dominating the cool woodland of Swilla Glen. Cross Manor Bridge to reach the eastern bank, through a gate and then over the Twiss again at Pecca Bridge to reach the first of the named falls – Pecca Falls.

An old quarry to the left does not detract from the Twin Falls – a double cascade – and the gushing Holly Bush Spout which empties into a deep plunge pool in the river down to the right. Emerging from the woodland, go past the old refreshment hut and out on to the sheep pastures beneath Constitution Hill. In the river below, Cuckoo Island heralds a right turn by the river, and the first sight of Thornton Force, embowered in trees and one of the great scenic glories of the Dales.

The River Twiss plunges over a lip of limestone having found a way around the glacial moraine of Raven Ray above, and crashes down in a cloud of spray onto the Pre-Cambrian slates of the Ingleton gorge. It is possible, with great care, to edge behind the fall and touch the limestone resting on the upturned edges of the slates. To be in contact with worlds which are more than three hundred million years apart is an awe-inspiring experience.

Leaving Thornton Force, the path leads up a rocky staircase left of the waterfall and leaves the river to contour round Raven Ray, crossing a footbridge to reach Twistleton Lane. Turn right here and follow the walled lane through a typical Dales limestone landscape with extensive views south towards the Forest of Bowland, through Twistleton Hall Farm, and a glorious view of the noble stepped profile of Ingleborough ahead.

Cross the minor road of Oddie's Lane, between Ingleton and Chapel-le-Dale, and then turn right on to the footpath which leads through Beezley's Farm, with its campsite, and then descends into the almost identical valley of

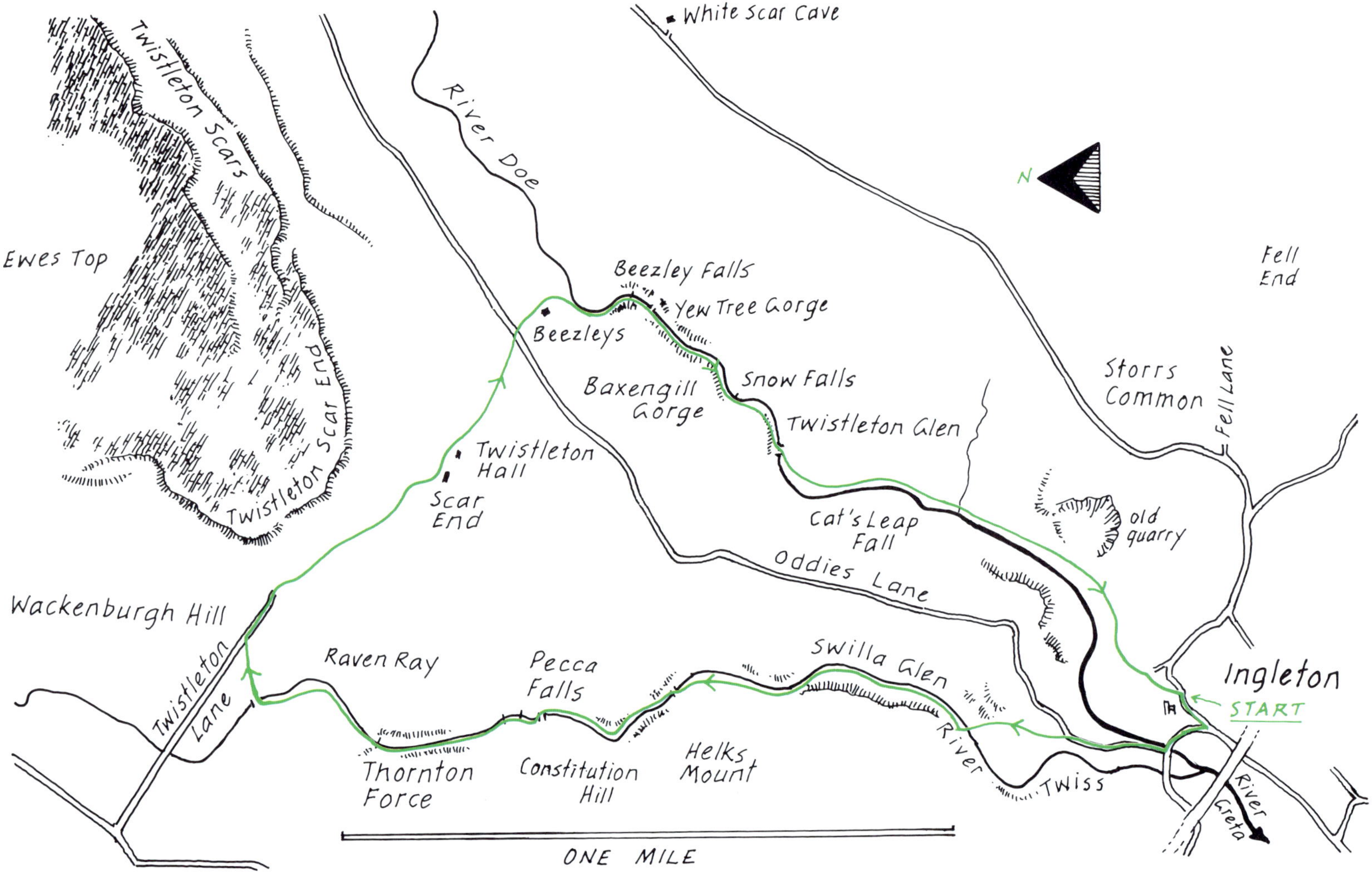
White Scar Cave
Twistleton Scars
River Doe
N
Ewes Top
Beezley Falls
Yew Tree Gorge
Beezleys
Fell End
Baxengill Gorge
Snow Falls
Storrs Common
Fell Lane
Twistleton Scar End
Twistleton Glen
Twistleton Hall
Scar End
Twistleton Scar End
Cat's Leap Fall
old quarry
Oddies Lane
Wackenburgh Hill
Twistleton Lane
Raven Ray
Pecca Falls
Swilla Glen
Ingleton
START
Helks Mount
River Twiss
Thornton Force
Constitution Hill
River Greta
ONE MILE

the River Doe. Almost immediately you enter the trees, the first of the Doe falls is encountered in the series known as Beezley Falls.

The path leads on down the right bank of the river into the Baxengill Gorge, where the lovely Snow Falls cascade in deep woodland. Then you enter the aptly named Yew Tree Gorge and into Twistleton Glen, crossing the river by a footbridge and running into what might be called the 'quarry belt'. Here, ancient and modern quarries have eaten into the delicately pastel-shaded slates, mainly for use as road aggregates. Over a stile, and you can seek out the last of the named falls just below the path at Cat's Leap – an elegant single long leap, reminiscent of a cat pouncing on a mouse.

You now re-enter limestone country, evidenced by a former quarry and an old limekiln on the left. Meal Bank Quarry is an ugly active scar on the left, as you re-enter Ingleton near the youth hostel, turning right past the church to return to the car park.

The noble, fort-crowned head of Ingleborough peeps over the shoulder of White Scars in this view from the drystone walls of Oddie's Lane, Ingleton. The picture illustrates perfectly the classic limestone-shale-gritstone geological succession of the Yorkshire Dales, with a mix of limestone, shale and grit in the walls in the valley of the River Doe, the upstanding scars of white limestone in the middle distance, and the resistant gritstone cap of Ingleborough in the background

BOLTON · ABBEY

Map OS Outdoor Leisure Sheet 10, Yorkshire Dales (Southern)

Start Cavendish Pavilion GR 076553

Length 8–9 miles

Time Allow 4–5 hours

Difficulty Easy moorland tracks with a modest rock scramble

TO SIMON'S SEAT

The romantic ruins of Bolton Abbey in the lower reaches of Wharfedale are a honeypot for the folk of Leeds and the West Riding towns. This is especially so on summer weekends, when the famous Stepping Stones can rival Dovedale's for sheer weight of numbers.

But the delightfully wooded surroundings of the former Augustinian priory (it was not actually an abbey) are beautiful, and the area is sensitively managed by the Duke of Devonshire as part of his Wharfedale estate. This enlightened regime has concluded access agreements covering Simon's Seat and Barden Fell east of the Wharfe, and Bardon Moor and Cracoe Fell west of the river, allowing the rambler free access for most of the year.

The summit tor of Simon's Seat in Wharfedale affords some of the finest views in the Dales

There are many very pleasant walks through the Bolton Abbey woodlands, both up and downstream of the priory. There is, for example, the delightful 4 mile stroll up to Barden Tower, the largely fifteenth-century remains of one of Lord Clifford's hunting lodges, a superbly situated three-storey tower house. This walk, on the Dales Way, passes one of the most famous sights along the Wharfe at The Strid. Here limestone buttresses force the river into a narrow channel only about two metres wide. Do not be tempted to leap it though, or you might end up like the fabled Boy of Egremond who was the first, but not the last, to be drowned here.

Our exploration of the Bolton Abbey estate makes the beautiful ascent of Simon's Seat, high above the woodlands and enjoying one of the great surprise views in the Dales.

Start from the car park at the Cavendish Pavilion off the B6160 north of Bolton Abbey, where refreshments are available, crossing the wooden footbridge over the rushing river and following the path upstream. After passing through gnarled oaks, the path emerges on to the narrow road at Posforth Bridge. Turn sharp left, doubling back up Lud Stream Brow to a gate on the left adorned by an access notice.

A good track winds up above wooded Posforth Gill, but a worthwhile detour can be made down to the gill itself, where Posforth Falls and an elegant waterslide higher up will add further interest to the ascent. Back on the main track, cross a tiny footbridge to enter the falsely named Valley of Desolation, so called after a violent storm some 150 years ago devastated the trees of Laund Pasture Plantation. The sandy track briefly enters this mature plantation and then reaches the open moor at Great Agill Bottom. This is a superbly managed heather grouse moor, best seen in late summer when it is a sea of purple.

The track crosses Great Agill Beck by a ford, and then rises steeply to a stone table where a shooter's track leads off to the right. Keep left here, following the path which crosses the headwaters of the beck and climbs steadily up to the first rocks at Truckle Crags, with Hen Stones across to the right. The summit crags of Simon's Seat (1,591ft/485m) are now visible on the skyline ahead, and only a few steps away.

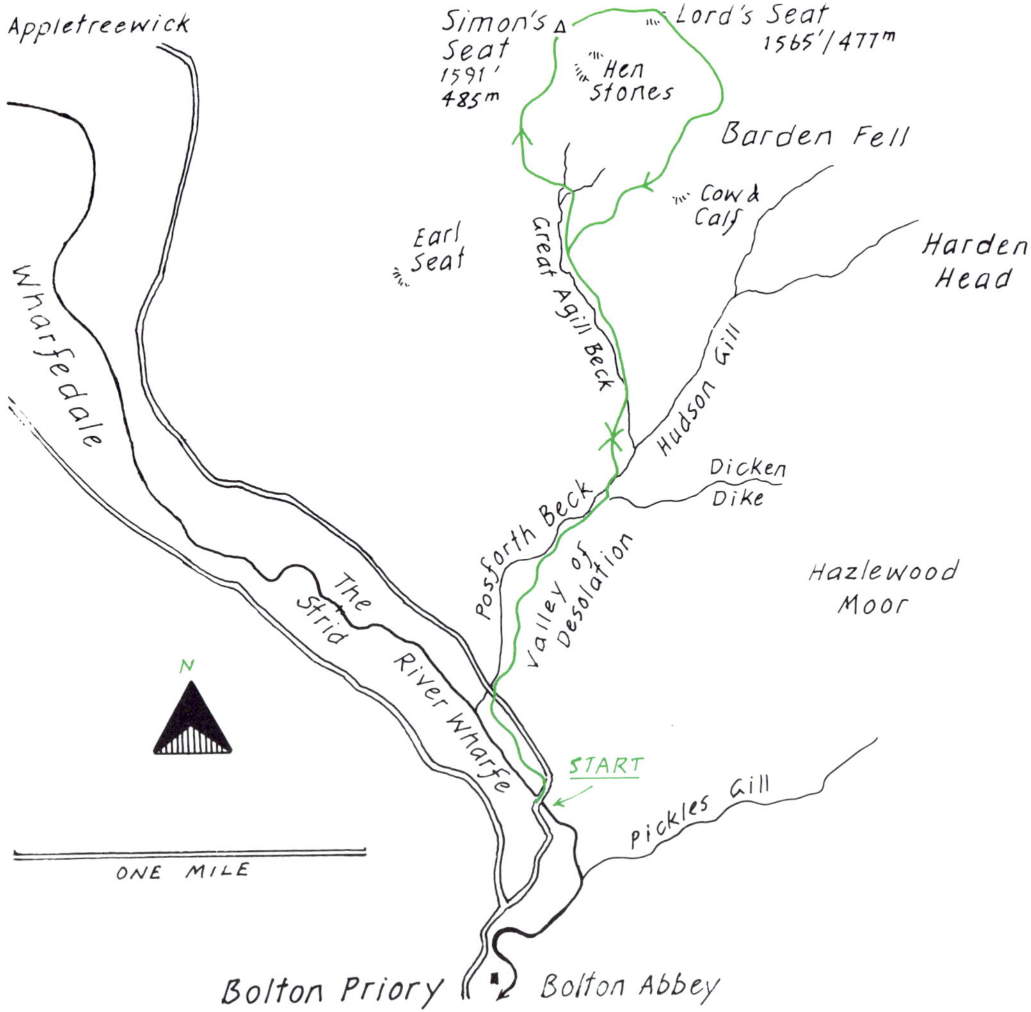

After a modest scramble to reach the highest point in the jumble of gritstone boulders which marks the summit, the surprise view mentioned earlier emerges. As you reach the incongrous white cemented-on trig point, the wonderful view northwards is suddenly revealed, showing the length of Wharfedale, with the conical reef limestone knolls around Appletreewick and Skyreholme and the deep gash of Trollers Gill prominent in the foreground. Beyond them, the view extends on a clear day southwest to Pendle Hill, with Fountains Fell, Buckden Pike and Great Whernside to the northwest.

After savouring the view, head east through the boulders to the subsidiary summit of Lord's Seat, (1,565ft/477m) which has its own interesting collection of summit tors. From here, follow the wall right which leads past a series of grouse butts to the shooter's track passed previously, which contours easily through the heather round the outcrop of the Hen Stones, high on the right.

After about half a mile, this regains the outward route by the stone table just below Great Agill Head. Retrace your steps down through the Valley of Desolation and Laund Pasture Plantation, perhaps visiting those waterfalls if you missed them on the way up, and eventually emerging back at the Cavendish Pavilion for some welcome refreshment.

The River Wharfe plunges through the awesome cleft of The Strid, near Bolton Abbey

GUNNERSIDE · GILL

Map OS Outdoor Leisure Sheet 30, Yorkshire Dales (Northern and Central)

Start Gunnerside village GR 983951

Length 10–11 miles

Time Allow 6–7 hours

Difficulty Good paths or tracks for most of the way, but rough moorland for the Rogan's Seat extension

THE LEAD LEGACY

When you look on the apparently unspoiled beauty of the northern Yorkshire Dales like Swaledale and Arkengarthdale today, it is hard to imagine what a hive of industry it was just over a century ago.

At the height of the lead-mining industry in the 1880s, about four thousand miners were burrowing under these now quiet hills. The hillsides echoed to the sound of men's voices, and smoke and explosions marked their quest to expose the rich veins of galena which ran in the limestone beneath the dales. These veins were given exotic names, like Reformers, Brandy Bottle, Moorhouse and Freeman's, and the names of the mines or 'levels' often referred to members of their owners' families, like the famous Sir Francis and Sir George levels in Gunnerside Gill, which were named after father and son Sir George and Sir Francis Denys.

The remains of their presence, now largely healed by Nature, are still to be seen in many a silent gill, and this walk up from the charming Swaledale village of Gunnerside reveals some of the finest reminders of this once-important industry.

From the car park by the bridge in the village, take the waymarked path which leads north up the eastern (right-hand) side of Gunnerside Gill. You soon pass the first evidence of lead mining in the form of a line of bunkers beside the path, used to store the 'bings' or large pieces of the precious ore.

The remains of the Sir Francis level can easily be seen across the gill, and the debris from two crushing mills used to separate the ore from the rock is visible on either side of the stream. The rusty old cast-iron cylinder on the opposite bank was once the air receiver for the mine's hydraulic engine, which pumped water out from the levels below. Flooding was one of the lead miners' greatest headaches, and much time and money was spent on draining mines to get at the lead veins.

Over a stile, the path leads off up the gill on a broad, grassy track across Swina Bank to the ruins of the Bunton Mine buildings, standing on a level shelf above the gill. You now cross three large shallow gullies which show an earlier method by which the miners excavated the ore. These are known as 'hushes' and are a common feature in the dalesides, often mistaken for naturally eroded streambeds as vegetation now covers their sides.

The method of 'hushing' involved the damming of a stream on top of the moor, thus creating an artifically high head of water, which was then suddenly released, sending a scouring force down the gill which it was hoped would reveal lead veins. The three seen here are known as the Bunton, Friarfold and Gorton hushes, and they are crossed by numerous paths. This is where the Friarfold complex of lead veins crosses the gill, and the Lownathwaite mines extend west from here until they meet the Swinnergill levels, higher up Swaledale. These mines were worked by Philip, Lord

The legacy of the lead industry at Bunton Mine, in Gunnerside Gill, Swaledale

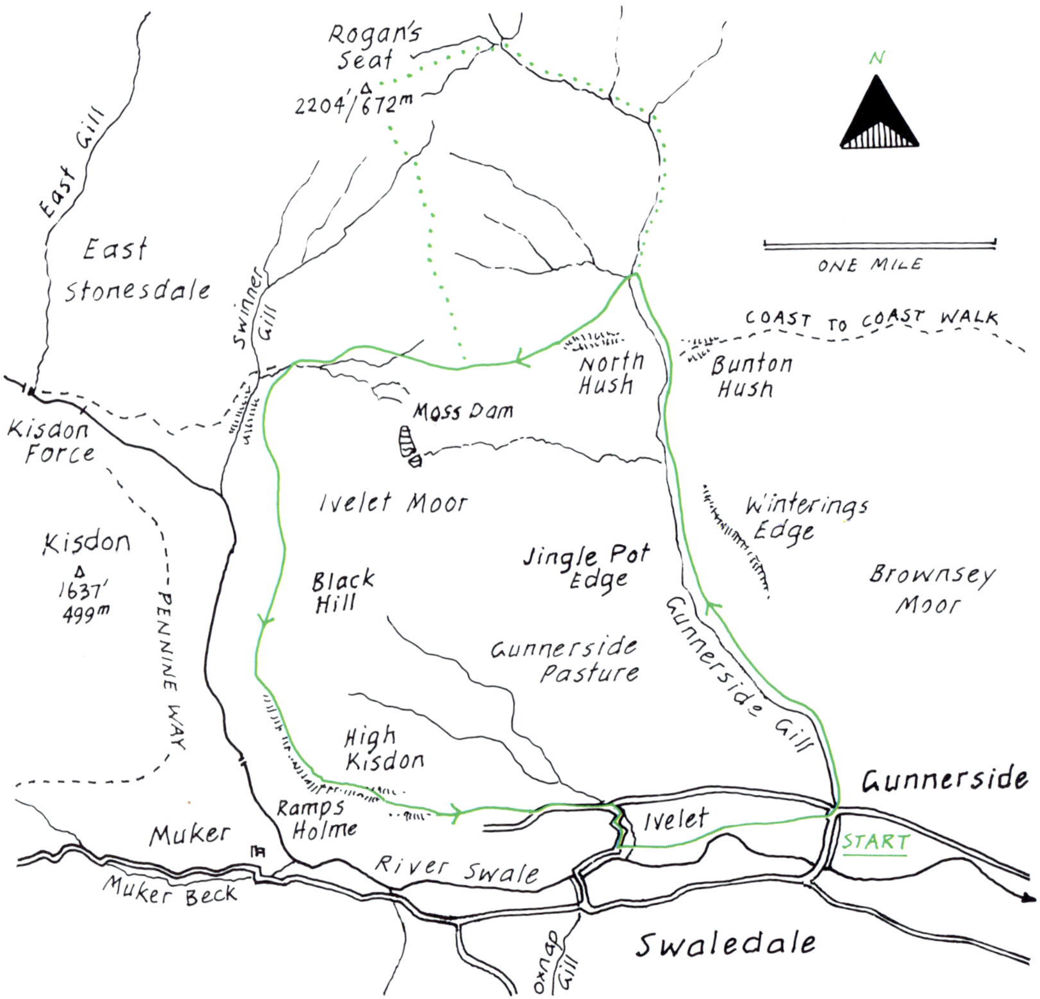

Wharton before 1670 and are therefore some of the oldest in the area.

To the east, paths up the hushes lead to the Old Gang mines and the Surrender smelt mill across Melbecks Moor in the valley of Hard Level Gill or Old Gang Beck. These well-preserved remains are usually reached from the village of Healaugh, lower down the dale.

A single-slab clapper bridge crosses the gill to reach the remains of the Blakethwaite smelt mill. Here the ore was burnt to remove impurities, and the four arches show where the peat fuel was stored before use in the process of smelting.

There is a choice of routes from here. Continuing up the increasingly steep-sided Gunnerside Gill will lead you to the impressive remains of the Blakethwaite lead mines. From here, by crossing the gill above a dam, you can reach the peaty summit of Rogan's Seat (2,204ft/672m) a rough mile across knee-deep heather, returning south to Swinner Gill across High Stone Man by an easy vehicle track.

Alternatively, cross the gill by the smelt mill and cross Lownathwaite Mea to follow another hush, this time called the North Hush, which leads due west past the prominent Woodward level tip and out on to the moor, descending by East Grain into Swinner Gill. This is an impressively deep, tree-lined gorge with its own set of lead mines, the oldest of which are the Beldi mines, near the junction with the Swale, which were sunk in 1771. Just up the Swale Gorge from here are the remains of Crackpot

Hall with a superb view down Swaledale, and the beautiful stepped falls of Kisdon, in a dramatic limestone gorge on the line of the Pennine Way.

Our route keeps to the main track heading south above the Swale and keeping just above the intake wall. This passes above Swinner Gill and Arn Gill Wood, crossing West Arn Gill and above Arn Gill Scar on a delightful and easy high-level path.

Over Arn Gill itself, the path contours along the slopes of Black Hill on Ivelet Boards above Ivelet Wood, with fine views of Kisdon Hill across the river. Ahead the peaty morass of Lovely Seat stretches to the south, as the path contours east round Ivelet Side and between High and Low Kisdon Scars.

On Cock Crow Scar, the track drops across Kisdon Bottom to meet the road at Shore Gill just above Gunnerside Lodge. Walk downhill to enter Ivelet village, where a footpath by the telephone box is signed to Gunnerside and leads pleasantly across riverside meadows back to the starting point.

Gunnerside is a typical Swaledale village, founded on the wealth created from wool and lead won from the surrounding hills. This view, from Satron Side on the southern side of the dale, shows the warm, grey gritstone village clustering at the confluence of Gunnerside Gill with the Swale. A mazy network of enclosure walls and barns spreads up to the unimproved moorland of Brownsey Moor (1,756ft/544m) beyond. In the foreground and in the sheltered dale and gill bottoms, a few trees cling tenaciously to life, but this is mainly a pastoral landscape shaped by the voracious teeth of Swaledale sheep

AYSGARTH

Map OS Outdoor Leisure Sheet 30, Yorkshire Dales (Northern and Central)

Start Aysgarth Falls car park GR 012887

Length 6 miles

Time Allow at least 4–5 hours

Difficulty Easy field paths

THE WONDERS OF WENSLEYDALE

Two of the 'musts' on any tourist's first visit to Wensleydale are Aysgarth Falls and Bolton Castle. Both are justly popular attractions, one a wonder of Nature and the other man-made.

Bolton Castle represents the finest medieval landmark in the Dales National Park, a remarkably well-preserved fortified manor house dating from the later years of the fourteenth century, while Aysgarth Falls, a couple of miles upstream, has attracted visitors for two centuries. This easy stroll takes in both places, and allows time for the proper exploration which both demand.

Start at the National Park car park at Aysgarth Falls, on the north side of the river by the side of the former Wensleydale Railway, built in 1874 by the North Eastern Railway Company to link Leyburn with Hawes. A visitor centre interprets the geology of the falls and the human and natural history of the surrounding countryside.

There are three main sets of waterfalls in the Ure at Aysgarth, each one reached by pleasant woodland walks and provided with convenient viewing platforms. Freeholders' Wood, through which the Middle and Lower Falls are reached, is one of the few broadleaved woodlands in the area which is still being coppiced in the traditional manner by the National Park authority. It is full of wildlife and a joy to behold.

The falls themselves are the result of the Ure gradually undercutting softer shale beds between harder beds of limestone, so creating the typical stepped appearance of the falls, also seen elsewhere in the Dales. The numerous cup-shaped hollows worn in the flat areas of limestone are tiny potholes created by small pebbles, swirled around in eddies when the river is in flood – a good time to see the falls at their finest.

After visiting each of the falls, return through Freeholders' Wood to the Lower Force where a signposted stile leads left away from the river on a waymarked path to Castle Bolton. This leads across the fields to Hollins House Farm. Pass to the left of the farm on a track, and after a few yards bear right, away from the track, with a post-and-wire fence on your right.

Reaching a wall, turn right over a stone stile and continue across the next field towards a group of farm buildings. At the wall, bear right over another stile and through a gap in a wall eventually reaching the ancient highway of Thoresby Lane, a green lane lined with hedges which leads to the farm of Low Thoresby, the site of a deserted village.

About 100 yards beyond the farm, bear left over a footbridge, turning left through a gap in a fence and, ignoring the ladder stile in front, turn right across a field towards a barn. Passing to the right of the barn, cross another field to emerge on a lane which leads directly to the village of Castle Bolton.

Castle Bolton is an unspoiled echo of feudal England; just one street of charming cottages, with a wide green and the tiny medieval St

Aysgarth Middle Falls, with the fourteenth-century tower of Aysgarth church in the background

Oswald's church nestling beneath the forbidding walls of the castle. The castle itself was built by Sir Richard de Scrope in 1378 as a fortified manor house. Local legend has it that ox blood was mixed with the mortar to give strength to the walls, which have stood the test of six centuries of Dales weather remarkably well. Mary, Queen of Scots, spent nearly a year of her unhappy captivity here.

The views of Wensleydale from the castle, which is still in private hands, are magnificent, but we continue our walk by taking the metalled lane which leads past the castle and its car park. Climb over a stile into a field, bearing left and following the yellow waymarks through the fields into the wooded valley of Beldon Beck. The stream is crossed by a footbridge.

The waymarked path passes to the left of the farm buildings of West Bolton, which have the remains of medieval strip lynchets (cultivation terraces) on the hillside behind them. Pass to the north of West Bolton Plantation, cross a stream and then gradually descend through several gates across the fields to East End Farm, turning right on reaching the lane to the village of Carperby.

This one-street village, granted the right to hold a market as long ago as 1303, was once an important centre of the Quaker movement, and boasts a fine, nineteenth-century Meeting House. Opposite The Wheatsheaf pub (where the celebrated veterinarian James Herriot spent his honeymoon) turn left through a gate and follow the path through the fields to cross Low Lane. Over the lane bear left, eventually re-entering Freeholders' Wood, so named because local freeholders still hold commoners' rights to use it. Regaining the road, turn left under the old railway bridge to return to the car park.

The south-west tower of Bolton Castle overlooks Wensleydale towards Hazely Moor

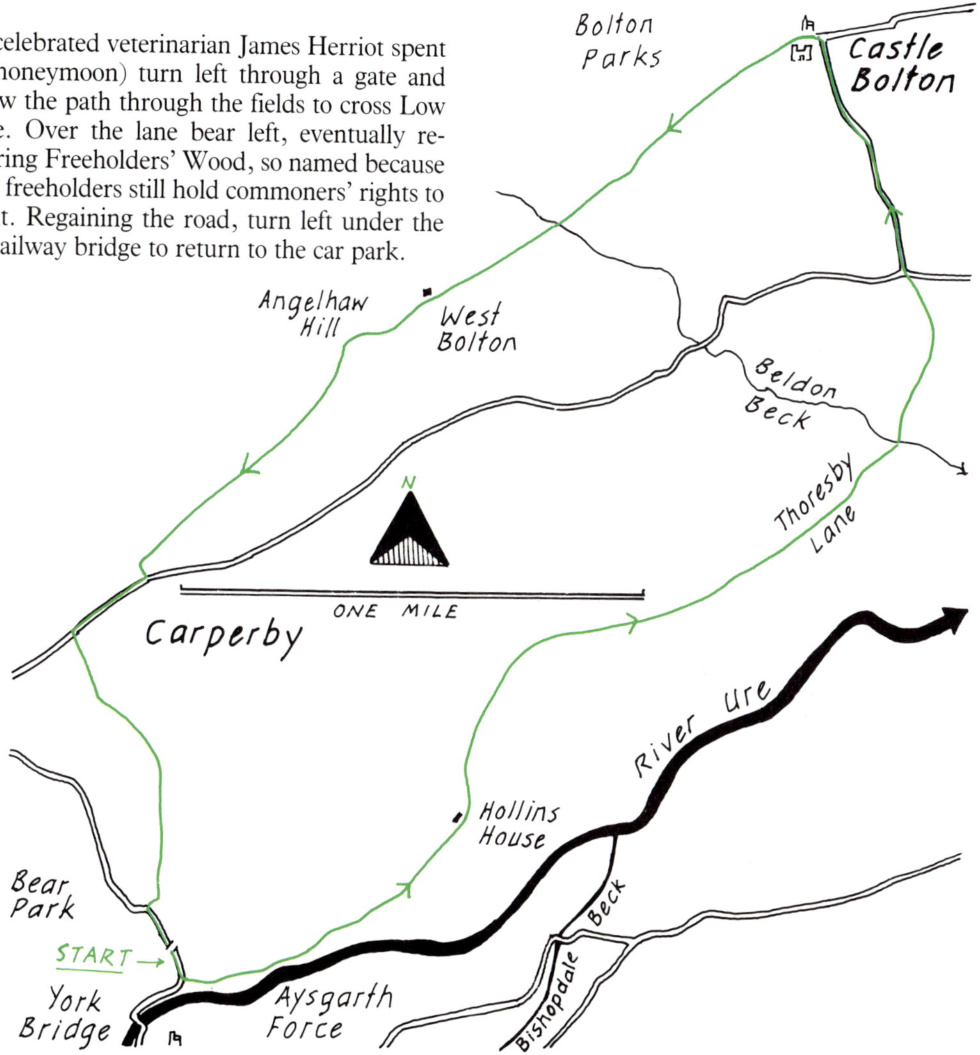

DENTDALE

Map OS Outdoor Leisure Sheet 2, The Yorkshire Dales (Whernside)

Start Dent station GR 764875

Length About 5 miles

Time Allow 2–3 hours

Difficulty Some steep gradients and rough moorland tracks

AROUND THE HEAD OF DENTDALE

Dentdale is *different* from the other Yorkshire dales. Its lush green countryside is parcelled up by hawthorn hedges and plentiful trees instead of the barren pastures and drystone walls which are such a common feature of the other dales. Although it is one of the northernmost dales in the National Park, you could just as easily be in southern England.

But at the head of the dale under the slopes of Great Knoutberry Hill (2,205ft/672m), it reverts to type, and this stroll from Dent station on the Settle to Carlisle railway explores the wilder upper reaches. It also provides one of the finest views in the Dales, down the length of Dentdale, uses an ancient packhorse route and passes under one of the greatest feats of engineering on the S&C at Artengill viaduct.

Descending Arten Gill below Great Knoutberry towards the graceful frieze of Artengill Viaduct

Start the walk from Dent station, but be warned, this highest mainline station is about 4½ miles from Dent Town itself and uphill most of the way. A common feature of the S&C was the distance the stations were built from the villages they served, a consequence of the tortuous, winding route the line had to take through the hills to take advantage of the lie of the land and the easiest gradients. Kirkby Stephen station is another example.

Dent station, just off the minor road which runs from Dentdale to Newby Head, is 1,150ft (350m) above sea level, so you have a good start to the day's climbing already. Take the road which leads out of the station past the little 'Midland-Gothic' style stationmaster's house, which was reputed to be the first house in England to be fitted with double-glazing. At this altitude, it was probably essential!

Turn right on reaching the road, and ascend steadily up the lane which is known as the Coal Road because it led from the coal pits on Shaking Moss down into Dent. It follows the line of Monkey Beck, past the plantations (left) which cover Dodderham Moss. This stiff climb brings you out on to Monkeybeck Grains, and a signposted broad bridleway which leads off to the right.

This is Galloway Gate, a name which echoes its former use as a drove road which brought cattle from Scotland down to the great cities of the North. The broad track, which gave the cattle plenty of opportunity for grazing en route, contours smoothly around the swelling slopes of Great Knoutberry at 1,700ft (518m) and when you reach Green Bank, below Pike's Edge, you get a fantastic, bird's-eye view down the length of sylvan Dentdale, with the smooth shapes of the Howgills beyond. To the left, the great whaleback of Whernside is prominent, with Gragareth beyond and Ingleborough to the south.

Galloway Gate bends round to the left, to drop down to a junction of tracks at the top of Artengill. Turn sharp right here on the rough and usually wet walled track between Great Knoutberry and Wold Fell.

The magnificent 600ft (182m) high Artengill viaduct now appears ahead, striding across the gill on eleven great arches. The track goes

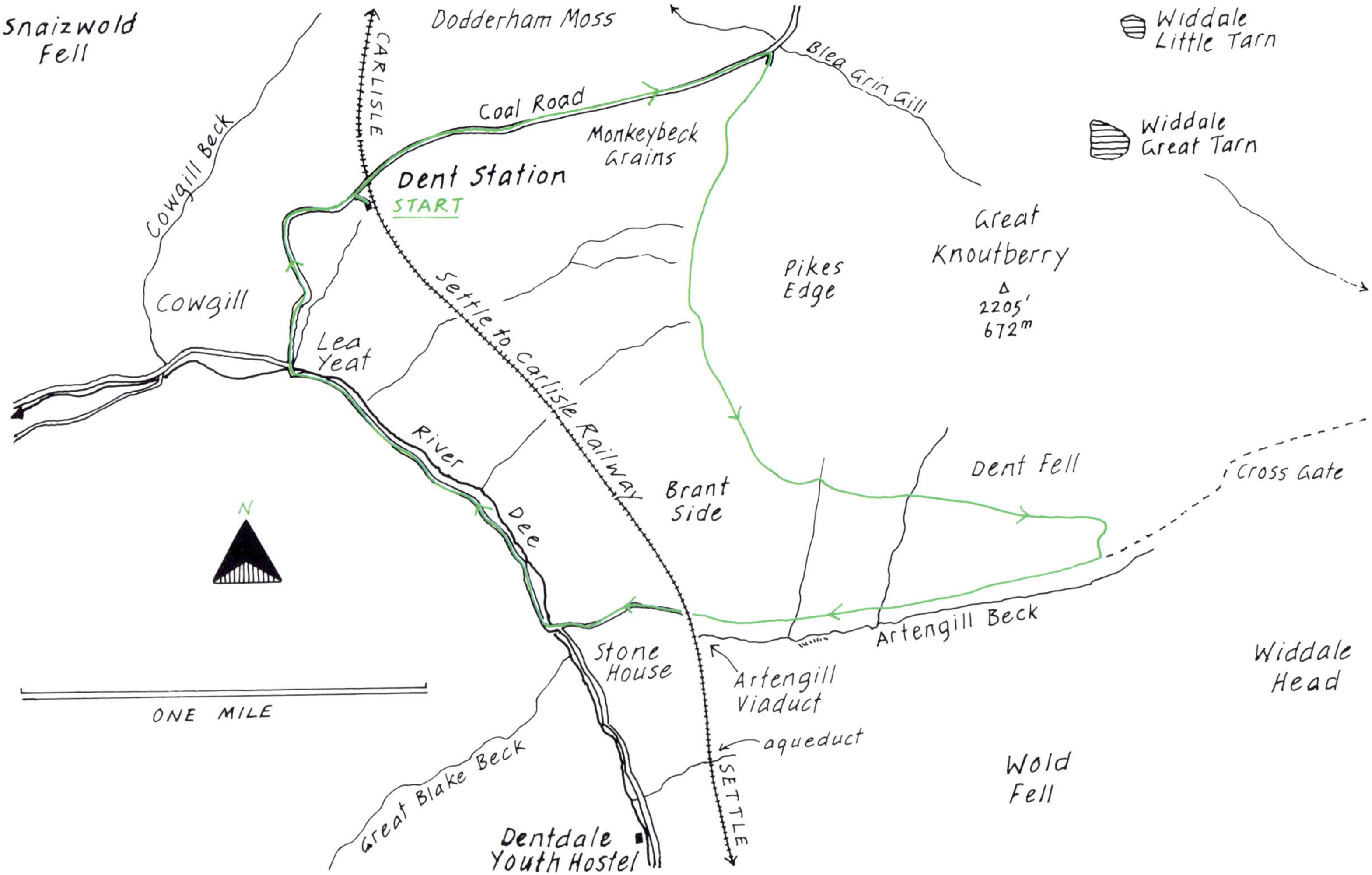
Snaizwold Fell
CARLISLE
Dodderham Moss
Widdale Little Tarn
Blea Grin Gill
Coal Road
Monkeybeck Grains
Widdale Great Tarn
Cowgill Beck
Dent Station
START
Great Knoutberry
2205′
672m
Pikes Edge
Cowgill
Settle to Carlisle Railway
Lea Yeat
River Dee
Dent Fell
Cross Gate
N
Brant Side
Artengill Beck
Stone House
Artengill Viaduct
Widdale Head
ONE MILE
aqueduct
Great Blake Beck
Wold Fell
SETTLE
Dentdale Youth Hostel

beneath it and passes the old workings above Stonehouse Farm where the prized Dent marble – a fossil-rich polished limestone – was produced in Victorian times.

Cross the bridge over the River Dee and turn right along the road which follows the river past the Sportsman's Inn near Cow Dub Bridge. Continue along this pleasant lane for about half a mile, with the river for company as it gurgles over limestone pavements and potholes, until you reach the bridge at Lea Yeat. Cross the bridge and turn right at the road junction which is signposted to Dent station and Garsdale.

There follows a stiff climb of about half a mile up the hairpins of Helmsike Hill back to Dent station. Across to the right (south) notice the superb engineering of the Settle to Carlisle line, defying Nature as it sweeps above Dentdale on huge embankments and across the impressive Dent Head and Artengill viaducts.

Walkers on the ancient drove road known as Galloway Gate, which contours round the western slopes of Great Knoutberry Hill at the head of Dentdale. Whernside (2,419ft/736m) is the dominant hill in the background. The name of 'Galloway Gate' gives a clue to its origin. It was one of a network of similar broad drove roads by which cattle were driven down from southern Scotland to markets in England, thus avoiding payment on the turnpike roads. These old drove roads were always as broad as this, providing ample roadside grazing for the passing herds of cattle. Another theory is that Galloway Lane gets its name from the Galloway horses which were used as packhorses to transport coal from the extensive mines in Garsdale to the north. It now offers a splendid promenade for walkers around the head of Dentdale, and some of the finest views on the Settle-Carlisle Way

BRIMHAM · ROCKS

Map Ordnance Survey Landranger Sheet 99, Northallerton and Ripon

Start Brimham Hall GR 223631

Length 4½–5 miles

Time Allow 3 hours

Difficulty Easy farm tracks and good paths

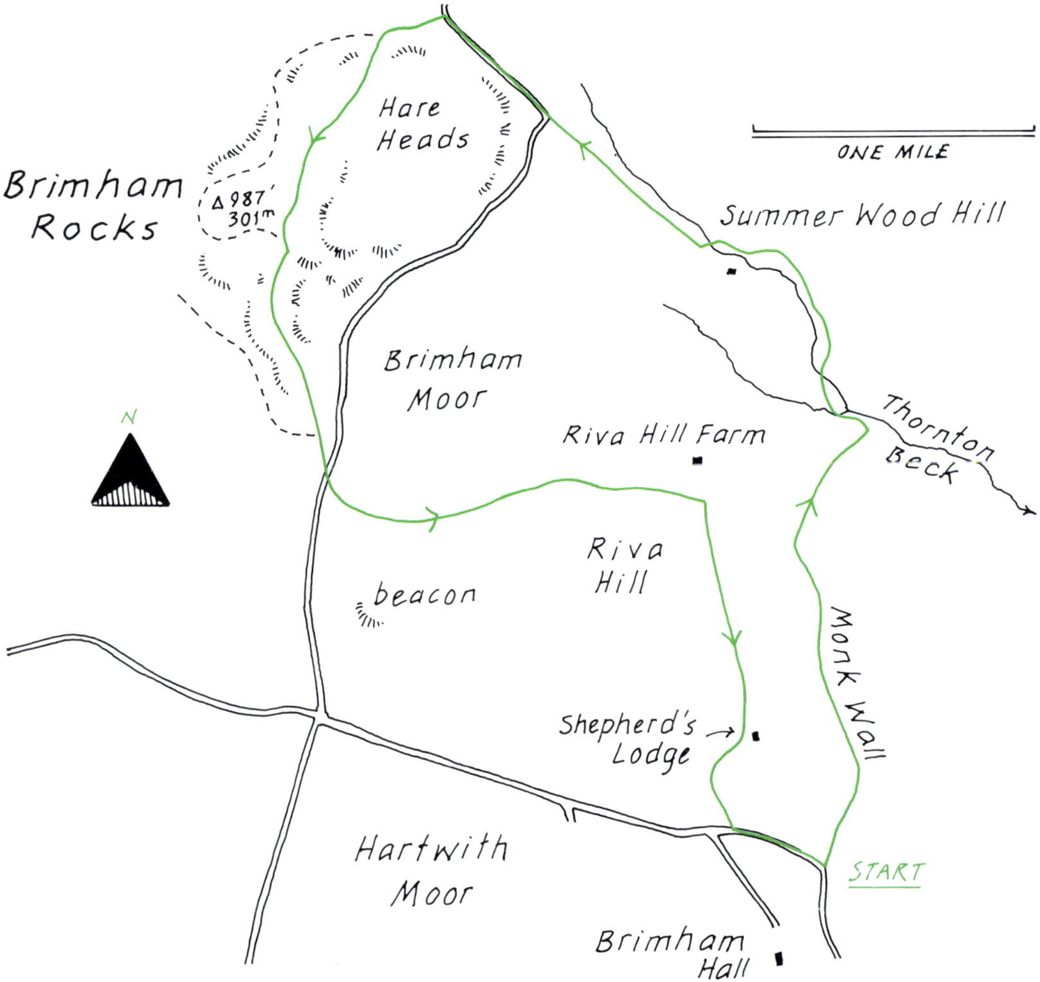

BRIMHAM'S SCULPTURE PARK

Brimham Rocks, the natural rock sculpture park three miles east of Pateley Bridge in Nidderdale, could have inspired the monumental works of the late Henry Moore. Nowhere in Britain is there a more fascinating collection of wind- and ice-sculpted gritstone tors in such a small area.

Early travellers could not accept that these had not been fashioned by human hands. After a visit to Brimham in 1786, the pioneer archaeologist Major Hayman Rooke reported to the Antiquarian Society his view that the rocks were the work of 'artists skilled in the power of mathematics'. Variously described through the ages as a Druid temple and even 'the world's most interesting collection of rocks', Brimham, now safely in the hands of the National Trust, continues to exert a powerful influence and makes a fine half-day outing.

Our walk to explore this amazing collection of rocks starts from Brimham Hall, which lies some 2 miles off the main valley road, the B6165, reached from the hamlet of Burnt Yates. Park carefully and follow the minor road north from the Hall, leaving it where it turns sharply left to follow the bridleway signposted Brimham and Warsil. On the right of this track is the ancient Monk Wall, associated with the vast estates of Fountains Abbey, lower down the dale near Ripon. At a cattle grid, the Monk Wall goes straight ahead, but our way bears left. Here, for the first time, Brimham's strange rock towers appear on the skyline ahead.

Turn right at the first road junction and descend on a concrete farm track towards Thornton Beck, embowered in trees. As you enter the wood, turn left on to a stony track which crosses the beck and go through a gate out of the trees near Summer Wood House. Go to the left of the farm, then follow the track uphill to the left directly to the easternmost outpost of Brimham Rocks – Hare Heads.

Cross the metalled road to reach a gate which gives access to the Rocks, which are set in a sea of purple heather in the late summer. You will need at least an hour to explore these weird and wonderful rocks, which have been lent such exotic names as the Dancing Bear, the Eagle, the Turtle and the Sphinx. It is fun to make up your own names for the outcrops, but do not miss the most spectacular outcrop of all, on the northernmost edge of the estate – the so-called Druid's Idol, a 200 ton rock perched on a pedestal only 12in (30cm) in diameter. The National Trust has set up a useful and informative visitor centre at Brimham House, a former shooting lodge at the centre of the 362 acre (146ha) estate, where there is also a tearoom and toilets.

From the car park at the southern boundary of the estate, head due east across the gorse and heather of Graffa Plain, where a large number of burial mounds have been excavated. The name is thought to mean 'the plain of the graves'. Pass between Riva Hill and the house of the same name. Reaching the concrete farm track again, turn right and retrace your steps alongside the Monk Wall to your starting place.

The Druid's Writing Desk – one of many bizarre rock formations at Brimham Rocks

WILD · BOAR · FELL

Map OS Pathfinder Sheets 617, Sedburgh and Baugh Fell and 607, Tebay and Kirkby Stephen

Start Garsdale station GR 789918

Finish Kirkby Stephen West station GR 763067

Length About 12 miles

Time Allow at least 6–7 hours

Difficulty A strenuous moorland tramp – choose a good day

WILDEST MALLERSTANG

According to the late Dr Eric Treacey, former Lord Bishop of Wakefield and affectionately known as 'The Railway Bishop', there were three wonders of northern England – Hadrian's Wall, York Minster and the Settle and Carlisle Railway.

His regard and affection for this incredibly optimistic piece of Victorian railway engineering is obvious, and a plaque on the down platform at Appleby station records his untimely and sudden death there while photographing trains in 1978. The S&C has accurately been described as the King Lear of British railways, a 72 mile route across some of the most difficult terrain in the country.

Built between 1869 and 1876 by the Midland Railway Company at a cost of £3.5 million, it includes 325 bridges, 21 viaducts and 14 tunnels, and features the highest English mainline station (Dent – 1,150ft/350m), the highest summit (Ais Gill – 1,169ft/356m), and the highest tunnel (under Shotlock Hill). The story of the public campaign to save 'the line that refused to die' after British Rail had tried to starve it of resources is well known, and the fact that today it carries more passengers than ever is a tribute to those campaigners.

Our route to explore some of the least-visited yet most dramatic summits of the western Pennines is one of only two linear routes in this book, and deliberately suggests the use of the S&C to get back to the starting point.

The forbidding escarpment of Wild Boar Fell is a popular and dramatic backdrop to photographs of steam locomotives pulling hard up the notorious 'Long Drag' from Carlisle to Ais Gill summit, and on this superb route, we traverse the entire Wild Boar Fell ridge, reputed site of the killing of the last wild boar in England.

This strenuous walk starts from Garsdale station, one of the most remote on any British main line. One of the great apocryphal stories of the S&C refers to the former turntable at Garsdale, on which a locomotive was alleged to have spun for several hours when it was caught broadside-on by one of the common windstorms which sweep across this part of the Pennines. It was only stopped by pouring sand into the well of the turntable, which was later protected from such disasters by the construction of a palisade of sleepers around it.

Take the road down to the main A684 Sedburgh–Hawes road, and cross it to the footpath opposite, which leads gently up over boggy ground across Garsdale Low Moor, with fine views into Grisedale and Baugh Fell to the left. Eventually, you reach the metalled road which serves Rowantree and Moor Rigg farms. After passing these, bear right contouring up the fellside of White Birks Common and across a line of shakeholes to reach the fence which marks the county boundary with Cumbria.

A stile gives access to the boggy slopes of

On the peaty summit plateau of Wild Boar Fell (2,723ft/708m), looking towards Mallerstang Edge

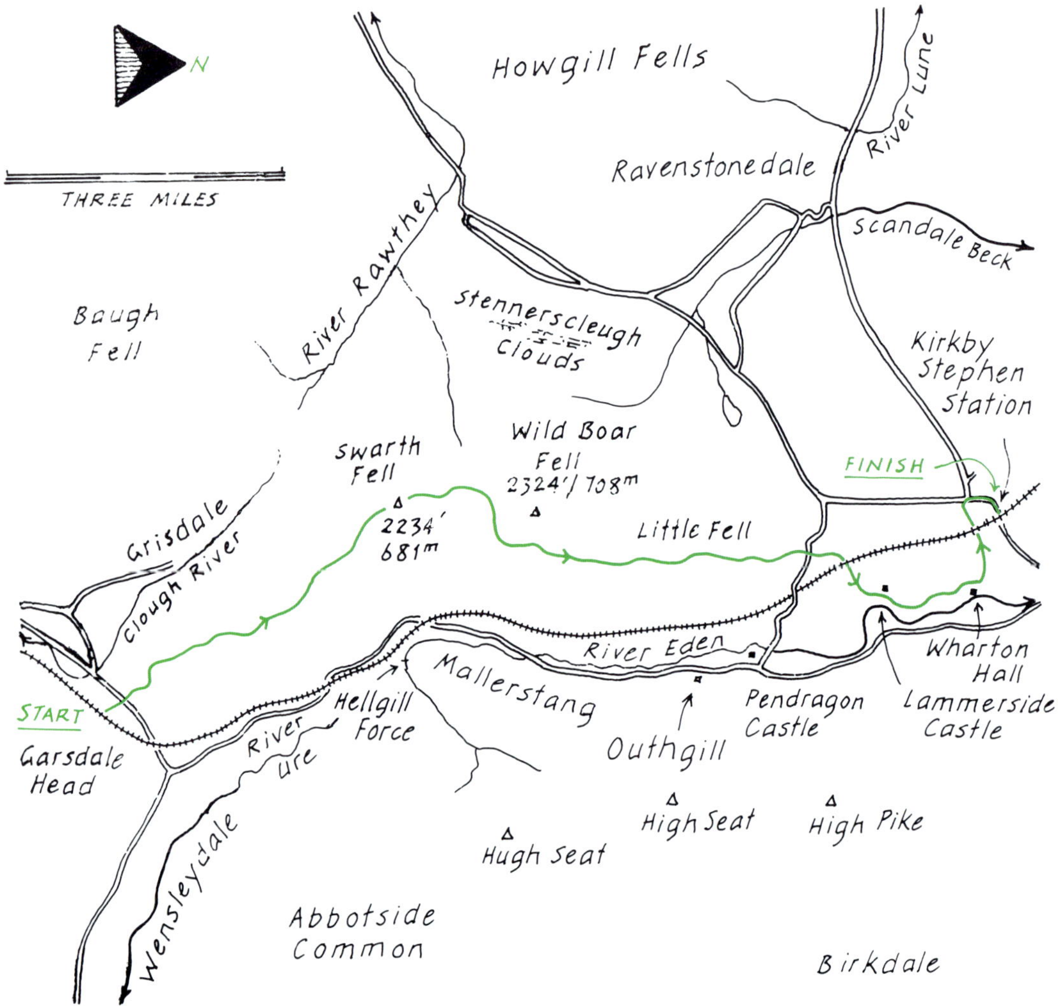

Swarth Fell, which is steadily climbed with increasingly fine views across the central Dales behind. Crossing a jumble of gritstone boulders, you quickly reach Swarth Fell Pike, the day's first summit and a fine viewpoint down the Mallerstang valley.

Walk along Swarth Fell's fine eastern escarpment to reach its reigning summit at 2,234ft (681m). The beautiful countryside at your feet down to Ais Gill and across to the broken escarpment of Mallerstang Edge is, unaccountably, not in the Yorkshire Dales National Park.

As you leave Swarth Fell's bold summit and descend to the col of Standard Brow with its fine linear tarn, you pass out of the National Park completely. The bold summit of Wild Boar Fell ahead is completely unprotected but surely merits inclusion. It is a stiffish pull up to the Wild Boar Fell plateau, but you can be heartened that this is the last real climb of the day.

You are soon on The Band above Ais Gill Head, and for the best views, follow the escarpment around High White Scar (with its crowd of 'stone men' cairns), Yoadcomb Scar and Blackbed Scar to reach the remains of the ancient burial cairn which marks the summit of Wild Boar Fell's Nab at 2,303ft (702m).

On a clear day, this is one of the finest viewpoints in the Pennines. Looking south, Yorkshire's famed Three Peaks are all visible: flat-topped Ingleborough, the sharp peak of Pen-y-Ghent, and Whernside closest on the right. Between them are the unmistakable whaleback of Pendle Hill and the dim outline of the Forest of Bowland, perhaps forty miles away in Lancashire. To the south and west, Morecambe Bay glistens followed by the seductively smooth rounded shapes of the Howgills. Beyond lie the central Lakeland fells, from the Langdales to Great Gable. Looking north, brooding Cross Fell dominates the fertile plains of the Eden Valley, with the Scottish hills beyond.

At your feet looking down into Mallerstang, you have a fine aerial view of the limestone pavements and line of potholes known as Angerholme Pots, and beyond them the wild escarpment of Mallerstang Edge. If you are really lucky, this marvellous panorama may be enhanced by the unforgettable sight of a steam locomotive breasting Ais Gill summit.

Leaving The Nab, carefully descend the delightfully named rocky staircase of the Scriddles, and follow the descending ridge across High and Low Dolphinsty and Little Fell to reach Tommy Road, a minor road leading up from Pendragon Castle. A bridleway leads you north beside a limestone wall, under the railway line and through Croop House Farm.

Descending towards the banks of the Eden, turn left to visit the remains of Lammerside Castle, a fortified medieval bastle house, and then continue on through the lush riverside meadows to the hamlet of Wharton. Wharton Hall is a fine example of a fourteenth-century manor house, fortified against once-frequent Scottish raids. The house is surrounded by fine sets of medieval strip lynchets, while numerous earthworks, bumps and hollows indicate a much larger settlement once existed here.

Take the bridleway from Wharton which leads left under the railway to Easegill Head, where you rejoin the road, turning right for a short stretch on the A685 to Kirkby Stephen West station, from where you can take the train back to Garsdale.

Lammerside Castle, a fortified medieval manor house or bastle, near Wharton

THE · HOWGILL · FELLS

Map OS Pathfinder Sheet 617, Sedburgh and Baugh Fell

Start Four Lane Ends, Howgill, 3½ miles from Sedburgh GR 633958

Finish Sedburgh GR 657922

Length About 8 miles

Time Allow 6–7 hours

Difficulty A hard day with plenty of climbing, but the going underfoot on the Howgills is easy. Do not attempt in mist unless skilled with map and compass

Howgill Fells seen from Shakla Bank near Sedbergh, with Arant Haw rising on the right

IN SEARCH OF THE BLACK HORSE

Everyone knows about the classic White Horses of southern England, but how many have seen the Black Horse of Busha, said to exist on the western slopes of Bush Howe?

The author of *Brigantia*, Guy Ragland Phillips, claimed that the horse was a 'dobbie' – a Celtic horse spirit described as 'a big, black, horrible misshapen thing that slips about', and that local people refused even to talk about it.

The winding, narrow Howgill Lane out of Sedburgh leads to the tiny hamlet after which the whole of this forty square miles of delectable Silurian slate hills is named. About half a mile before Howgill hamlet is Four Lane Ends, which is where the walk begins.

Alfred Wainwright described the walk from here to The Calf, the 2,219ft (676m) summit of the Howgills, as 'beautiful . . . one feels really amongst the hills, intimately so'. As you leave the metalled road at Castley Farm, turning left on a walled track which winds around Castley Knotts and drops down into the valley of Long Rigg Beck into the heart of the hills.

Ahead lie the rounded, typically Howgill heights of Fell Head, Bush Howe and White Fell, your next objective. The central mass of Bram Rigg and The Calf lies out of sight beyond. The celebrated Black Horse soon comes into view on the upper slopes of Bush Howe, although some would say that the patch of naturally formed dark slatey scree looks much more like a short-legged dachshund.

Fording Long Rigg Beck, you begin the long, arduous ascent of the western shoulder of White Fell, with tremendous views down the Lune Valley with its viaducts and the glint of Lily Mere opening up behind.

Approaching White Fell Head you may well see some *real* black horses – the wild Fell ponies which inhabit these hills. From the top of the ridge, turn right along the flat, grassy track which contours around the deep scree-lined valley of Calf Beck to gain the trig point on the summit of The Calf.

From here, turn south and follow the bridleway which runs into the col and up to Bram Rigg Top (2,204ft/672m), then along the ridge to Calders, where the post and wire fence which runs round Hobdale is one of the few enclosures you will find anywhere on the Howgills. From Calders, the bridleway runs clear and true along Rowantree Grains, with views across Hobdale to Middle Tongue, and down into Garsdale and Dentdale beyond. Skirting below the top of Arant Haw, the track leads unerringly towards Winder (1,551ft/473m) via Green Mea.

Winder is a fine viewpoint, overlooking the little town of Sedburgh and the Rawthey Valley, with the hills of the Yorkshire Dales beyond. Drop down off the ridge to follow the bridleway which winds diagonally down to Lockbank Farm, entering Sedburgh via Howgill Lane.

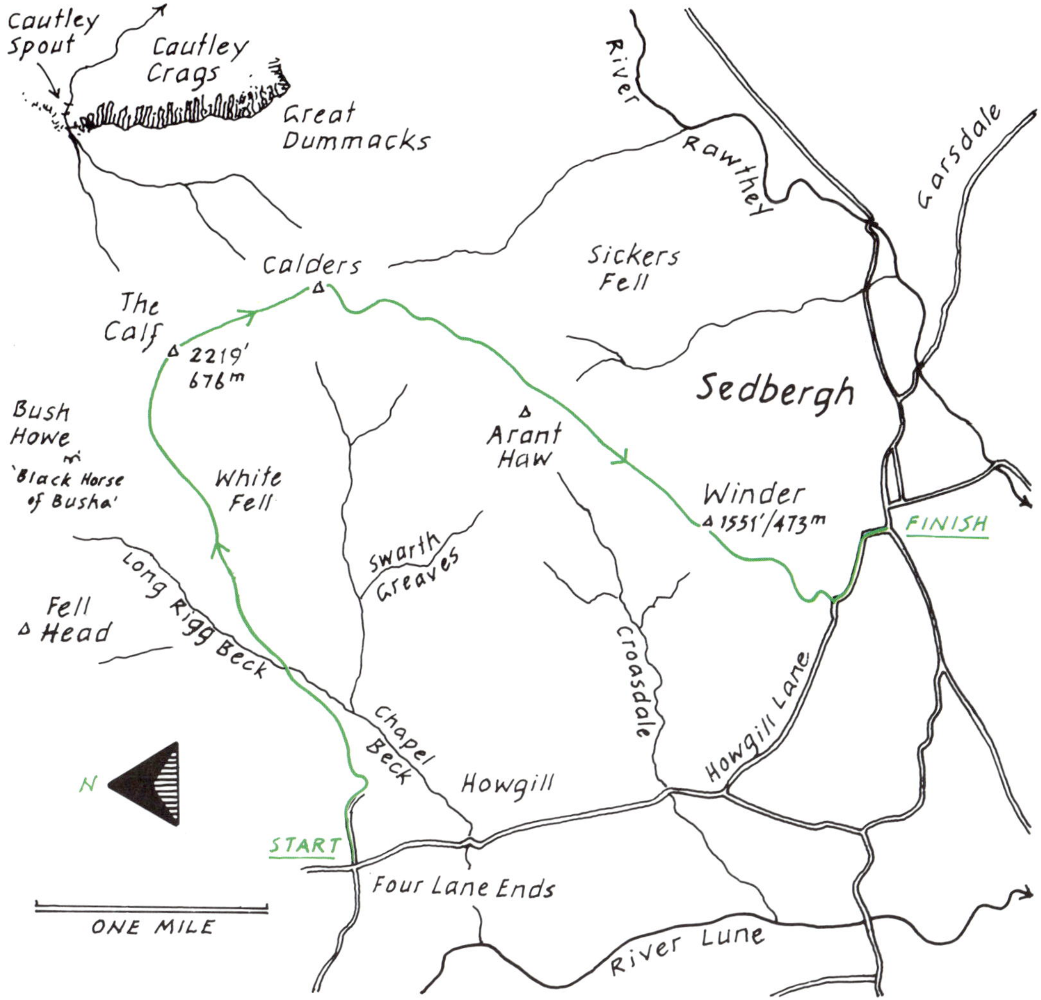

CAUTLEY · SPOUT

Map OS Pathfinder Sheet 617, Sedburgh and Baugh Fell

Start The Cross Keys Inn, Cautley GR 698969

Length 4–6 miles, depending on your chosen route back

Time Allow about 4 hours

Difficulty A quite strenuous fellwalk, which could present difficult navigational problems in mist

THE WATERFALLS OF CAUTLEY SPOUT

From most angles, the Howgill Fells present a gentle, smoothly rounded appearance, resulting from their formation in evenly eroding Silurian slates. This geological fact means that, strictly speaking, they are not part of the Pennines at all but belong more comfortably to the Lake District. However, local government has placed the southern Howgills firmly within the Yorkshire Dales National Park.

The exception to the geological 'rule' of the Howgills, and perhaps the scenic highlight of the range, is to be found at Cautley on their eastern slopes. Here alongside a mile-long cliff of broken crags, a dramatic gash has been gouged in the gentle grassy slopes by a spectacular series of waterfalls some 700ft (213m) high known as Cautley Spout.

The usual approach to Cautley Spout is from the Cross Keys Inn, a temperance hotel on the A683 Sedburgh to Kirkby Stephen road. There is usually enough roadside parking here for you to leave your car safely.

Drop down to the elegant little footbridge which crosses the River Rawthey, and turn left at the top of the bank on the other side. The clear, but often muddy path leads round the slopes of Ben End and is joined from the left by another track coming up from Low Haygarth, a perfect Pennine farmstead sheltered by a belt of trees.

As the Cautley Holme Beck valley opens up to your right, follow the clear path which leads over a number of fords with increasingly fine views into the heart of the hills ahead. To the left, the great broken escarpment of Cautley Crags – the biggest exposure of naked rock in the Howgills – dominates the scene. The summit of Great Dummacks (2,160ft/658m) is to the left and the view down the valley is dominated by the huge bulk of Baugh Fell. Ahead, Cautley Spout is revealed in its tree-fringed gorge between Yarlside to the right and the end of Cautley Crag to the left.

The valley becomes more and more impressive as the path climbs through a belt of bracken and into its deepest confines. As you approach the steep slope up to the falls, take the path which leads closest to the gorge, which is made even more beautiful by the rowans which overhang its vertiginous depths. Take care here, because it is a long drop to the waters of Force Gill Beck. There are two sets of falls, the main one and an upper one nearest the moor top. Follow the path to the Upper Falls, which are possibly the most beautiful because of their fan-shaped cascade.

You now have a choice of routes. You may wish to continue up Swere Gill to meet the bridleway coming up from Bowderdale to the reigning summit of The Calf. You can then follow the ridge to Bram Rigg Top and Calders, turning west at the fence over Little Dummacks to Great Dummacks and the steep descent right of Pickering Gill and Cautley Crags back to Cautley Holme Beck and your outward route.

A shorter alternative is to turn right and take the sheep trod which crosses the grassy saddle

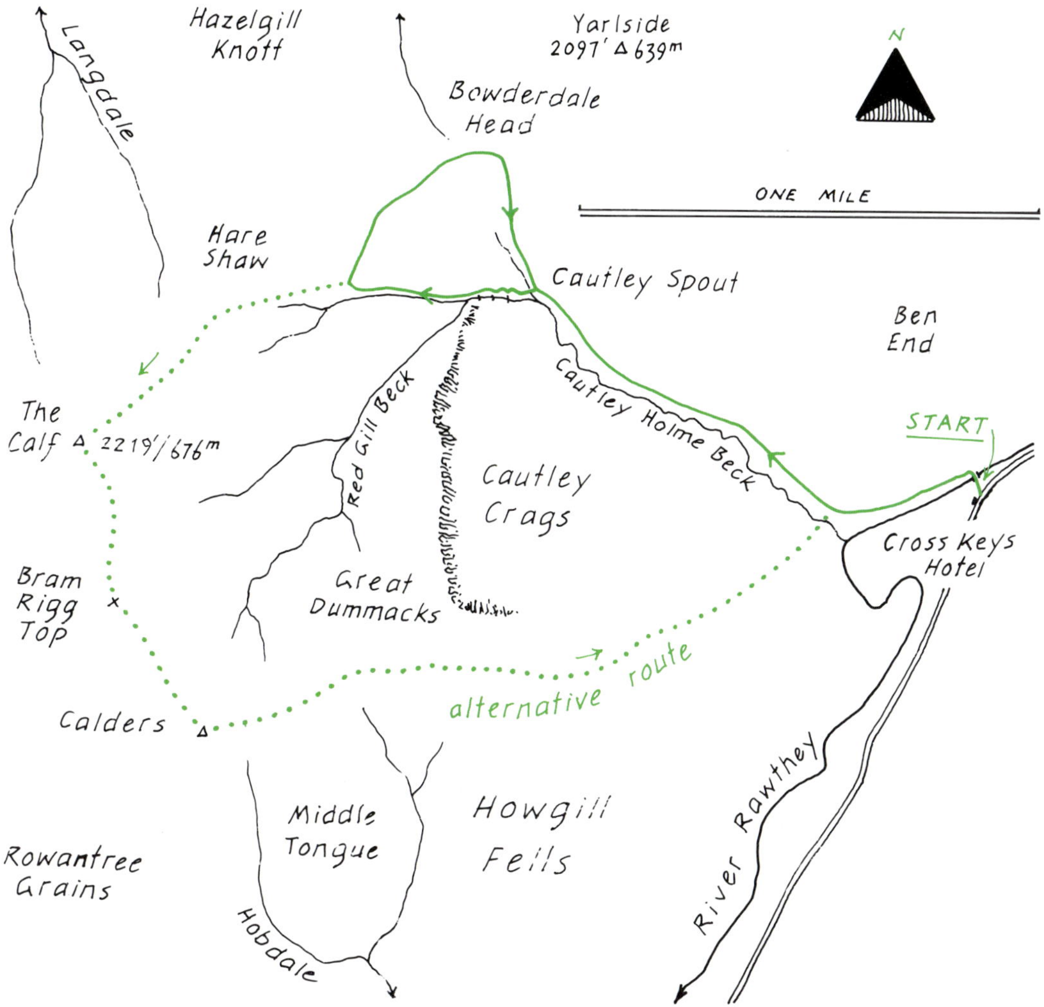

The lace-like Upper Falls of Cautley Spout, on the western slopes of the Howgill Fells

of Bowderdale Head between the two highest summits of the Howgills: The Calf and Yarlside. This joins a path (right) which contours gently down through the screes of Yarlside to rejoin your approach route just past the foot of the waterfalls. It is now a simple walk back down the valley to the Cross Keys Inn.

5

THE·NORTH·PENNINES

ENGLAND'S·LAST·WILDERNESS?

In modern touristspeak, the North Pennines are 'England's Last Wilderness', sandwiched between 'England's Green and Pleasant Land' to the west and the 'Land of the Prince Bishops' to the east. That is how the glossy brochures spawned by a vigorously awakening tourism industry describe the last of the Pennines before Hadrian's Wall, with the Eden valley to the west and Durham on the eastern seaboard.

Officially, however, this land is designated Britain's largest Area of Outstanding Natural Beauty (AONB), and contains a National Nature Reserve (NNR), 28 Sites of Special Scientific Interest (SSSIs), an Environmentally Sensitive Area (ESA) and an internationally important Biosphere Reserve. When John Dower was writing his seminal report on National Parks in England and Wales in 1945, the North Pennines were relegated to his reserve list, along with the North York Moors, the Cheviots, the northern Yorkshire Dales, and the Broads, all of which have since been given full National Park status and protection.

But the North Pennines never quite made it, an omission which is doubly hard to understand, because the contrasting and not always compatible forces of emergent tourism and ecological officialdom both seem to have acknowledged the undoubted quality of this forgotten and still largely undiscovered land.

A settled wilderness. Walls and barn at Bow Hall Farm on the track from Dufton to High Cup Nick

To the walker, the 772sq miles (2,000sq km) of moorland and mountain, spectacular landforms and fascinating history between Stainmore and the Tyne valley offer some of the finest wild walking left in the Pennines. Unsullied by the trippers who throng the honeypots of the Yorkshire Dales to the south and Hadrian's Wall to the north, the North Pennines are perhaps the least spoiled of the northern landscapes, despite over five thousand years of human industry.

Whether they should truly be termed 'England's Last Wilderness' – a phrase which seems to have been coined by Professor David Bellamy, a Teesdale resident and one of the area's most enthusiastic protagonists – is seriously open to question.

It is true that Cross Fell, the strange, barren moonscape which is the highest point of the Pennines, or the awesome, raw power of High Force or Cauldron Snout, can certainly give a very good impression of a wilderness. That breathtaking moment when you seem to emerge on the very edge of the world at High Cup Nick on the Pennine Way is another of Britain's finest wilderness moments; and wandering through the glorious flower meadows of Upper Teesdale can easily conjure up an impression of Ice Age Britain. But every landscape in the North Pennines has to a greater or lesser extent been materially altered by humankind. Some scenes, such as the lead-poisoned landscape of Weardale, or the sad, abandoned cottages of Upper Allendale, leave the walker in no doubt as to their tortured industrial past.

The old industries of lead and silver mining may have declined, leaving their relics to be reclaimed inevitably and silently by Nature, but the new-found discipline of industrial archaeology has generated a revival of interest in their crumbling remains. The Killhope Wheel Lead Mining Centre in Weardale was recently made a World Heritage Site, and its 40ft (12m) diameter cast-iron water wheel is the centrepiece of a fascinating interpretive display reflecting the past industry of the area.

While the town of Allendale's pagan Tar

Barling festival evokes memories of an older religion, Blanchland's ancient abbey walls remind the walker that the power of the medieval Church even spread high up these remote and apparently inhospitable dales.

But for most walkers, the true spirit of the North Pennines is to be found in the spectacular landforms and dazzling flower meadows of Upper Teesdale. Here, in what has been called 'the valley of the ice flowers', the advance of agribusiness has not yet reached the neat, uniformly whitewashed farms of the Raby estate, and national rarities such as blue gentian, bird's eye primrose, alpine rue and alpine bistort, and the area's own Teesdale violet, are allowed to flourish in meadows which are a riot of colour in early summer.

Underlying this Ice Age flora is a unique geology which has been shaped as much by fire as ice. The intrusive basaltic Whin Sill surfaces here to give us the outstanding landforms of High Force, Cauldron Snout and High Cup Nick, and the heat it generated literally baked the rock through which it was forced, so creating the crumbly 'sugar' limestone of the upper part of the dale. Rich in minerals, this sugar limestone created the fertile subsoil needed to support the growth of these floral rarities.

Vast tracts of the North Pennines are out of bounds to the walker, either preserved as grouse moors or, in the Murton Fell, Scordale, Hilton, Tinside Rigg and Mickle Fell areas, excluded as part of the enormous Ministry of Defence Warcop Training Range. Here public access is only permitted during periods when the range is clear – usually on Mondays – and walkers cross these areas at their own risk. Details of access arrangements can be checked by ringing the Warcop Range Officer's Department of the MoD on Brough (07683) 661.

Bombarded by artillery, scarred by industry and restricted by official designations, the North Pennines can sometimes seem to be a landscape under seige. But they have survived all these pressures to give the seeker after solitude some of the loveliest and loneliest walking in England.

Travelling north on his journey through Great Britain in 1725, Daniel Defoe described the 'terrible aspect' of the western escarpment of the Northern Pen-nines from the Vale of Eden as looking 'like a wall of brass'. And that is exactly how they can appear when the rays of the setting sun seem to ignite the forbidding crags of Melmerby High Scar, Wildboar Scar and High Cup.

It is then that the land of the seven dales, which gives birth to three of the greatest northern rivers – the Tyne, the Tees and the Eden – can truly resemble 'England's Last Wilderness'.

The massive 40ft (12m) diameter water wheel at the Kilhope Lead Mining Centre in Weardale

A deserted farmstead on Allendale Common, above High Shield, Allenheads

CROSS · FELL

Map OS Landranger Sheet 91, Appleby

Start Blencarn village GR 636312

Length 11 miles

Time Allow at least 6–7 hours

Difficulty A tough, challenging fellwalk, which should not be attempted unless the weather is clear and you are properly equipped with map and compass

ON TOP OF THE PENNINES

To Pennine Wayfarers, Cross Fell is usually a long, boring slog en route from Dufton to Garrigill, approached over the only slightly lesser heights of Great and Little Dun Fells to the south. In truth, this is hardly the best approach to the highest point of the Pennines.

The following route was suggested by my friend the North Pennine connoisseur Paddy Dillon, and pays due regard to Cross Fell as a satisfying summit in its own right – which it surely deserves.

Cross Fell, capped by cloud, as seen from near Crewgarth in the Vale of Eden

Cross Fell, at 2,930ft (893m), is a mountain of myth and mystery. It is said to have been given its name following a visit by the early Christian missionary St Paulinus during the seventh century. Before this, it was known as Friend's Fell, and was the haunt of devils. St Paulinus held a mass on the bleak, windswept summit to drive out the demons, and erected a cross there to mark the exorcism. Some of those exhausted Wayfarers might be excused for wondering whether he succeeded, and local people in the Eden valley below know that at least one devil still remains in the form of the vicious Helm Wind.

The Helm has the distinction of being the only wind in Britain to have been given a name. It occurs when a northeasterly wind blows up and across the Pennines, tumbling with amazing force over the western escarpment near Cross Fell and into the Eden valley below, causing all kinds of havoc. It is presaged by the Helm Cap – a bank of cloud building over the escarpment – and the Helm Bar – which forms in the resulting vortex of wind.

Cross Fell is also famous for a bewildering geology which, in addition to the traditional Pennine mix of limestone, shale and grit, includes intrusions of the Whin Sill and coal, silver and lead mines. It is also a National Nature Reserve, part of a World Biosphere Reserve, and a Site of Special Scientific Interest on account of its rare sub-Arctic flora, more akin to the Cairngorms than the English Pennines. All this means that Cross Fell is a very special place, and a worthy summit to crown the Pennines.

Our expedition to the roof of the Pennines starts from the East Fellside village of Blencarn, a backwater settlement grouped protectively around its green at the foot of the hill. A corridor of unenclosed rough pasture – perhaps used to bring sheep and cattle down from the hill for protection in times of trouble – leads to a bridleway out from the southern end of the village and towards the foothills.

This old trackway soon crosses the ancient Maiden Way, a Roman road which may have been used to take the precious lead ore from the Pennines to the lowlands. Then, as it enters open country, it passes to the south of the isolated farm of Wythwaite, a typical Norse settlement.

Looking north from this gradually ascending track, you may be able to make out a series of ancient cultivation terraces below Ranbeck Farm. These are somewhat romantically

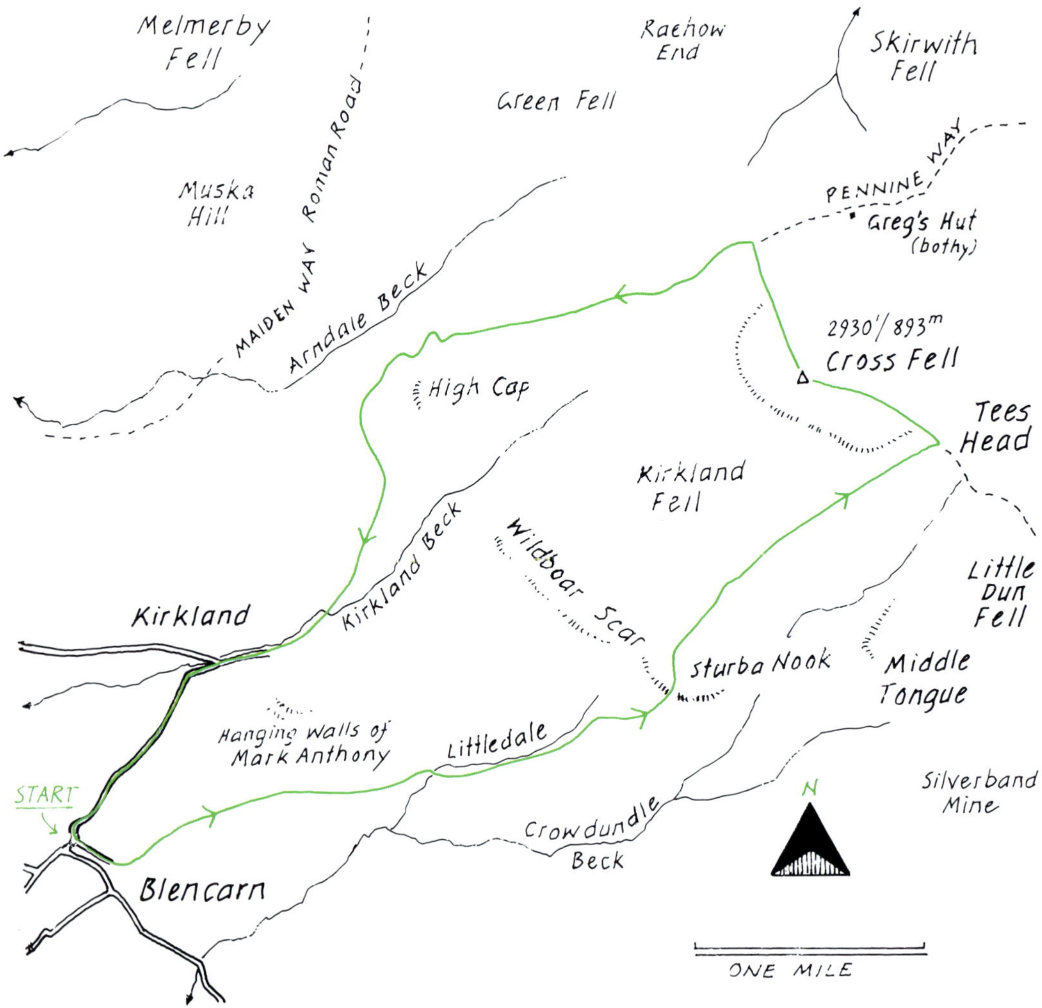

known as 'The Hanging Walls of Mark Anthony', although what Mark Anthony was doing building walls on these bleak northern hills has not been explained.

The old grassy trackway leads on steadily up the slopes, passing to the left of Grumply Hill on the banks of a small beck and then, by a narrow track, through the screes and crags of Wildboar Scar at 1,985ft (605m). A sketchy path runs northwest from here to Tees Head, on the col between Little Dun Fell to the right and Cross Fell to the left. This boggy patch of peaty moorland is the undistinguished birthplace of the mighty River Tees, which grows in strength just across the hill in Upper Teesdale.

Our route now joins the badly eroded Pennine Way for the final approach to Cross Fell's extensive summit plateau. The summit itself is marked by a collection of furniture which includes a trig point, a cross-shelter and several cairns. The western edge of the plateau has some superb views across the Vale of Eden to the not-so-distant Lakeland hills, and beyond them, the Scottish Southern Uplands. It is a grand viewpoint on a clear day, as you would expect at such an altitude.

Leave the summit by the Pennine Way (northbound), past Crossfell Well (a spring) and The Screes. Half a mile east from here is Greg's Hut, an often welcome bothy for tired Pennine Wayfarers. Our route however, turns left (west) from a large cairn and heads down the fellside on a stony and often wet track across the broad western shoulder of Cross Fell. This

Sunset over the Vale of Eden from Cross Fell

was the old 'Corpse Road' – one of the highest in the country – by which bodies were carried from Garrigill to be buried in the consecrated burial ground of St Lawrence's, Kirkland.

After some soggy going, you pass the remains of some small coal pits, just above the top of High Cap (1,794ft/547m). The track, which appears to have served the coal pits, improves from here, and descends the steep slopes of High Cap by some well-engineered zig-zags.

The gradient eases as you approach the valley of Kirkland Beck and enter the village of Kirkland by the lane which leads up past Kirkland Hall. Looking south from here there is another view of the Hanging Walls of Mark Anthony. It is now a mere mile along the minor road past the small Blencarn Reservoir, back to Blencarn village.

UPPER · TEESDALE

Map OS Outdoor Leisure Sheet 31, Teesdale

Start High Force Hotel GR 885287

Length 12–13 miles

Time Allow 8 hours

Difficulty A really tough moorland walk over some of the roughest and most remote places in the Pennines. Not for the inexperienced

WILDEST TEESDALE

Upper Teesdale is a place apart, a unique reminder of Ice Age Britain reflected in landscapes and in a flora which echoes twelve thousand years of natural history.

The Ice Age flowers of Upper Teesdale – the startlingly blue spring gentians, delicate pink bird's eye primroses, yellow mountain saxifrages and the creamy-white candles of alpine bistort – are internationally important and strictly protected in a National Nature Reserve.

Approaching remote Widdy Bank Farm in Upper Teesdale, with Cronkley Scar on the left

Quite apart from the precious alpine and arctic plants which adorn the surrounding hills, the restless, rushing waters of the Tees have carved out some of the most spectacular landforms in the Pennines. High Force must be one of the most brutally powerful waterfalls in the British Isles, while the 'Devil's cauldron' of Cauldron Snout, a few miles upstream, is one of the most impressive, in its wild and remote setting. This is one of the few walks in this book which follows the over-used line of the Pennine Way, but Tom Stephenson's magnificent route along the banks of the Upper Tees past High Force, Falcon Clints and Cauldron Snout really cannot be bettered.

Start from the High Force Hotel, where there is a large car park and toilets. Ignore the crowds heading across the road to the woodland walk which leads down to the waterfall via the north bank of the river, and instead turn left and walk down the road for a couple of hundred yards to the gate and steps which lead down to Holwick Head Bridge, and another botanical wonder of Teesdale. Over the bridge, turn right and ascend on the easily graded path to enter the Teesdale National Nature Reserve at a stile with an English Nature sign.

The path above Keedholm Scar passes through one of the largest remaining juniper woods in Britain. The scented trees are mostly stunted into low bushes, but there are others which grow tall and slim like cypresses. Their wood, known as savin, was once used to make the best quality charcoal.

The thunderous roar of High Force leads you on until you get your first glimpse of this tremendous cataract through the junipers. The ferocious fall plunges 70ft (21m) over a black outcrop of Whin Sill dolerite into the dismal pool beneath, sending up plumes of spray. Usually, there are two falls dropping either side of a central buttress. It is always an impressive sight, but perhaps especially so in spring when the peat-stained river is in spate, swollen by melted snow.

The path leads on through the stunted woodland to the top of the falls and then on past the ugly Middleton Quarry on the opposite bank (beware of blasting) to the short ascent of Bracken Rigg, with its fine views down to the tiered rocks of Dine Holm Scar opposite. The river makes a sweeping curve here, turning north towards Forest-in-Teesdale, and the path follows it faithfully, descending past Cronkley Farm and across the water meadows to the bridge across the Tees.

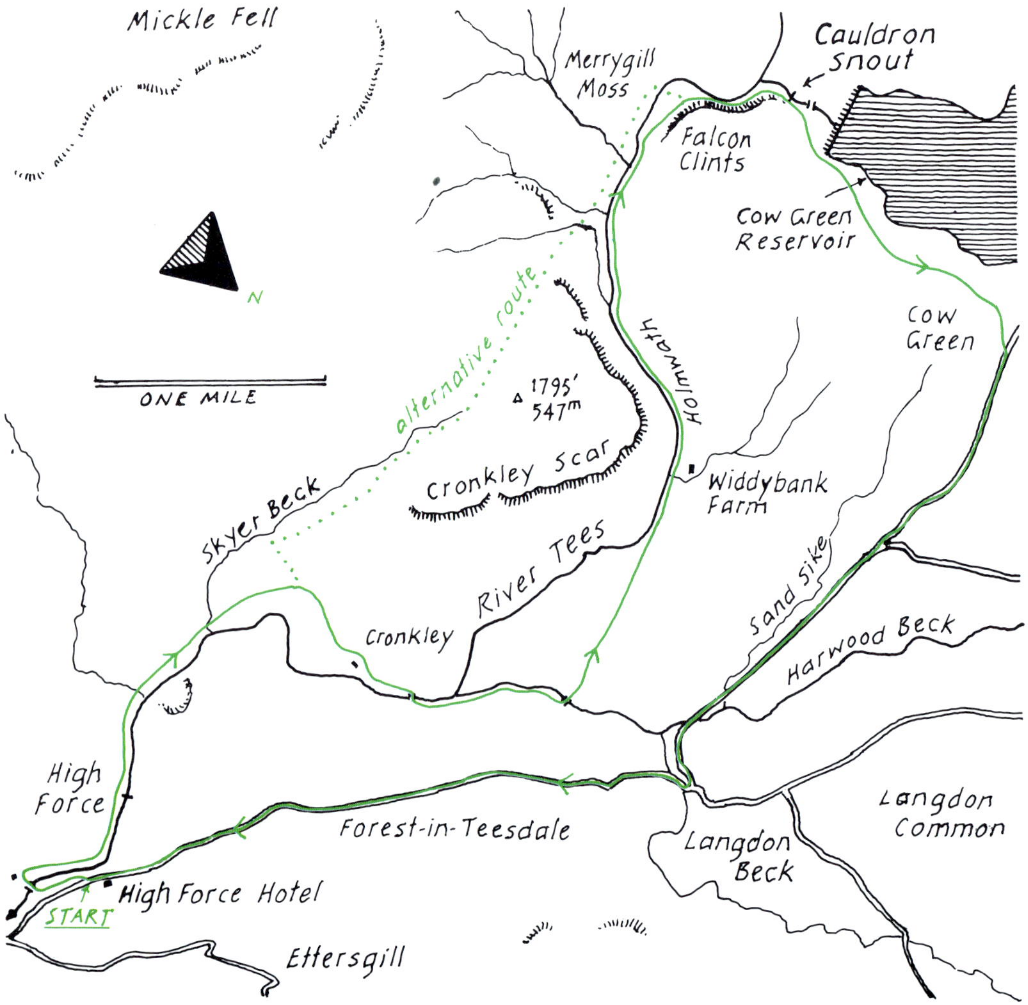

Turn left over the bridge and follow the footpath beneath Haugh Hill to Saur Hill Bridge, which crosses Langdon Beck and leads up to Sayer Hill Farm. Pass to the left of the farm and over a step stile on to the open fellside of Widdybank Pasture.

A sign by another stile tells you that you are entering the National Nature Reserve as you head towards the wild, broken escarpment of Cronkley Scar across the river, the former location of the Widdy Bank Pencil Mill which made slate pencils from an outcrop of Devonian shale. A diversion on to a farm track leads you to white-painted Widdy Bank Farm, part of the massive Raby estate and surely one of the most remote farms in the Pennines.

The route now returns to the riverside, winding between the high fells and crossing increasingly rough ground over a long series of duckboards designed to help the walker and protect the delicate vegetation of the area. A strenuous scramble across boulder fields and scree below the cliffs of Falcon Clints is a real test of agility and footwear. This is most definitely mountain-boot country!

Eventually, the path leaves the whinstone boulders, turning north towards the sound of another River Tees highlight – Cauldron Snout. Nothing can prepare you for your first sight of the thunderous fan of boiling white spray which issues from a narrow cleft in the glistening black wall of the Whin Sill high above. This view from the foot of the Snout is one of the great surprise sights of the Pennines, and a very welcome one on the often monotonous Pennine Way.

Climb carefully up the rocky staircase on the right of the waterfall, emerging at the top to another, less pleasant, surprise. The great white concrete wall of the Cow Green Dam greets you, and you realise that the power of Cauldron Snout is no longer entirely natural, being controlled by the dam. Cow Green was the scene of an epic battle between environmentalists and developers in the 1960s. The result was a defeat for the conservationists and the construction of the massive Cow Green Reservoir, which flooded many of the riverside meadows on which the rare flowers of Teesdale flourished.

You now have a choice of return routes. You can either retrace your steps down past Cauldron Snout, carefully ford the river and return sticking closely to the southern bank, or cross desolate Cronkley Fell via Man Gate, White Well Green, Thistle Green and Birk Rigg on the bridleway back to Bracken Rigg, rejoining your outward route back to High Force.

Another option is to take the metalled waterworks road which leads up right past the dam wall and round the eastern shore of the huge reservoir, built to supply water to Teesside's thirsty industry, following what the water company euphemistically calls a nature trail. Unfortunately, it does not show the rich heritage which was lost when the waters flooded in, including the fabled 'Wheel of the Tees', a great meander which used to swing almost full-circle through the flower-rich meadows.

Walkers on the Pennine Way in remote upper Teesdale

The road is followed until it reaches the minor road which leads down to the main car park at Cow Green. Turn right here for a lonely 2 mile road walk across the wastes of Widdybank, crossing Langdon Beck to reach the hamlet of the same name and the main valley road B6277, which is followed for another two miles to the High Force Hotel.

The view from the lip of High Force, England's greatest waterfall

HIGH · CUP

Map OS Outdoor Leisure Sheet 31, Teesdale

Start Dufton village GR 690250

Length About 10 miles

Time Allow at least 6 or 7 hours

Difficulty A steep climb on a good track, followed by some tough moorland walking. Map, compass and boots essential

HIGH DRAMA AT HIGH CUP

The Great Whin Sill, an igneous intrusion through the regular sedementary geological successions of the Pennines, creates some of their most impressive landforms. It was utilised by Hadrian as the natural foundation for his monumental frontier fortification; it created the spectacular waterfalls of High and Low Force and Cauldron Snout; and it is responsible for perhaps one of the most exciting landscapes in the Pennines at High Cup Nick.

The Whin Sill crags of High Cup, looking east from Nichol's Chair

The glaciated valley of High Cup bites deeply into the western scarp of the Pennines above Dufton, but what gives High Cup its unique character is the upstanding horseshoe-shaped frieze of dolerite crags, formed of the Whin Sill, which rims the canyon.

High Cup Nick comes as a spectacular highlight on the Pennine Way, and a welcome relief to the weary Wayfarer plodding the long moorland miles from Cauldron Snout across Golden Mea and the soggy valley of Maize Beck. Suddenly the world is at your feet.

Our route to High Cup Nick reverses the Pennine Way by starting from the pretty red sandstone village of Dufton, clustered around its green and watched over by conical Dufton Pike in the verdant Eden valley.

Head out from Dufton past Dufton Hall as if to take the Pennine Way north, but go straight on where a bridleway sign indicates High Scald Fell. This narrow track leads steadily uphill past Pusgill House on the right, heading directly towards Dufton Pike, one of a line of conical slaty hills beneath the Pennine scarp. The track contours right around the back of this shapely 1,578ft/481m hill, above the unpleasantly named Pus Gill and past some old pit workings on the left. At the back of Dufton Pike, the now-stony track enters the steep defile of Great Rundale, between Bownber Hill on the left and Bluethwaite Hill on the right.

This valley has been scarred by industry in the past when it was the scene of much mining activity for lead and barytes. Various workings, levels and, on the opposite bank, distinctive 'hushes', where water was used to expose lead veins, are visible. Recently, there have been attempts to reactivate this industry, using this old track which has been extended higher up the hillside. However, the valley is silent again now, and a steep climb brings you out through a line of shakeholes in the limestone to the flat of High Scald Fell.

Directly ahead (due east) is Great Rundale Tarn, a peaty pool overlooked by an old shelter hut. The tarn, one of several on this boggy plateau, does not, in fact, drain into Great Rundale but sends its waters east into Maize Beck and eventually into the North Sea via the Tees. Follow the outlet to the tarn and head downstream, keeping to the northern (left hand) bank for a boggy mile and a half.

Eventually, you will emerge at the footbridge which crosses the northern end of Maizebeck Scar. You then pick up the well-worn track of the Pennine Way through the limestone

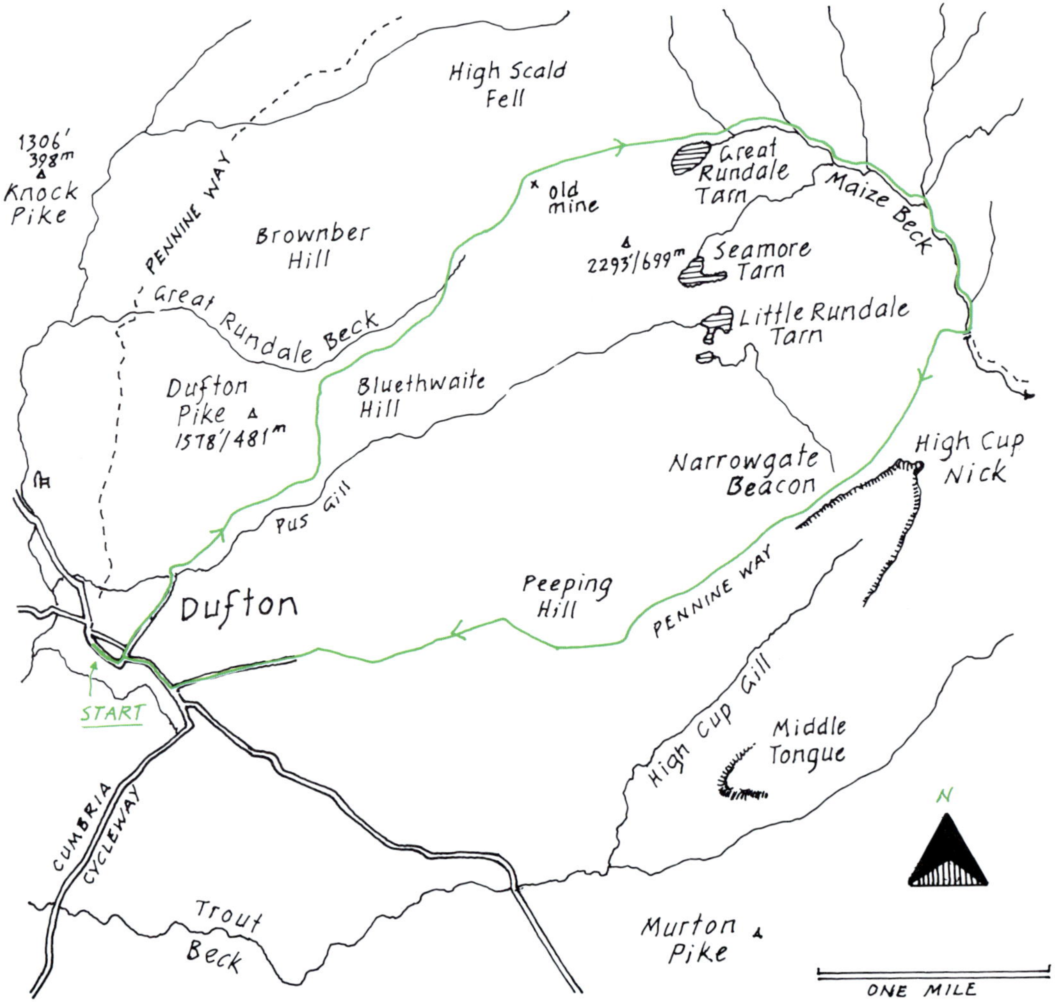

outcrops of High Cup Plain. Within half a mile the stupendous chasm of High Cup Nick fairly explodes into view at your feet. Strictly speaking, the 'Nick' only refers to the apex of the re-entrant, where the tiny High Cupgill Beck flows down into the yawning gulf of High Cup, flanked on the left by High Cup Scar and on the right by Narrowgate Beacon. The colonnade of dolerite stands up like a collar around the rim, and the view down into the depths of the gill is truly breathtaking. In good weather the view extends across the Eden Valley to the blue, misty hills of Lakeland.

Our return route to Dufton follows the Pennine Way around the northern rim of High Cup by the Narrow Gate path. See if you can spot the isolated pinnacle of Nichol's Chair among the rocks along this side; it is supposed to have been named after a Dufton cobbler who not only climbed to its top, but soled a pair of boots while sitting there.

Hannah's Well, a clear spring on the rocky path beneath Narrowgate Beacon, is the next landmark, and the route leads easily down through outcrops of limestone and shakeholes around the disused Peeping Hill quarry. The walled track bends sharply left across Dod Hill and passes Bow Hall to re-enter Dufton at Town Head by Billysbeck Bridge, where you must turn right to return to the centre of this charming fellside village.

Looking back from Great Rundale towards conical Dufton Pike

BLANCHLAND

Map OS Landranger Sheet 87, Hexham and Haltwhistle

Start Blanchland GR 965504

Length About 9 miles

Time Allow about 4 hours

Difficulty A moderate moorland and forest walk on good tracks most of the way

JEWEL OF THE DERWENT

The beautiful stone-built village of Blanchland in the Upper Derwent Valley is surrounded by some fine heather moorland, some of which we explore on this walk.

Blanchland was based on a Premonstratensian abbey, founded here in 1169. The monks, never more than a dozen in number, were members of an order which was an offshoot of the white-robed Cistercians – hence the name meaning 'white land' – who always sought out remote places for their devotions.

Blanchland village, showing the old abbey gatehouse, now the Post Office

BLANCHLAND

Map OS Landranger Sheet 87, Hexham and Haltwhistle

Start Blanchland GR 965504

Length About 9 miles

Time Allow about 4 hours

Difficulty A moderate moorland and forest walk on good tracks most of the way

JEWEL OF THE DERWENT

The beautiful stone-built village of Blanchland in the Upper Derwent Valley is surrounded by some fine heather moorland, some of which we explore on this walk.

Blanchland was based on a Premonstratensian abbey, founded here in 1169. The monks, never more than a dozen in number, were members of an order which was an offshoot of the white-robed Cistercians – hence the name meaning 'white land' – who always sought out remote places for their devotions.

Blanchland village, showing the old abbey gatehouse, now the Post Office

Legend relates how a band of Border raiders, intent on sacking the abbey, became lost in fog near Grey Friars Hill. The overjoyed monks unwisely rang the abbey bells in celebration, thus giving away their position. Dead Friars, below Bell's Hill on Blanchland Common, perhaps hints at the result of their action.

The village today is largely based on the plan of the abbey's outbuildings, and is dominated by the squat tower of what remains of the abbey church. The gatehouse is the post office and the abbot's lodge is now the Lord Crewe Arms.

Our walk starts from the gravelled square in the centre of the village. Take the lane which leads to the hamlet of Shildon, and is soon replaced by gravel track. Notice the ruins of the large former lead mine, but do not be tempted to explore: the buildings and shafts are in a dangerous condition.

The clear track continues to climb quite steeply for just over a mile until a gate is reached giving access to the open Blanchland Moor by the charmingly named Pennypie House. It is said to have taken its name from the fact that drovers and lead miners using the track could stop and buy a pie for a penny here.

The track now levels off below War Law Hill and then descends to enter the fringe of the extensive Slaley Forest, one of the Forestry Commission's monotonous and alien 'tree factories' which cloak so many of our northern hills. Turn left along a track on the edge of the forest which passes through a newly planted area and then into more mature forestry.

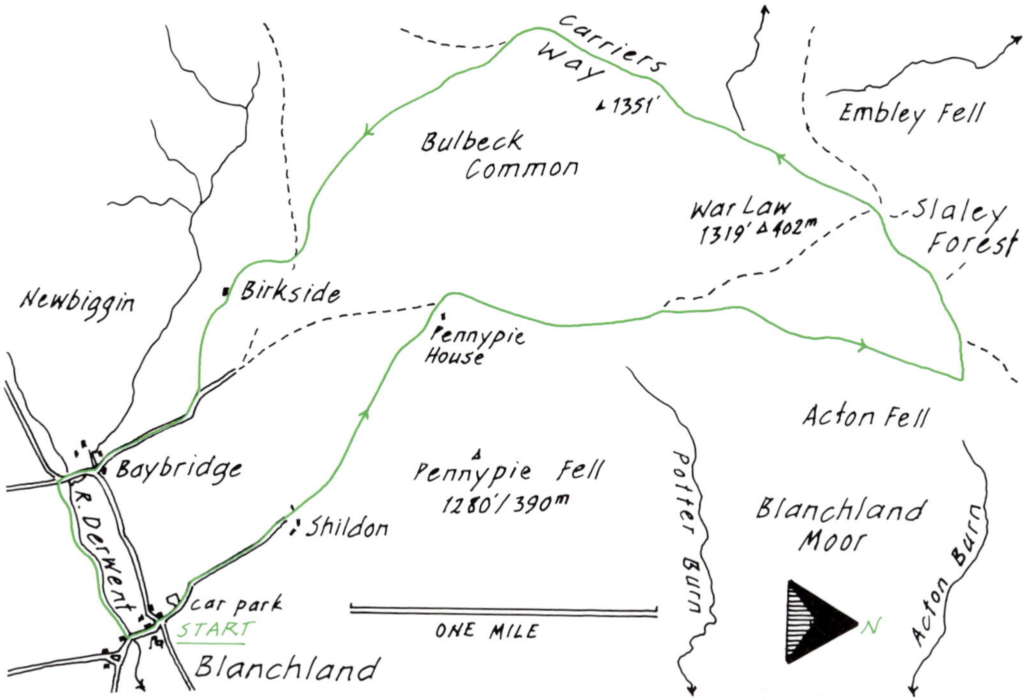

When the track swings right, take the ride on the left which leaves the forest by a gate. Bear a little left of the main track across the open moor, to walk slightly uphill and meet the Carrier's Way, an ancient packhorse route hollow-way winding through the heather.

Follow this track around War Law, which gives good views of Devil's Water down in the valley, until it descends to a gate and a wooden post, where you turn left past another post to pick up a track which leads off the moor and down to the farm of Birkside. The road to the farm gives access to the road, which descends to the village of Baybridge.

From Baybridge, cross the river and turn left on a pleasant woodland path which follows the river for the half-mile back to Bridge End, Blanchland. Turn left to re-enter the village.

6

NORTHUMBERLAND

THE·LAND·OF·FAR·HORIZONS

The Romans called the site of their temporary marching camps at Chew Green in the wild, wet wilderness at the head of the Coquet Valley in the Cheviot Hills *Ad Fines*, which freely translated means 'the end of the world'.

At the time this was the northernmost extremity of the Roman Empire, and to the poor legionaries posted to this most inhospitable spot, it must truly have seemed the last outpost of civilisation.

Even today, the faint lines in the wilderness which mark the embankments of grass-covered stones near the Cheviot Border Ridge at Chew Green are still evocative of the all-conquering power of Rome. To the well-known authority, Professor Sir Ian Richmond, they were quite simply 'the most remarkable visible group of Roman earthworks in Britain'.

Surely one of the most imposing monuments to Roman military might in Europe is Hadrian's Wall, built across the neck of England between the River Tyne and the Solway Firth under order of the Emperor Hadrian in AD120. It took a labour force of ten thousand men eight years to construct, and for nearly three hundred years was garrisoned and patrolled by generations of Roman soldiers and auxiliaries.

That sense of being at the edge of civilisation has always marked the Northumbrian Pennines, and it is interesting to note that when the vast Redesdale Army Training Area, now known as the Otterburn Camp, was set up in 1911, the first camp near Rochester was still known as Ad Fines.

Northumberland is still England's empty quarter. The population of the 405sq mile (1,049sq km) Northumberland National Park (which includes Hadrian's Wall country, the Simonside Hills and the Cheviots to the north) is just 2,200 – the population of a typical Dales village. The number of visitors – an estimated one million per annum – is the smallest to any of Britain's eleven national parks.

A fifth of the National Park is still a military zone occupied by the Ministry of Defence, where unwelcoming signs inform the walker: 'Danger. Military Target Area. Do not touch anything; it may explode and kill you.' When the red flags are flying on the Otterburn ranges, the rule is 'keep out', surely an incongruity in an area set aside for public recreation.

A further fifth of the National Park is owned by the Forestry Commission, whose serried ranks of conifers cloak the once open hillsides. The unnatural landscape of Kielder to the southwest of the Park, is the largest man-made forest surrounding the largest man-made lake in Europe.

Peeping out from the bottle-brush conifers of the Kielder, Wark, Wauchope, Falstone and Redesdale forests are moorland heights with names which give a clue to the sometimes violent past of these hills. Places like Bloodybush Edge, Oh Me Edge, Deadwater Fell, Blackman's Law and Gallow Lane hint at the bad old days.

Wherever you go in the Northumbrian Pennines, it is hard to escape that feeling of being on a border. Perhaps it is an echo of the bloody past of these watching hills, for throughout their history, the Northumberland uplands have always been 'debatable land'.

This was never more so than during the three hundred years of the Anglo-Scottish Border reivers, between the late thirteenth and mid-sixteenth centuries, when cross-border raiding was rife. It was a time, according to its most

On the edge of the Empire: Hadrian's Wall marches west along the crest of Housesteads Crags

eloquent chronicler, George MacDonald Fraser, when 'no man who lived between the Scottish Southern Uplands and the Pennines could walk abroad unarmed in safety; no householder in all the Marches could go to sleep secure; no beast or cattle could be left unguarded'.

The Border reiver, or 'steel bonnet', was a unique figure, a kind of rustic gangster who might come from any social class and who abided by no law other than his own. History books, coloured by the romantic ballads of Sir Walter Scott and others, have tended to impart a false chivalrous gallantry to the Border reiver but, according to Fraser, he was a professional cattle-rustler who was also a skilful fighting man, and 'a guerrilla soldier of great resource to whom the arts of theft, raid, tracking and ambush were second nature'. He left murder, plunder and destruction in his wake.

The effect of all this is still evident in the small, isolated Northumbrian settlements like Elsdon, the 'capital' of Redesdale, built protectively around a green where cattle could be herded in times of trouble. Elsdon, a perfect little Border village, also has one of the best examples of a vicar's pele tower, a fortified house which could double as a mini-castle when the steel bonnets called.

Elsewhere in the countryside the remains of so-called bastle houses can still be found. These were similarly fortified farmhouses, where the upper floor accommodated the farmer and his family, and the lower his cattle or stock. Good examples are to be found at Black Middens in North Tynedale, and Gatehouse in the valley of the Tarset Burn a few miles northwest of Bellingham. With a few exceptions, all bastle houses occur within twenty miles of the border, a zone stipulated for their construction under an Act of Parliament of 1555.

The reivers also left their mark in the English language, where the word 'bereave' still reminds us of one of their stocks-in-trade; and 'blackmail' another: the word originally referred to the illegal rent or protection money paid by Border residents to powerful reivers in order that they should be left alone and protected against other raiders.

No such protection was available to the native Brigantian tribes when the might of Rome drove north as far as Northumberland. A string of hillforts, settlements and field systems especially on the northern foothills of the Cheviots show that the area was relatively highly populated by the time of the Iron Age, when the Roman legions arrived.

The most important of these hillforts is Yeavering Bell, where a wall of tumbledown stones still marks the boundary of an extensive 17 acre (7ha) hillfort in which up to 120 hut circles have been identified. It is also one of the finest viewpoints of the northern Cheviots, with commanding views over the rolling 'White Lands' of the Cheviots to the south and the valley of the Tweed and Lammermuir Hills across the border to the north.

In the valley of the River Glen immediately below the heather and bilberry-clad heights of Yeavering Bell, a rather incongruous monument marks the site of Ad Gefrin, the Anglo-Saxon palace of Aethelfrith and Edwin, successive kings of Northumbria in the seventh century, and where Paulinus restored Christianity to the area. Roman roads, such as Dere Street, Gamel's Path and The Maiden Way, still thread the hills.

Hadrian's Wall came after several abortive attempts to establish a strong northern border to the all-conquering Empire. It utilised the rolling crest of the Great Whin Sill, an igneous intrusion of basalt which provides a natural line of defence facing to the north, and it remains one of the best places in northern Europe to appreciate the glory that was Rome.

The 73 mile Wall, soon to become an official National Trail, has attracted travellers and antiquaries for centuries. In 1801 William Hutton, a businessman, walked the 600 miles from Birmingham along the length of the Wall and back again, at the age of 78. It is obvious from reading his charming and humorous account, written as an antidote to the dry-as-dust reports of contemporary antiquaries, that Hutton was in love with the Wall. Others have since followed in Hutton's footsteps, and more still will come when it becomes an official trail, but few have imparted as much wit and wisdom on their tour. Jessie Mothersole, whose *Had-*

Enigmatic cup-and-ring markings score boulders on Garleigh Moor. The Simonside Hills can be seen beyond

The classic Vicar's Pele at Elsdon, Redesdale

rian's Wall (1922) is a charmingly illustrated account, was another great Wall enthusiast.

Hadrian's Wall is still one of the great historical walks of Britain, and the boggy but beautiful Border Ridge of the Cheviots, is one of the great wilderness experiences.

Strictly speaking the Cheviots are not part of the Pennines. They were formed by volcanic action about 380 million years ago, when magma was forced up through the Silurian strata via a series of circular vents, spewing out lava flows which cooled to form the andesite which now covers about 350sq miles (900 sq km) of the Cheviot Hills. The chemical makeup of these andesites supports pale grassland rather than the dark, chocolate-brown heather of the acid-rich Pennines, and it is this which gives the dissected plateau of the Cheviots its local name of 'the White Lands'.

Later volcanic action saw massive intrusions of magma which formed the hard, granite core of the Cheviots, such as The Cheviot itself and Hedgehope Hill. This crystalline rock is perhaps best exposed at the graceful waterfall of Linhope Spout, below Great Staindrop in the Breamish Valley.

In contrast to the White Lands are the cementstones and fell sandstones seen in the gorge of the Coquet above Alwinton and in the Simonside and Harbottle Hills to the south and east of the Cheviots. These were formed from the gravelly deposits of great prehistoric rivers which flowed from the north and eventually gave us the darker, heather-covered moorland known locally as 'the Black Country'. This is much more like the rest of the Pennines, with rolling grouse moors terminating abruptly in steep, gritty escarpments.

Early man favoured these drier moorlands, and the flat sandstone boulders of the Simonside Hills above the attractive market town of Rothbury display some of the first works of art to be executed in Northumberland. The enigmatic cup-and-ring markings, perhaps best seen near Lordenshaw on Garleigh Moor east of the crest of the Simonside Hills above Rothbury, remain a Pennine mystery. They are exactly like those on Ilkley Moor and elsewhere in the Pennines, but no one knows who carved them or why. An Early Bronze Age date is usually given for these intricate carvings.

Just up the hill from Garleigh Moor are the extensive remains of one of the many commanding Iron Age hillforts which dot these hills, and they bring us neatly back to the coming of the Romans. The best-preserved examples of the might of the Roman occupation are often found in the wildest, least hospitable spots, protected by their very isolation. The main despoilers of the Wall, who so upset William Hutton during his traverse, have not been major developers but local farmers and landowners who used it as a convenient quarry for building stone. Close inspection of many farms and barns near to the Wall, will often reveal pieces of Roman work incorporated in them.

Northumberland – the empty quarter – has always been off the beaten track, and the huge expansion of the Border Forest around Kielder by the Forestry Commission has tended to concentrate visitor activity in that area. Kielder Water, a 2,684 acre (1,070ha) reservoir controversially built to meet the water requirements of the Northeast into the twenty-first century, has become a centre for water sports, while the surrounding coniferous forest attracts motorists and mountain bikers, who enjoy the dark, mainly monotonous forest rides.

Walkers, however, mourn the loss of open moorland. For them Northumberland is still what the great Northumberland-born historian and rambler, G. M. Trevelyan, called 'the land of far horizons'. In a famous essay, *The Middle Marches*, published in 1926, he encapsulated the essence of Northumberland:

> In Northumberland alone, both heaven and earth are seen; we walk all day on long ridges, high enough to give far views of moor and valley, and the sense of solitude far below ... It is the land of far horizons, where the piled or drifted shapes of gathered vapour are for ever moving along the furthest ridge of hills, like the procession of long primeval ages that is written in tribal mounds and Roman camps and Border towers, on the breast of Northumberland.

The Cheviots across the valley of the Till, as seen from Lyham Hill near Wooler

THE · CHEVIOT

Map OS Landranger Sheet 74, Kelso, Pathfinder NT 82/92

Start Mounthooly GR 882225

Length About 8 miles

Time Allow at least 5–6 hours

Difficulty A serious expedition, with some tough bog-trotting

THE CRAGGY HEART OF THE CHEVIOT

Most walkers approach the boggy plateau of The Cheviot (2,676ft/815m) from the south on the well-worn route via the Pennine Way, or from the east via Langleeford and the Harthope Burn. By doing so, they miss two of the great scenic wonders of the massif: the remote, hidden valley of the College Burn and the mysterious craggy ravine of Hen Hole.

Like so many great routes, this approach from the north is difficult of access, but it more than repays the determined rambler with a superb wilderness experience and a true taste of the wildest Cheviots.

Vehicular access to the upper reaches of the College Valley beyond Hethpool is by permit only, and only twelve cars a day are allowed to take the single track mountain road which winds the 3 miles into its hidden recesses. You should apply to John Sale and Partners, agents for College Valley Estates, at 18–20, Glendale Road, Wooler for your permit, which is not normally available in snowy conditions (no skiing is allowed) nor during the lambing season, from 12 April to 12 May. No dogs are allowed and no fishing is permitted in the College Burn. Walkers are always welcomed, but that extra 6 mile round trip without a permit should be carefully considered if you are aiming for the summits.

Park just before the isolated shepherd's bungalow at Mounthooly, and take the farm track which leads off through the farmyard past a shelter belt and into the broad, glaciated trough of the College Burn.

This is the Cheviots at their wildest, where, with only the hardy Swaledale sheep and the bubbling College Burn for company, the track leads on into the heart of the hills. The unsightly coniferous plantations which cloak the sides of The Schil to the west and West Hill to the east are the only signs of human presence, apart from a series of circular drystone stells (sheep enclosures) which are passed en route. There are fine views back down the valley to the twin hills of Housedon and Coldside, across the valley of the Bowmont Water to the north.

The main track leads up steeply from the last sheep stell towards the nick in the skyline ahead formed by Red Cribs, which takes its name from the red colour of the bare slopes of soil. This old trackway or drove road was mentioned in 1597 as 'Gribbheade, a passage and hyeway for the theefe', a reference to its use by the robbing Border reivers. A good grassy track leads off right from Red Cribs to the rocky summit of The Schil, one of the best viewpoints on the Cheviots. This small, lichen-encrusted tor is a remnant of the metamorphic aureole which surrounded the former volcano represented by the reigning summit of The Cheviot.

Our route, however, bears left away from Red Cribs, and the real drama begins as the great gash of Hen Hole is gradually revealed, with the smooth summit of The Cheviot beyond. The Hen Hole gorge was carved out of

The name of Birnie Brae tells the Pennine Wayfarer he's nearly in Scotland. Looking north down the length of the College Valley

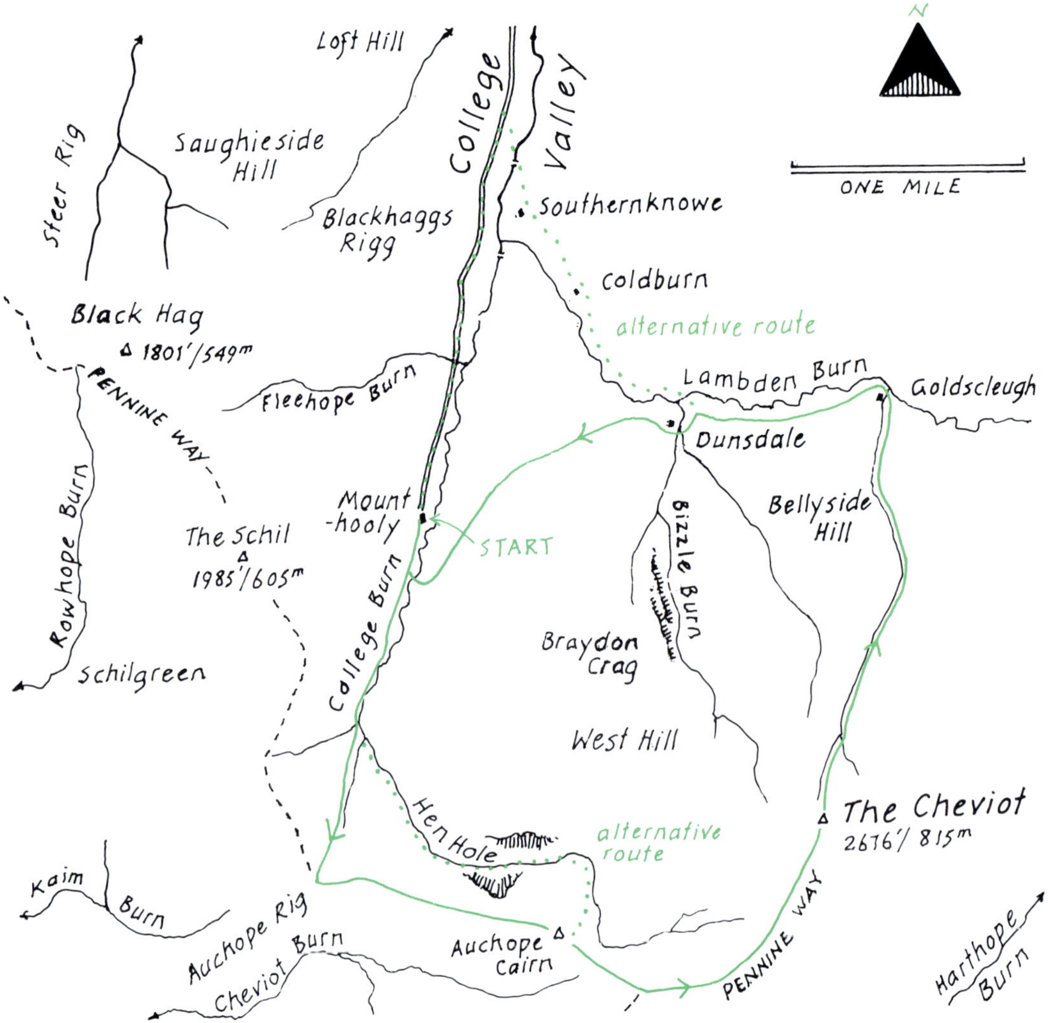

the hard, volcanic andesite rocks by the rushing waters of a melting glacier at the end of the Ice Age, ten thousand years ago.

The College Burn rises in the boggy glacial cirque or corrie at the head of the Hen Hole, and cascades down between the beetling walls of rock in a series of impressive cascades and waterfalls.

There is a track of sorts into Hen Hole which will tempt the more adventurous scrambler into the heart of the gorge, for a *direttissima* assault on The Cheviot, but be warned, this is a route for experienced hillgoers only. More pragmatic ramblers should head up the side of the gorge to meet the Border Fence and the well-worn track of the Pennine Way on the skyline.

At the fence, turn left and follow the Pennine Way through the tussock grass up and down past the mountain refuge hut just across the border in Scotland, on the long col between The Schil and Auchope Cairn. Once a dilapidated railway carriage stood here, incongruously placed on one of the highest and wildest cols in England, and was a life-saver to many walkers caught out on the gruelling 25 mile slog across the Cheviots near the end of their marathon. It was replaced by this purpose-built wooden refuge in 1988, the structure being airlifted in by helicopter from Mounthooly. It is managed by the Northumberland National Park authority.

Walk up over increasingly boggy ground to the exposed summit of Auchope Cairn, and then, still following the Pennine Way, reach a stile in the morass which leads across the worst peat bogs the Pennine Wayfarer has encountered since Kinder Scout, Bleaklow and Black Hill in the Peak. The path leads to the left across Cairn Hill and Scotsman's Cairn to the summit of The Cheviot. It is, as one guidebook succinctly puts it, 'a climb only for the record, not for pleasure, nor the view'. Indeed, there are often times when the concrete mushroom of the Ordnance Survey trig point is inaccessible to the walker because of the appalling conditions underfoot.

There is a choice of return routes from the summit of The Cheviot. You can retrace the boggy path back to Red Cribs, or alternatively continue east to a prominent cairn where a track leads off north after about half a mile. This follows the east bank of the burn which runs across Bellyside Hill down through a forestry plantation to the farmhouse of Goldscleugh. From here a path leads off left along the Lambden Burn through Dunsdale and back to Mounthooly, or to Hethpool via Coldburn, Southernknowe and Sutherland Bridge.

Looking north down the College Valley in the wild heart of the Cheviots, towards white-painted Fleehope cottage, near Mounthooly. This winter view gives an idea of the harshness of this uncompromising borderland, the home country of the steel-bonneted Border reivers, and a place of almost constant internecine warfare for three centuries. The trackway which leads out of the head of the valley via Red Cribs was still known as 'a passage and hyeway for the theefe' as late as 1597

HEDGEHOPE · HILL

Map OS Landranger Sheets 80, The Cheviots and 81, Alnwick and Rothbury

Start Hartside GR 975162

Length About 8 miles

Time Allow 4–5 hours

Difficulty Very rough going on tussocky moorland; not for the inexperienced

LINHOPE SPOUT AND HEDGEHOPE

Many Pennine Wayfarers have looked longingly south and east from the ankle-sucking peat bogs of their route across the Cheviots towards the inviting and apparently untrodden rounded, grassy hilltops of Hedgehope, Dunmoor and Comb Fell. This route is for those wishing to enjoy the unrivalled freedom that these lovely, lonely fells can impart.

It starts from the beautiful Breamish Valley, one of the major eastward-flowing tributaries running off the granite masses of the Cheviots. Approach on the minor road which runs west from Ingram and park on a wide verge at Hartside, where there is a farm gate which is usually locked.

The private road beyond leads west up past ancient earthworks between conifer plantations to Linhope, a collection of estate cottages and a large house nestling among banks of rhododendrons. ('Hope' usually, as here, indicates a strip of better land in a narrow valley.)

Beyond the buildings, a signed track leads up steeply right alongside the plantation boundary. After about half a mile, at the corner of the plantation, a sign indicates a footpath crossing the moor above the deep ravine of Linhope Burn towards Linhope Spout, which is just visible through a cluster of trees.

Linhope Spout is a most attractive 40ft (12m) waterfall embowered in trees yet set among barren open fells. Here the Linhope Burn shoots down from the crystalline granite core of the Cheviot massif in a single graceful leap.

Above the Spout, follow the burn to a bridge before contouring up the tussocky slopes of Great Staindrop to reach the spectacular twin-peaked 1,782ft/534m summit, from where there are fine views down the Breamish Valley to the east, and northwest towards the less than imposing summit of The Cheviot. The view northwards is dominated by our objective, Hedgehope Hill.

Turn north to follow the narrow path on the east side of the fence along the ridge of Staindrop Rigg (Old Norse for ridge) to the col between Great Staindrop and the lovely, conical shape of Hedgehope Hill which lies directly ahead. It is now very steep and rough going up the slopes to the summit, as the fence bears away to the right.

Although Hedgehope Hill at 2,342ft/714m is 330ft/100m short of The Cheviot, in almost every other respect it is a finer hill. It dominates the Upper Breamish Valley, and stands aloof from the surrounding summits of the Cheviot 'White Lands', surely the most shapely and satisfying of all the Cheviot summits.

If you are lucky enough to visit the summit of Hedgehope on one of the Cheviots' rare clear days, you will be rewarded by one of the finest viewpoints in the far north of England. The beautiful Northumberland coastline is visible to the east beyond Alnwick, and the low-lying Farne Islands and Lindisfarne (or Holy Island) can sometimes be made out to the northeast, basking like whales on the grey surface of the North Sea.

The broad southeast ridge of Hedgehope leads off, following a fence and a path of sorts over very rough, peat-hagged terrain down to Dunmoor Hill, our next objective. A huge

Linhope Spout occupies a secluded, tree-filled hollow in the hills above Hartside

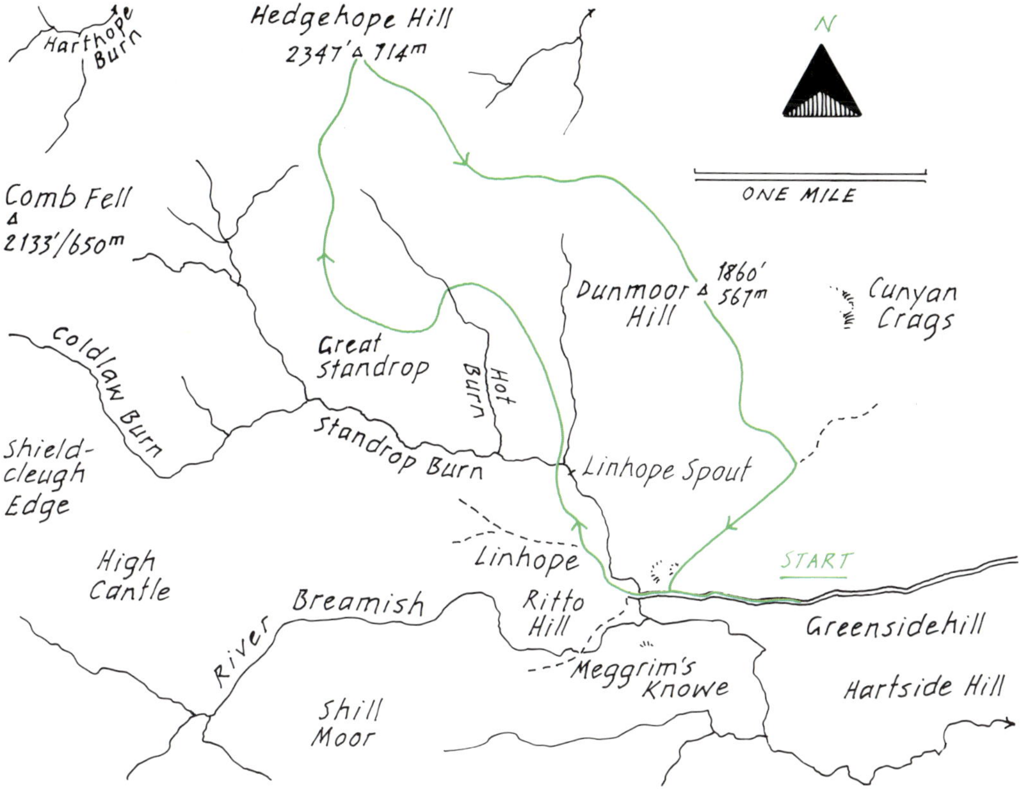

forestry plantation spreads up the hill from Kelpie Strand, Threestone Burn and the Harthope Valley in the north, but our route skirts this by descending to the often boggy col between the two hills.

Climb up to the cairn on the top of 1,860ft/567m Dunmoor Hill for some fine views down the Breamish Valley and to the ancient settlement sites of Hartside Hill opposite.

Descend the tussocky slopes of Dunmoor, between the rocky outcrops of Cunyan Crags to the east and Long Crag to the west to rejoin the bridleway leading left, back to Linhope and Hartside, which is screened by its shelter belt of trees.

STEEL · RIGG

Map OS Landranger Sheet 87, Hexham and Haltwhistle

Start Steel Rigg car park GR 751677

Length About 8 miles but can be lengthened

Time Allow 5–6 hours

Difficulty Mostly good paths, but can be wet in places. Boots and waterproofs recommended

A WALK ALONG THE WALL

Hadrian's Wall, at the northernmost extremity of the Empire, remains one of the most impressive examples of Roman military might in Europe. This walk gives a taste of what it must have felt like to be a defender, or attacker, of this final frontier.

Start from the car park at Steel Rigg, just off the B6318 west of Housesteads. The car park itself is actually built on the line of the Wall, which was used by local farmers and builders as a convenient source of building stone for many centuries. From the car park, turn right along the road for about 200 yards, to a gateway and signpost on the right which indicates the way to Hotbank Farm.

There are increasingly good views of the Wall perched on the top of the great igneous wave of the Whin Sill of Peel Crags as you approach the mixed woodland of Peatrigg Plantation on your left. This is the intimidating view of the Wall that would have confronted invading barbarians.

Passing the barns at Peatrigg and Long Side, there are fine views, looking east, of the successive waves of hills marking the intrusion of the Whin Sill. The glacial lake of Crag Lough nestles like a moat beneath the grey rocks of Highshield Crags. Continue along this waymarked route, crossing a stile near a sheepfold and a ditch. Reaching a second stile, take the farm track left to follow the low ridge which was probably once a drove road linking Hotbank Farm, to the right, with King's Wicket, our destination to the east.

Passing a cross-shaped stell (sheep shelter) on your left, continue east on this ridge until you reach the remains of a limekiln. Cross the line of the Pennine Way, coming north from Rapishaw Gap between Cuddy's and Hotbank Crags to your left, and continue east to pass a circular stell to your right. Continue on, passing through a hollow, to a small plantation via two stiles until you reach the gate and stile of King's Wicket in the dip between King's Hill and the rising ground to Sewingshield Crags to the north.

If you are feeling fit, it takes about half an hour to reach the summit of Sewingshield Crags (1,066ft/325m), one of the highest points and finest viewpoints on the Wall, and the legendary resting place of King Arthur and his knights.

Our route turns west at King's Wicket and the appropriately named Busy Gap – a break in the basalt ridge used with great frequency by the Border reivers of the sixteenth century. Climb up over King's Hill and Clew Hill along the line of the Wall (now an ordinary-looking field wall) heading for the woodland of the Housesteads Plantation ahead.

Cross the Knag Burn by the stone bridge and head up the steep hill to Housesteads Fort, the most impressive and extensively excavated of all the forts on the Wall. Known to the Romans as Vercovicium, it covers 5 acres (2ha) and contains the remains of barracks, granaries,

The view looking east from Cuddy's Crags towards tree-topped Housesteads Crags on the Wall

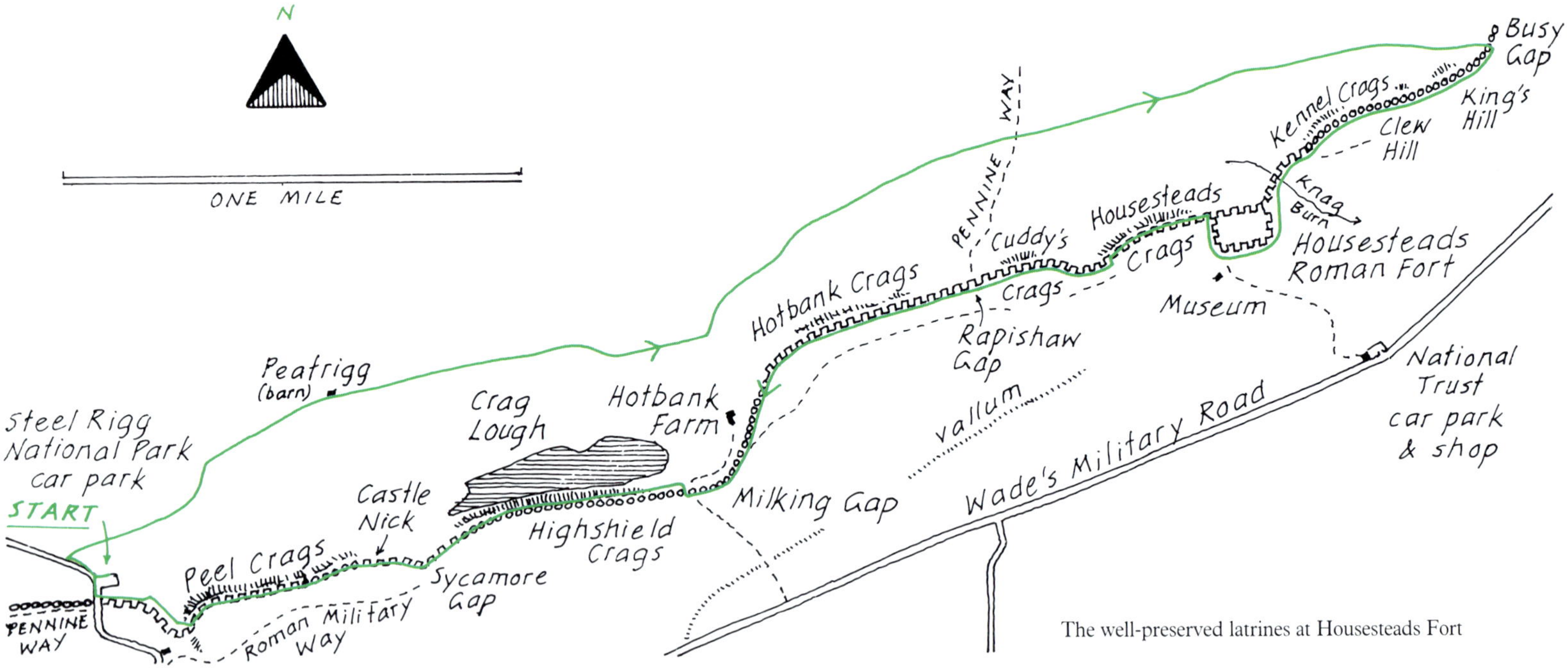

The well-preserved latrines at Housesteads Fort

latrines and what appears to have been a Roman hospital. There is an interesting museum on the site, jointly run by the Northumberland National Park authority and the National Trust.

After a thorough investigation of this fascinating site, head west along the top of the Wall into the Scots pines in the wood at the top of Housesteads Crag.

Continue on to Cuddy's Crags – which take their name from the nickname of Northumberland's favourite saint, Cuthbert – and then steeply down to the Rapishaw Gap. This is one of the most heavily used parts of the Wall and forms part of the Pennine Way. Climb up the other side, past the remains of Turret 37, to the Whin Sill crest of Hotbank Crags. The summit of Hotbank Crags is another fine viewpoint, with four of the loughs (lakes) of Northumberland visible: Greenlee, the largest, Broomlee, Crag and Grindon, the smallest. The views also extend south to heather-covered Barcombe Hill, where the Romans quarried much of the stone for the Wall, and further to the southwest, Cross Fell and Cold Fell, two of the highest points of the Pennines. Beyond them on a clear day, Skiddaw and Blencathra in the northern Lake District can sometimes be seen.

Crag Lough comes into view again as you descend to Hotbank Farm, sheltered by a belt

of trees. Through the farmyard, Milecastle 38 is visible, and a panel gives information. The track runs down to Milking Gap, where you cross a ladder stile to reach a farm track.

Turn right over a stile beside a cattle grid on the north side of the Wall. Continue west over another ladder stile and into the mixed Scots pine and sycamore trees of the Crag Lough woods. There are tantalising glimpses of Crag Lough below to the left; tufted duck and goldeneye can sometimes be seen in these waters.

Walk carefully along the crags, and then descend to the next gap, or 'nick', which is known as Castle Nick because of the well-preserved remains of Milecastle 38. Here the two gateways and officers' quarters are clearly visible.

Continue along the well-defined footpath alongside the Wall to Cat Stairs and Sycamore Gap, which featured in the film *Robin Hood, Prince of Thieves*. The old tree from which the gap took its name was dying, so, to perpetuate the name, the National Trust planted another in 1989 in the odd circular walled enclosure.

There is a steep climb to the final escarpment of Peel Crags, where the huge pillars of basalt which form the Whin Sill are well exposed. Walk alongside the Wall across the top of Peel Crags past the remains of Milecastle 39, following the footpath down the steep western end via the steps. Follow the small valley to the right, through a wicket gate and back to the Steel Rigg car park.

WALLTOWN · CRAGS

Map OS Landranger Sheet 86, Haltwhistle, Bewcastle and Alston

Start Walltown car park GR 674664

Length About 5 miles

Time Allow about 3 hours

Difficulty Easy wall-walking but some steep ascents and descents. Boots recommended as it can be muddy

ACROSS THE NICKS OF THIRLWALL

This is a route alongside Hadrian's Wall to Great Chesters Fort across some of the Nine Nicks of Thirlwall. It is recommended by the Northumberland National Park authority as being less busy than the Housesteads section.

Start from the car park at Walltown, east of Thirlwall with its ruined fourteenth-century castle built almost entirely from Roman wall stones. Walk up the hill to the Wall, turning right to head east past the well-preserved Turret 45A, which, in its commanding position overlooking the Haltwhistle Burn, may have served as a signal station and probably predates the Wall.

Continue along the line of the Wall behind Walltown Farm and the site of Walltown Tower. Walltown Crags, which drop steeply to the north (left) were split by nine 'nicks' or gaps in the rock, and although some have since been quarried away, as at Walltown Quarry, most remain a feature of the landscape.

The next nick is Walltown Nick, where a steep climb down the slope leads you to King Arthur's Well. Cross the stile and continue east along the Roman Military Way, built to give easy access between the vallum and the forts on the Wall. The Way climbs up past tree-sheltered Allolee Farm on the right to the heights of Muckleback Crag and on to the Scots pine plantation of Cockmount Hill, where a Roman milestone taken from the Military Way doubles as a gatepost on the left.

View east along the Wall from Cawfield Crags

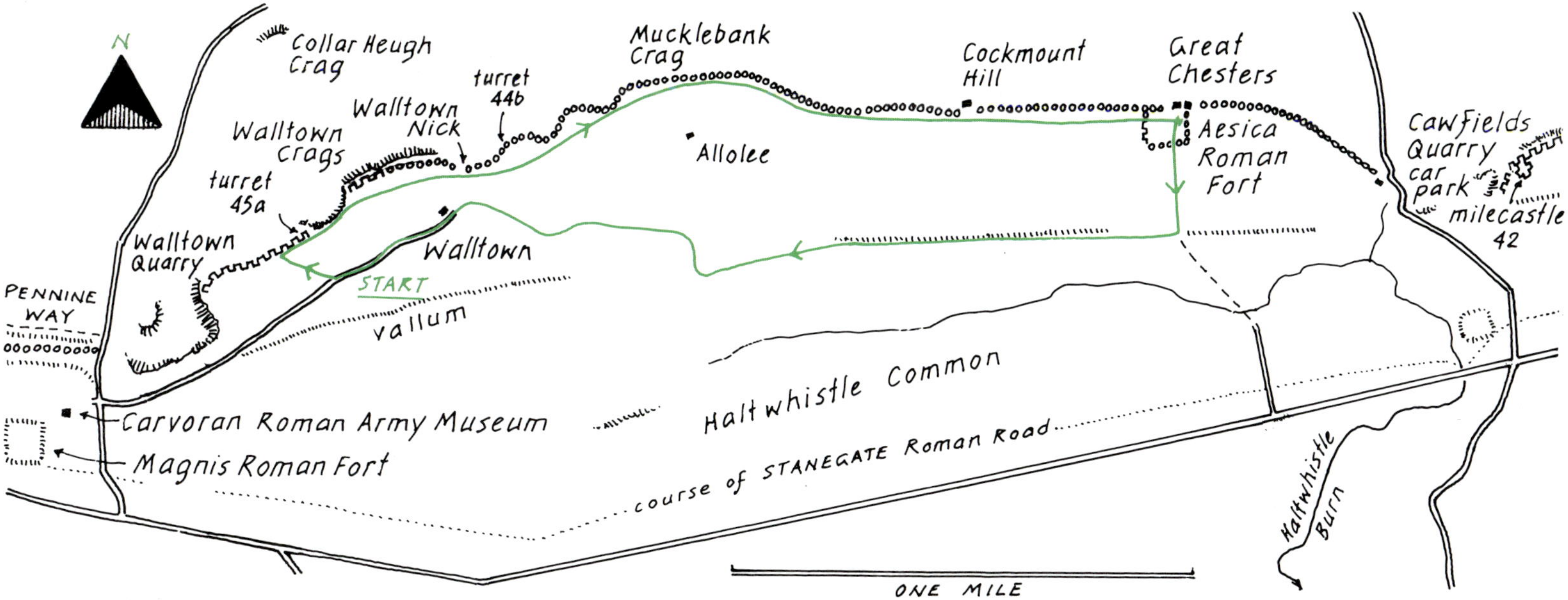

Leaving the plantation by a ladder stile, walk past Cockmount Hill Farm towards the fort of Great Chesters, which was known by the Romans as Aesica. The fort, which included gates, towers, administrative offices, a granary and an underground strongroom, was built about AD128 and guarded the Caw Gap with a force of about five hundred infantry soldiers.

At Great Chesters Farm, turn right and descend the farm track to a metalled road, where you turn right again following the gated track back towards Walltown along the line of the Roman vallum. The vallum forms the southernmost limit of the Wall fortifications, and runs parallel with the Wall for the whole of its 73 mile (117km) length. Its purpose was thought to be to mark the official limit of the military zone in Roman times. There is a very well-preserved section of the vallum on your immediate right at the start of this section of the track, and you traverse a series of crossing points in the vallum, with visible gaps in both banks.

The outlines of cultivation terraces can be seen on the hillside below Cockmount Hill to the right, but these are more likely to be medieval than Roman.

After passing through the fourth gate, the track bends right, crossing the line of the vallum, and goes over a cattle grid. Through the gate, you pass the site of a British earthwork. To the right are the remains of a limekiln, which was served by the worked-out face of a small quarry behind.

Passing the site of Walltown Tower, once the home of the brother of Nicholas Ridley, a Protestant martyr burnt at the stake alongside Bishop Latimer in 1555, you are soon back to the Walltown car park.

THE · SIMONSIDE · HILLS

Map OS Landranger Sheet 81, Alnwick and Rothbury

Start Rothbury Forest car park GR 042992

Length About 8 miles

Time Allow 5 hours

Difficulty Easy moorland and forestry track walking

THE SIMONSIDE RIDGE

The Simonside Hills are a heather-clad, 5 mile ridge of fell sandstone running across the eastern border of the Northumberland National Park between Elsdon and Rothbury. The characteristically dark heather moorlands have given the name of the 'Black Lands' to these and the Harbottle Hills, in contrast to the 'White Lands' of the grass-covered Cheviots.

The finest one-day excursion in the Simonside Hills is the 4 mile traverse of the main ridge, from Garleigh Moor to the reigning summit of Tosson Hill (1,443ft/440m). Taken during late August when the heather is at its best, this is an outstanding outing, with fine views in every direction, especially across the fertile Coquet Valley to the distant Cheviot Hills in the north.

On the crags of Raven's Heugh at the western end of the Simonside ridge, looking towards the Cheviots

Park in the Forestry Commision's car park and picnic area below Simonside summit south of Rothbury. Turn right to walk back up the road and out of the trees towards the col between Garleigh Moor and The Beacon.

Before starting west across the ridge, it is worth spending a few minutes locating the numerous mysterious 'cup and ring' marked boulders which litter the slopes of Garleigh Moor below its reigning Iron Age hillfort. A particularly fine example overlooks the road and is marked by a Ministry of Public Buildings and Works sign. Dating from the Bronze Age, these concentric rings and hollows still baffle archaeologists.

Back on the road, an easy track leads up through the heather to the first summit on the ridge, The Beacon, which is reached by turning right at the top of the col, leaving the main track which descends over Caudhole Moss. There is a fine view east from this 1,181ft/360m summit across the rich archaeological sites of Garleigh Moor, with an aerial view of the concentric rings of its crowning hillfort. Looking north, the roofs of Rothbury sheltering beneath the tree-clad crag of Addyheugh are prominent in the middle distance, with the mock-Tudor façade of Cragside peeping out of the trees to the east.

From the large cairn on top of The Beacon, follow the broad track westwards down and then up again to the prominent outcrop of Dove (or Dough) Crag. Facing north across the thick forestry plantations of Rothbury Forest directly below, the sandstone rocks of Dove Crag are reminiscent of a Peakland 'edge', with rolling miles of sweet-scented heather moorland stretching down to the south.

Another mile through the heather brings you to the first of the eponymous summits of Simonside, known as Old Stell Crag. Indeed, if you look down from your lofty vantage point you may be able to make out several stells, or ancient circular sheep pens.

The name of Simonside itself is thought to have been derived from Sigemund's Seat, and is recorded as Simundesette in 1279, 'sett' denoting a settlement or dwelling in Old English. The views from the westernmost 1,407ft/428m summit of Simonside are superb

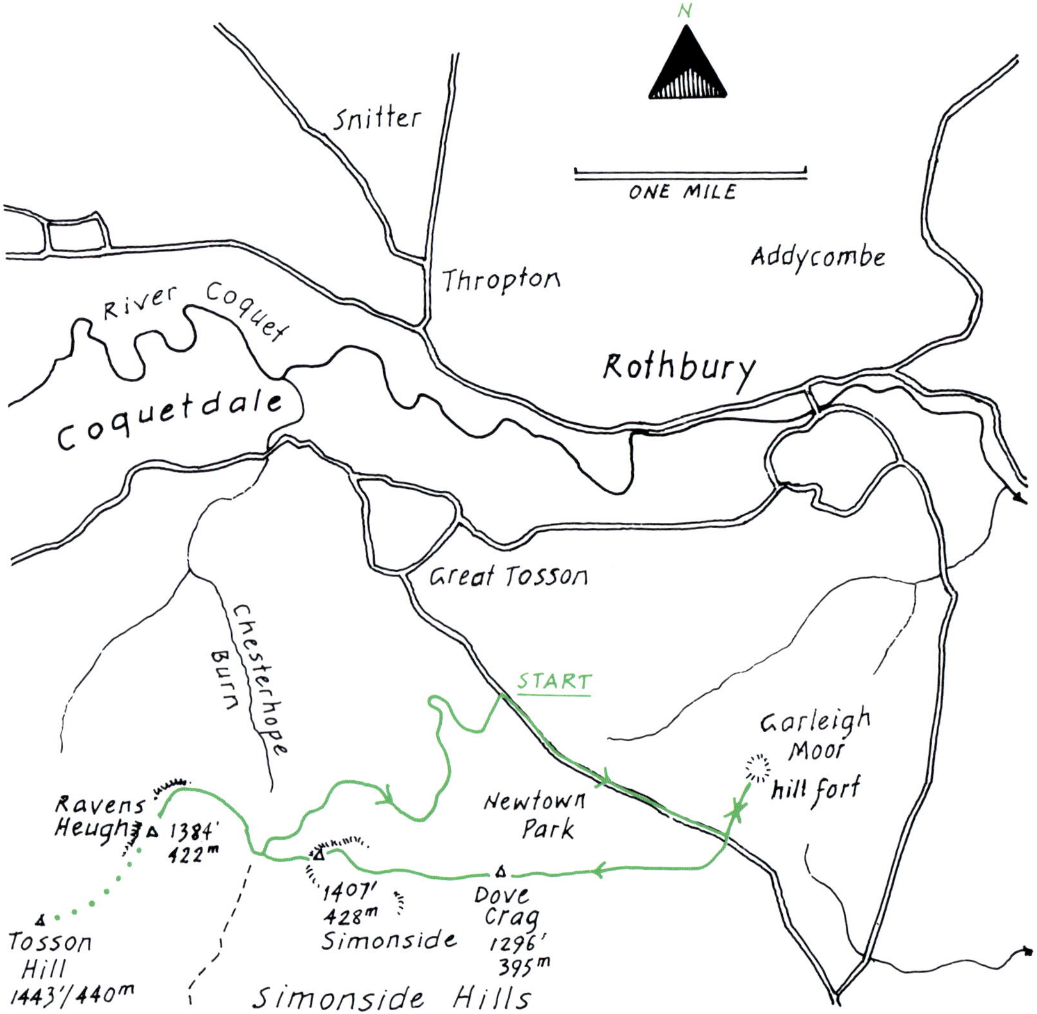

– one of the best viewpoints in the whole of Northumberland.

It is a steep descent through the shattered sandstone crags at the western end of Simonside, where there is some rock-climbing on the coarse fell sandstone. At the foot of the crags, you meet up with the forestry track which leads down to the right through the trees of Rothbury Forest and eventually back to the car park.

To complete the ridge, however, head up again towards the narrow neck of land between the trees and over the stile to the impressive crags of Raven's Heugh (1,384ft/422m). Here, there is a fine raven's-eye view between the curiously detached crags across the meandering Coquet to the lakes of Caistron far below. A perfect circular stell lies in the bracken-covered slopes directly beneath the crags of Raven's Heugh ('Heugh' is the local name for a hill which ends abruptly).

Another mile through the heather finds Tosson Hill, at 1,443ft/440m, the highest point on the Simonside Hills. There is no official access, but the circular drystone-wall shelter on the summit offers nothing like the views you have already enjoyed on the eastern summits.

Retrace your steps to the gap between Raven's Heugh and Simonside and turn left to follow the waymarked forestry tracks which eventually lead back to the car park in Rothbury Forest.

The author approaching the summit of Simonside, with the ridge extending to Dove Crag behind

ROTHBURY

Map OS Landranger Sheet 81, Alnwick and Rothbury

Start Cragside entrance GR 067034

Length 5 miles

Time Allow 3½ hours

Difficulty Easy walking in woodland and on heathery moorland

A ROTHBURY ROUND

Rothbury, the undisputed capital of Coquetdale, is an attractive little market town with a long history. It was first recorded as Routhebiria, or Routha's town, in the twelfth century, and has been visited by three English kings: King John in 1201, Edward I in 1275 and Edward VII (then Prince of Wales) in 1884. This is an easy walk through the woods and moorland which enclose Rothbury to the north.

Take the B6341 Alnwick road north from Rothbury for about 1¼ miles and park opposite the northern entrance to Cragside. This was Lord Armstrong's former baronial home, now in the care of the National Trust.

Walk west along the drive to Debdon, through a gate and bear left downhill and over the bridge to Primrose Cottage. Here leave the road through a gate on the right and walk up the track beside the mixed plantation to your left.

At a crossroads of tracks, go straight on through pleasant woodland and eventually out on to the open moorland. The land here is part of Lord Armstrong's Cragside estate, and the tracks you are using were used by the family as carriage drives, to be enjoyed by visiting guests.

The track curves round to the left, below the summit of the hill up to your left. The views now open up towards the distant Cheviot, on the right, and shapely Hedgehope to the left. The red stone quarry in the distance is Harden Quarry at Biddlestone, where the red felsite is extracted for roadstone. Down to the right, close to the edge of the moor, are the ruins of Cartington Castle, where Queen Margaret of Scotland lodged in the sixteenth century. It was later besieged by Parliamentary forces during the Civil War in 1648 and badly damaged.

The track passes a circular sheepfold and prehistoric cairn on the hilltop to the left before contouring around the 816ft/249m summit of Brae Head, topped by an Ordnance Survey triangulation pillar and fire-watching tower. There are good views of the north-facing sandstone escarpment of the Simonside Hills, with Raven's Heugh to the right and Dove Crag to the left, rising around the Forestry Commission plantations of Rothbury Forest.

At a fork in the track bear left passing on your right the tall television transmission mast, erected in 1980 to improve the reception for the people of Rothbury. Ship Crag rises to the left, a fine viewpoint across the little township nestling in the Coquet Valley.

Continue on this track round the bilberry-clad hillside until just before a gate leads into a plantation. Turn left here on a narrow path and follow it downhill over well-managed heather moorland to a gate. You will probably hear the distinctive 'go-back, go-back' call of the red grouse as you pass through the heather.

Continue on in the same direction for about 500 yards until the path leads to a stile in the angle of a plantation. Enter this overgrown plantation and then turn right along the forestry track to a stile at a T-junction. Turn right here and descend back to Primrose Cottage.

From Primrose Cottage, retrace your steps to the starting point down the Debdon road, emerging again on the B6341 opposite the entrance to Cragside.

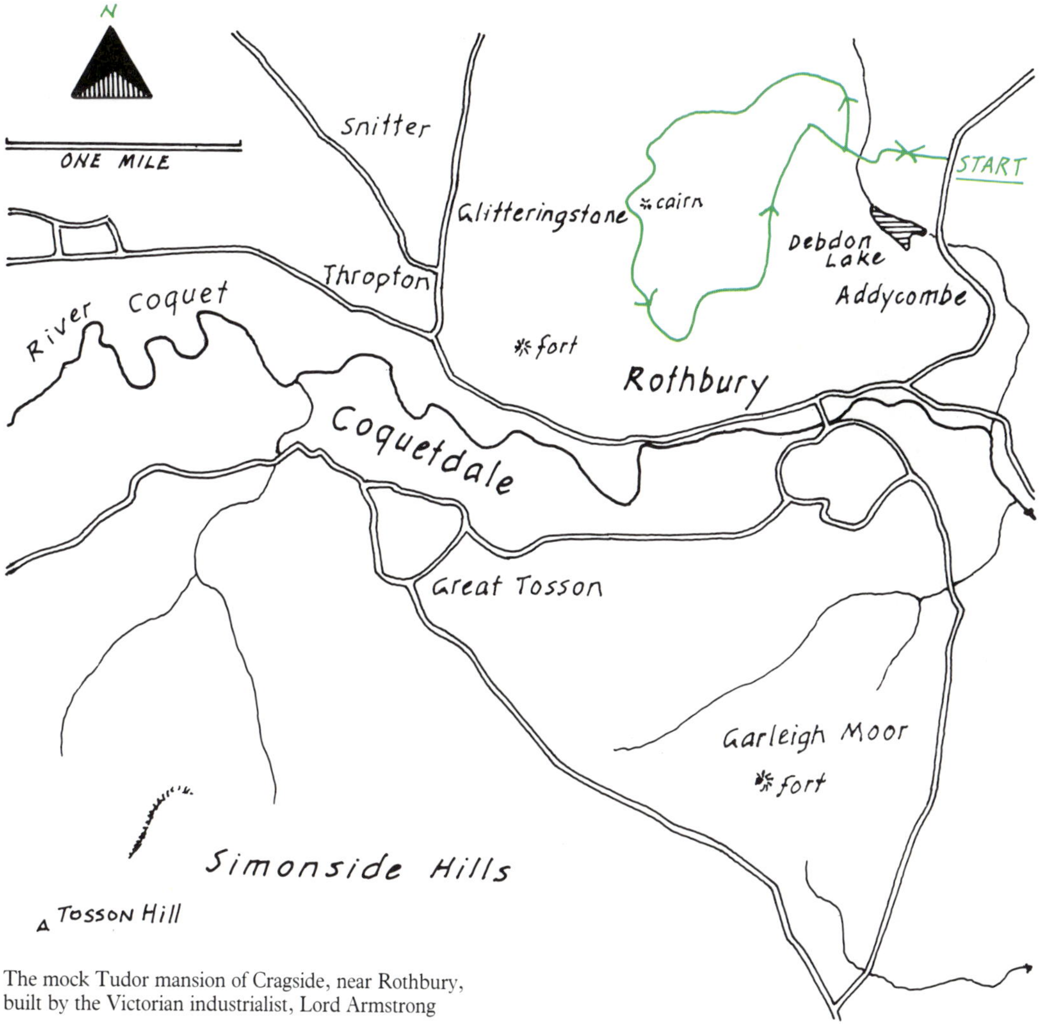

The mock Tudor mansion of Cragside, near Rothbury, built by the Victorian industrialist, Lord Armstrong

TOWER · KNOWE

Map OS Landranger Sheet 80, The Cheviot Hills and Kielder Forest

Start Tower Knowe Visitor Centre car park GR 699868

Length About 2 miles

Time Allow about 1½ hours

Difficulty Partly gravelled paths with easy gradients, but can be wet

AN ARTIFICIAL 'WILDERNESS'

The 200sq miles (520sq km) of Kielder Water and the Border Forest represent the biggest single man-made landscape in Europe, and most conservationists turn up their noses at this entirely artificial scene, mourning the tragic loss of the open moorland. But the fact remains that this artificial 'wilderness' is one of the most popular visitor attractions in the Northeast.

Most visitors to Kielder Water gravitate to the popular Tower Knowe Visitor Centre, run jointly by Northumbrian Water and the Northumberland National Park authority. This short walk is based on the centre, and shows something of what was lost when the extensive tree planting began after World War I, and the shallow valley of the River North Tyne was flooded in 1982.

Banks of meadowsweet and rosebay willowherb decorate the shores of Kielder Water, near Tower Knowe

Leave the main car park and walk north on the gravelled path, crossing a small footbridge, to reach the low exposed headland of Tower Knowe, which overlooks the eastern reaches of the reservoir with the dam wall to the right.

Tower Knowe – the word Knowe comes from the Norse and means a small hill – gives some idea of what the surrounding countryside was like before afforestation took place. The heather, rushes, sedges and purple moor grass would have given sparse grazing for the cattle and sheep of the Celtic farming community which lived here eighteen hundred years ago.

Tower Knowe is the site of a Romano-British settlement, the remains of which can just be made out on the eastern side of the promontory. The site was extensively excavated as the waters of the reservoir began to rise, and it is thought to date from the first century. Unfortunately, the northernmost stockyard which was excavated is usually flooded when the water level is high, and the formerly thatched hut circles are no longer visible. The Tower Knowe settlement may have housed as many as twenty people in its heyday around AD200.

A large cairn incorporating a plaque, commemorating the inauguration of the Kielder Water scheme in 1976, and an Ordnance Survey trig point crown the summit of Tower Knowe. Having admired the view, continue on the waymarked path and return to the Ferry car park, following the gravel path behind the visitor centre to reach the Waterside car park. Continue on the shoreside path past the indistinct remains of a former drift coal mine on the slopes to the left.

Walk on through the heather and bilberry, passing large blocks of lichen-covered sandstone, to an inlet where a stream comes in from the left and runs into what was once the Whickhope Valley, now mostly submerged beneath the smooth waters of the reservoir. There are more trees now, as the rowans and birches are gradually colonising the moorland slopes.

Reaching the top of the moor, just before a large plantation, the waymarked route turns back towards the visitor centre on a higher route above the reservoir shore. There are fine views towards the nearby Bull Crag peninsula, and of the tree-covered Wind Hill and Belling peninsula on the opposite shore.

The path continues between the shore and the North Tyne road (right), gradually descending towards the visitor centre. As you approach the centre, it passes through the site of the former Shilburnhaugh Colliery, one of a number opened in the area in the early nineteenth century. It was worked off and on until 1940, when it finally closed. At its height, it employed four men and produced about 500 tons of coal annually. Within a few steps of the drift mine site, you are back at the visitor centre car park.

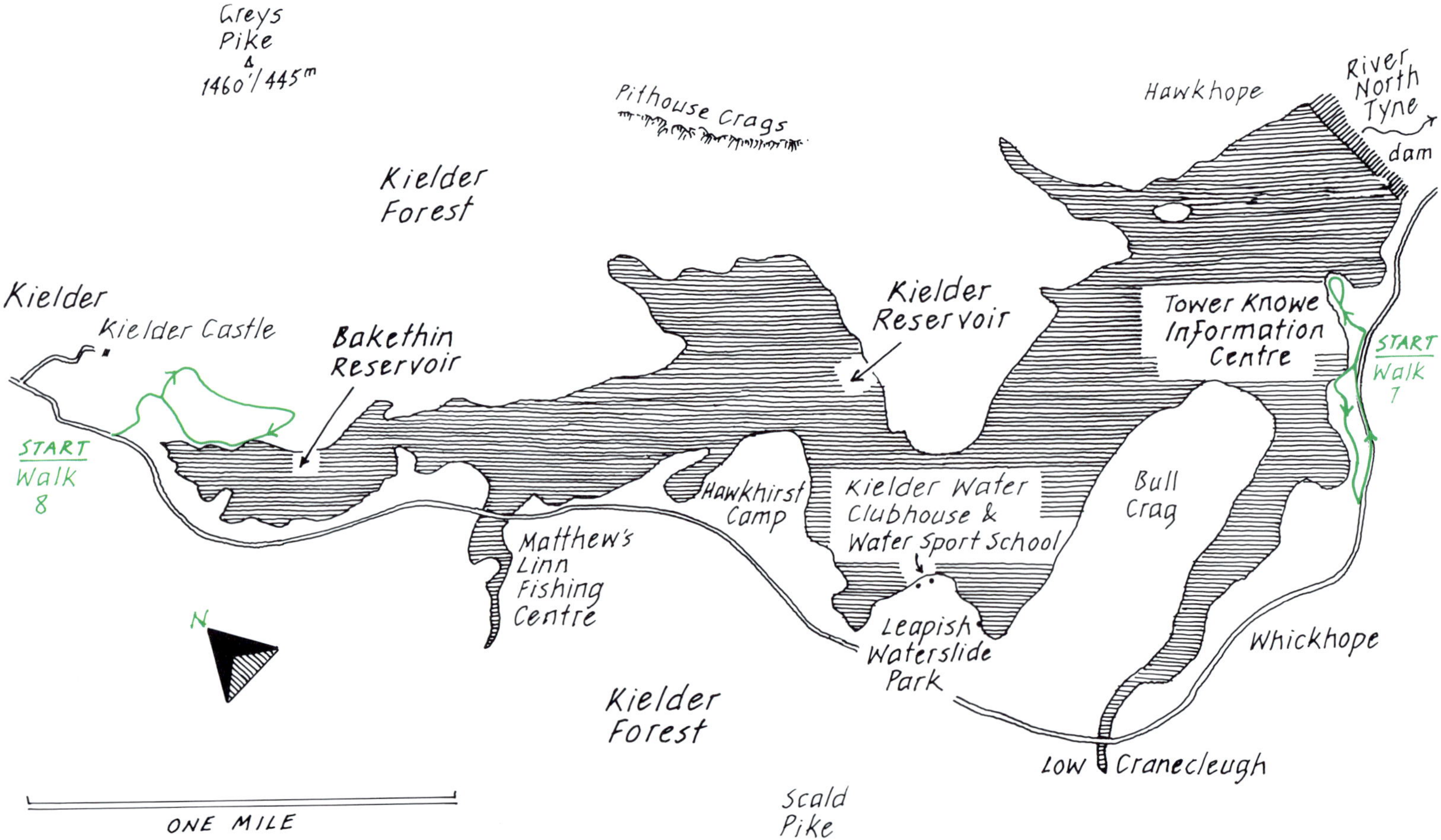

BAKETHIN · RESERVOIR

Map OS Landranger Sheet 80, The Cheviot Hills and Kielder Forest

Start Fishermen's car park, Kielder GR 632927

Length About 2 miles

Time About 1½ hours

Difficulty Easy going on forestry and former railway tracks

DOWN IN THE FOREST...

Bakethin is the upper of the two reservoirs which make up Kielder Water, and is separated from the main lake by a weir designed to ensure that silting up does not occur when the water level is low.

This easy circular walk takes you into the depths of the Kielder Forest south of the estate village of Kielder itself. It reveals several examples of former settlements which existed here before the march of the spruce. The walk

The flower-decked embankments of the former Border Counties Railway at Bakethin Reservoir

follows a self-guided trail provided by Northumbrian Water.

Start from the Fishermen's car park south of Butteryhaugh Bridge (which is south of Kielder village). Turn left and walk beside the River North Tyne through birch and sycamore trees to reach the quaintly named bridge.

Here turn right on to the Forestry Commission's North Haul forestry road, and climb steadily up to reach the brow of a hill, at which point the trees start to crowd in on both sides of the track.

Turn left here and go through the gate at the bottom corner of a field. Walk up the edge of this field – a clearing in the dense forestry all around – to reach the remains of Camp Rigg, a small Romano-British settlement named as a 'Homestead' on the OS map. All that remains is a grass-covered oval of stony bank which extends into the forest. This was the wall of the stockyard for the domestic animals kept on the site.

Carry on past the settlement site to a small wooden gate in the fence to your right. Go through this and enter the plantation via a waymarked, grassy track. Fork left in the trees, pass through a gap in a drystone wall and continue until you come to a firebreak. These are designed to limit the spread of forest fires, and there are many throughout the Kielder Forest, often providing the only feasible way to walk comfortably through the dense trees.

At the grassy firebreak, bear left and climb up to a narrow forestry road, where you must turn right. After a few yards, you pass an area where the spruces have been clear-felled. At the far end of this cleared area, a large cairn of moss-covered stones can be seen, up against the forest. This is known as Deadman Cairn, and is the remains of a circular Bronze Age burial mound, where a chieftain was buried perhaps four thousand years ago.

Back on the forestry track, pass a disused quarry on the left, where you bear right and continue down the tarmac road. A little further on, another firebreak enters from the left. This leads to another ancient circular enclosure, known as the Druid's Circle or Shilling-put. It is probably another Bronze Age ritual site, a common feature in this area, indicating that a sizeable population once lived in this now tree-choked wilderness.

At last, the track breaks out into the open again, and the blue waters of the Bakethin reservior are visible. At the crossroads, turn right and walk back along the North Haul road for a short way. Turn left where some steps lead down towards the lake shore, and go along the footpath almost at the edge of the reservoir. The farm on the hillside to the left is Gowanburn, which is close to the site of a medieval farmstead now lost in the forest.

The footpath meets up with the grassy track of the former Border Counties Railway. This railway originally ran from Hexham through the valley of the North Tyne and across the border into Scotland. This stretch was built in 1862, and finally closed in 1958. To the left, the line of the railway track is swallowed up by the waters of the reservoir.

Turn right and follow the line of the track through cuttings and over embankments decorated with silver birch and willow back to Kielder village. There are fine views of the Bakethin reservoir to the left, especially from the embankments, and you may spot goosander, teal and great crested grebe on the water in summer, and adders basking on the trackbed at your feet.

The railway track eventually crosses the spectacular Kielder skew-arch viaduct, where information plaques explain its history. A few hundred yards after crossing the viaduct, a path on the right leads off down steps and back into the Fishermen's car park, immediately below the embankment.

Alternatively, you can turn off the track where the stone parapet of the viaduct begins, walking down the slope to the burn and following the path through the mixed woodland. After crossing a small stream, carry on through conifers before bearing right to follow the waymarked route up the hillside. When you rejoin the North Haul roadway, turn left and return down the road across the Butteryhaugh Bridge to the Fishermen's car park.

The famous skew-arch Kielder Viaduct spans the North Tyne River near the northern end of Bakethin Reservoir

BIBLIOGRAPHY

Ainsworth, Harrison. *The Lancashire Witches* (Routledge, 1854)

Allen, Bob. *Escape to the Dales* (Michael Joseph, 1992)

Bellamy, David and Quayle, Brendan. *England's Last Wilderness* (Michael Joseph, 1989)

Boyd, Donald. *On Foot in Yorkshire* (Maclehose, 1932)

Boyd, Donald and Monkhouse, Patrick. *Walking in the Pennines* (Maclehose, 1937)

Brown, A.J. *Moorland Tramping in West Yorkshire* (Country Life, 1931)

Byne, Eric and Sutton, Geoffrey. *High Peak* (Secker and Warburg, 1966)

Collins, Herbert. *The Roof of Lancashire* (Dent, 1950)

Davies, Hunter. *A Walk Along the Wall* (Weidenfeld & Nicolson, 1974)

Defoe, Daniel. *A Tour Through the Whole Island of Great Britain* (Penguin, 1971)

Derry, John. *Across the Derbyshire Moors* (Loxley, 1926)

Dillon, Paddy. *Walking in the North Pennines* (Cicerone, 1991)

Fiennes, Celia (ed. Christopher Morris) *The Illustrated Journeys of Celia Fiennes* (Webb & Bower, 1982)

Fraser, George MacDonald. *The Steel Bonnets* (Barrie and Jenkins, 1971)

Hannon, Paul. *80 Dales Walks* (Cordee, 1989)

Hannon, Paul. *Freedom of the Dales* (Hillside, 1992)

Harding, Mike. *Walking the Dales* (Michael Joseph, 1986)

Harding, Mike. *Walking the Peak and Pennines* (Michael Joseph, 1992)

Hill, Howard. *Freedom to Roam* (Moorland, 1980)

Hillaby, John. *Journey through Britain* (Constable, 1968)

Hodges, Richard. *Wall to Wall History* (Duckworth, 1991)

Hopkins, Tony. *Northumberland National Park* (Webb & Bower, 1987)

Hughes, Glyn. *Millstone Grit* (Gollancz, 1975)

Marsh, Terry. *The Pennine Mountains* (Hodder & Stoughton, 1989)

Mitchell, W.R. *Wild Pennines* (Hale, 1976)

Monkhouse, Patrick. *On Foot in the Peak* (Maclehose, 1932)

Mothersole, Jessie. *Hadrian's Wall* (Bodley Head, 1922)

Muir, Richard. *The Dales of Yorkshire* (Macmillan, 1991)

Phillips, Guy Ragland. *Brigantia* (Routledge & Keegan Paul, 1976)

Poucher, W.A. *The Peak and Pennines* (Constable, 1966)

Priestley, J.B. *English Journey* (Heinemann, 1934)

Raistrick, Arthur. *The Pennine Dales* (Eyre Methuen, 1968)

Raistrick, Arthur. *The West Riding of Yorkshire* (Hodder & Stoughton, 1970)

Redfern, Roger. *Portrait of the Pennines* (Hale, 1969)

Richards, Mark. *High Peak Walks* (Cicerone, 1982)

Richards, Mark. *White Peak Walks, The Northern Dales* (Cicerone, 1985)

Richards, Mark. *White Peak Walks, The Southern Dales* (Cicerone, 1988)

Rothman, Benny. *The 1932 Kinder Mass Trespass* (Willow, 1982)

Sellers, Gladys. *The Yorkshire Dales, A Walker's Guide* (Cicerone, 1984)

Sellers, Gladys. *Walking in the South Pennines* (Cicerone, 1991)

Sellers, Gladys. *Walks on the West Pennine Moors* (Cicerone, 1979)

Smith, Roland. *First and Last* (PPJPB, 1978)

Smith, Roland. *Peak National Park* (Webb & Bower, 1987)

Smith, Roland. *Walking the Great Views* (David & Charles, 1991)

Smith, Roland. *Wildest Britain* (Blandford, 1983)

Speakman, Colin. *A Yorkshire Dales Anthology* (Hale, 1981)

Stephenson, Tom. *Forbidden Land* (Manchester University Press, 1989)

Stephenson, Tom. *The Pennine Way* (HMSO, 1969)

Sutcliffe, Halliwell. *The Striding Dales* (Warne, 1929)

Unsworth, Walt. *Portrait of the River Derwent* (Hale, 1971)

Wainwright, A. *Pennine Way Companion* (Westmorland Gazette, 1968)

Wainwright, A. *Walks in Limestone Country* (Westmorland Gazette, 1970)

Wainwright, A. *Walks on the Howgill Fells* (Westmorland Gazette, 1972)

Waltham, Tony. *Yorkshire Dales: limestone country* (Constable, 1987)

Waltham, Tony. *Yorkshire Dales National Park* (Webb & Bower, 1987)

Wright, Geoffrey N. *The Northumbrian Uplands* (David & Charles, 1989)

Wright, Geoffrey N. *The Yorkshire Dales* (David & Charles, 1986)